Scar Tissue

and other stories

First published by Clan Destine Press in 2019

PO Box 121, Bittern
Victoria 3918 Australia

Copyright © Narrelle M Harris 2019

All rights reserved. No part of this book may be reproduced or transmitted in any form or by any means, including internet search engines and retailers, electronic or mechanical, photocopying (except under the statuary exceptions provisions of the Australian Copyright Act 1968), recording or by any information storage and retrieval system, without prior permission in writing from the publisher.

National Library of Australia Cataloguing-In-Publication data:

Harris, Narrelle M.

SCAR TISSUE: and other stories

ISBN: 978-0-6482937-8-1

Cover Design © Willsin Rowe
Photos: © Narrelle M. Harris
Design & Typesetting: Clan Destine Press

Clan Destine Press

www.clandestinepress.com.au

SCAR TISSUE

and other stories

NARRELLE M. HARRIS

CLAN DESTINE PRESS

INTRODUCTION

This collection is inspired by two ideas: hidden histories (both real and imagined) and scars. Those ideas can be separate or intertwined.

Walking around any town, any village, any city, I'm always aware of its small-picture unknown history. Who has walked this way before me? What worker, thousands of years ago, paused at the foot of this same pyramid, when it was still being piled stone upon stone? What Roman soldier took a breath as he stood by this wall when this great city was Londinium?

Hidden histories aren't just separated from me by time. People walk past every day, and I wonder who they are and what their story is. That woman who is smiling as she talks on the phone; that lost looking man, that anxious teenage boy: what everyday histories are unfolding for them?

And sometimes, the world at large leaves unexplained artefacts behind: articles of clothing, jewellery, buttons, books, locks and keys. Signs of some other story of which I can only see a single sentence, or perhaps only a punctuation mark in what could be a comedy, a tragedy, or a bizarre adventure.

Found objects lack context, allowing the finder to imbue them with any number of meanings.

I always wonder how these items were parted from their owners, and whether the separation was amicable. I wonder, too, whether the separation left scars.

Almost everyone has scars. Some are physical and some are emotional or psychological. Some are deep and hurt every day. Others only ache when the weather changes or something reminds us of the wounds when they were fresh.

But scars are also a sign of survival. The dead don't heal. If we have scars, and carry that pain and the memory of suffering, we also carry our survival with it. Precarious as that sometimes feels, here we are.

Here are some stories, old and new, about secret histories, invented stories, and the scars that show that we survived.

Narrelle M Harris
2019

Scar Tissue

Lachlan knocks on the door. He means to sound confident, bold, like he has a right to be here, but the sound is diffident. He's not sure he's welcome. He doesn't feel like he should be.

Clara opens the door and her expression flickers before she smiles. 'Lachie!' She reaches out to kiss him on one cheek. He shoves flowers into her hands, and it's awkward, but she manages to rescue the bouquet – gerberas and baby's breath and delicate fern fronds – and put it right side up. She has grace, does Clara. 'That's lovely, Lachie, you shouldn't have.'

It's what people say, "you shouldn't have", but Lachlan knows it was the right thing to do. He's relieved. It doesn't make up for much, but it shows willing. He wants to make amends. He's six months clean, and he intends to make it six months more. Six years more. Six decades more, and six lifetimes at least, if the Buddhists are right. His time with the needle is done. Whether the needle is done with him may be another matter, but he's worked hard – is still working hard – to build a new life.

'Jayden's giving Amelia her bath,' says Clara, leading Lachlan into the living room. 'He won't be long.'

This is when Jayden comes into the living room, dressed only in his pyjama pants, barefoot and bare-chested, though his torso is mainly obscured by the little bundle wrapped in a soft blanket. Jayden's infant daughter, held across his body, hides the scar.

For the briefest second, Lachlan can pretend it doesn't exist. Only, of course, he can't. Not *even* for the briefest second.

'Who soaked Daddy's shirt through with bathwater, hmm?' Jayden asks the infant, who claims responsibility by squealing happily and wriggling in her swaddling. 'Who's my little mermaid?' Amelia's gummy mouth opens and with a shout of 'YAH!' claims that title as well.

Jayden rubs Amelia's tiny button nose with his own, and he makes ridiculous 'ooop-PAH, ooop-PAH' sounds at her, while she waves her hands and squeals at the game.

Then Jayden shifts his baby in his arms and the scar is on display.

Jayden is unselfconscious about the puckered lines where plate glass had become embedded in his shoulder. He'd nearly bled to death, and he still doesn't have full mobility. For a long time, he'd felt awkward about the damage. He made up stories to explain it when he couldn't hide it. But here, in his home, with his family, he acts as though it's not important. It's become assimilated with all the other, smaller, insignificant scars he's accumulated: the one from gashing his knee falling out of a tree while at a school camp, the triangular mark on his wrist from when he tried to iron his own shirt when he was eight and slipped with the iron; the dent from when he and his best mate played swordfights with steak knives and they managed to actually stab each other.

Lachlan stares at Jayden's scar while trying not to stare at it, hoping, as always, that somehow the ruined and lined skin will disappear and shift. Lachlan could easily take another scar on his own body. He has a map of them, all significant. The one in his scalp from when Dad clobbered him with the beer bottle for interfering with his little brother's punishment. The one on his mouth from being pushed face first into garage wall for getting lippy in Jayden's defence. The long line across his ribs from the knife, the day they finally got someone to *do* something about the old bastard.

Those tiny puckers in his inner elbow, a memento of how, after the brutality stopped, it really hadn't.

Lachlan's scars, large and small, are part of the landscape of who he is, now. Whatever regrets and sorrow they came with, they have other meanings too. They comfort him, sometimes. Once upon a time, he'd done better.

Jayden was never meant to be marked. Lachlan spent his whole life protecting his little brother, only to fail at the last. Jayden's terrible scar is all Lachlan's fault, and Lachlan can never, ever take it back. He can only try to make amends. To be better than he was. To not fail again.

Jayden grins at his brother, though, for all the world as if there was nothing to forgive.

He forgives me, Lachlan thinks, as Jayden sprawls on the floor beside the sofa, unwraps the baby and lays her on his belly.

'And whose Uncle is going to fetch your sleep suit after Daddy left it in the bedroom, hmm?' Jayden says to Amelia, who slaps her little fists against his chest. Jayden laughs, holding onto his daughter so she doesn't roll off. She lists to one side, still held securely, and her baby fist is thrown out in Lachlan's direction.

Lachlan obeys the command without a second thought, fetching the little green sleep suit, and thinks that one day Amelia's body will bear marks and maps of its own. It can't be helped.

But he will help it if he can. He failed to protect Jayden, from either their father or from himself. But if it is humanly possible, he will not let the world scar her at all.

Clara hears the pair of them squabbling in the hall for a good minute before one of them manages to get the key in the lock. She'd have opened it, but the brothers have a way of fighting that is way too entertaining to miss.

'What part of "don't jump!" did you miss, you idiot?' Jayden's tone is impatient.

'What part of "don't throw that!" did *you* miss, blockhead? Oh, that's right. *All of it.*' Lachlan is scathing.

The key turns in the lock and the door opens with a bang, accompanied by irritated huffing and squelching noises. Jayden turns an apologetic look on his wife.

'Sorry, baby. We had a mishap.'

'Date night is off, I take it?' She'd been looking forward to a night out – dinner, maybe dancing – while Lachlan took care of Amelia, but to be honest, whatever this is, it looks hilarious.

'Until I wring the Yarra out of my underwear at least.'

'I lost my goddamned phone into the goddamned *river*,' Lachlan complains, dripping murky water on the welcome mat. Much good the mat does; there's quite a lot of water.

'You didn't have to dive in to save me,' says Jayden, stifling a laugh. Jayden is dripping a matching pool of scummy river water, off to the left of the mat.

Lachlan scowls.

'What kind of moron jumps into a river with their *phone* in in their pocket?' Jayden smirks.

'The kind of moron who has to move in a hurry because his blockhead fishing partner is about to go arse over tit over the side of the goddamn boat.'

'I was just fine.'

'Yeah, right. Until you *fell arse over tit* over the side of the *goddamn boat*.'

'Of course. It's all *my* fault now.' Jayden's back to not feeling reasonable.

'That we're *both* soaked through?' Lachlan says. 'Hell, yes.'

The argument continues while Jayden and Lachlan peel off outer layers and start into the flat, heading for the bathroom.

Clara wonders at the edge in Lachlan's voice – Jayden seems to think it all funny but his brother is clearly upset – but the point becomes clear as Lachlan rounds on Jayden with a blistering: 'I thought you could *swim*.'

Jayden's good humour evaporates. 'You utter *dick*. The water was freezing. I *cramped*. You *know* that shoulder doesn't have full mobility.'

Silence descends so suddenly it's like the stillness after a crash. The blood drains from Lachlan's face and he holds his breath.

'Shit,' says Jayden. 'Shit, Lachie, I didn't mean… it's okay. It was just the shock of the water, you know? I was on my way back up when you grabbed me.'

Lachlan does this thing, this pursing of his mouth and a glance away down and to the side, and Clara reads the shame in it. She doesn't know if Jayden has seen it, and Lachlan shifts back to a defiant posture quickly.

They have reached the bathroom and the brothers stride in, after a tussle at the doorway, and disappear inside. There's the sound of running water and some crashing about while two grown men fight over who gets first shower.

There's a sound from Amelia's bedroom and she leaves the men to it while she fetches her daughter. She returns to the hall with three-year-old Amelia in her arms. Amelia chews a knuckle, stares at the door.

'Bath time for Daddy and Unca Lachie,' she observes.

'Yes, baby, Silly Daddy and Silly Lachlan are all muddy.'

The complaints about the state of Jayden's clothes, the state of Lachlan's hair, the *oh my god what is this in my pants? Is that a leech? Fuck, well, it looks like one. I don't care if it's just vegetable matter, Lachie, this is* **unacceptable!**

Amelia grins. 'Puck a leeeeeeech!' she says.

'Puck it completely,' Clara agrees.

More shouting, more complaints, a shower running, stopping, running again, thumping, what seems to be a tussle over the towels, someone crashing into the wash basket and then Jayden apparently collapsing into helpless laughter. A deeper voice joins him, and Clara knows that they're all right.

Clara and Amelia make a strategic withdrawal as the door opens and Jayden, a towel around his waist, darts down to the bedroom for clean clothes.

Lachlan emerges with his hair a wild tangle. He's wrapped in Clara's long silk robe, tied tightly at the waist. The right side of the robe bears the motif of a Bird of Paradise plant, stridently orange and pale green against the dark green background.

Lachlan tugs the robe around more closely and gives Clara a defiant look.

'Oh, be my guest,' she says, with a grin.

He rolls his eyes at her, then stops to give Amelia a kiss hello.

'Muddy Unca Lachie needs a clean!' says Amelia.

'Muddy Lachlan needs a change of clothes,' he says in reply.

'I like that,' Amelia points emphatically at the robe. 'It's pretty. You look pretty.'

'Thank you,' he says solemnly. 'You look nice, too.'

Jayden joins them, dressed in jeans but shirtless, towelling his hair dry.

'Daddy!'

'Baby girl!'

Father-daughter kisses are exchanged and Jayden scoops his girl up for a hug. He carries her to the sofa and drops down on it. Amelia manages a controlled landing so she ends up standing on his thighs. She pats his face while he kisses her fingers, then pats his chest.

She becomes fascinated by the scar on his left shoulder. She's familiar with it of course, but it's almost like it's the first time she's really noticed it. She pats the healthy skin, then the ridge of scar tissue. She traces her fingers over and over the puckered edges of it.

Clara wonders if she should distract the child, but Jayden is just watching her explore his skin. Clara can see Lachlan watching them too. There's that shame again, at what he'd done. After their father's imprisonment, Jayden had thrived and Lachlan, who'd been strong for so long, fell. So far.

He'd been high – again or still – and Jayden had tried to take care of him, and to get rid of his brother's stash. In the struggle, Lachlan had shoved Jayden through a plate glass sliding door. He'd nearly died. Lachlan had been beside himself with horror and grief, and had checked himself into rehab as soon as he knew Jayden would survive.

Four years clean now. Clara is proud of him, of how he's worked to climb back up again, and be strong again, for himself as well as Jayden. And he dotes on his niece, as though that little girl were his salvation.

Amelia, meanwhile, prods the marks on her father's chest, the skin and muscle, then pats at them with her soft, chubby hands.

'Daddy has an ouch,' she says. It's the term she's been using lately.

'A big ouch, yes.'

Amelia's eyes are large with curiosity and concern. 'Does it hurt?'

'Not any more.'

'Are you all better?'

'All better now.'

'It gets stiff some days,' Lachlan supplies suddenly. 'Especially when it's cold like today. I... forget, sometimes.'

The look Jayden gives Lachlan is a complicated thing, part forgiveness, part irritation, part affection, part exasperation. The way that brothers do.

'Poor Daddy's ouch,' says Amelia. 'I'll kiss it better,' and she plants a sloppy kiss on the smaller scar, the way her parents give her kisses to make it better when she falls or bumps her head. She draws back and pats the hard tissue again. 'It feels funny.'

'If you get a big ouch and then it gets better, sometimes the skin goes pale and hard like that,' Jayden says, his voice low and even. 'It's called a *scar*.'

Amelia considers this information. 'Mummy has a scar on her tummy and Lachie has a scar on his head and his side and his mouth. Unca Lachie has lots of scars. I'll kiss them better too.'

Jayden flicks a glance at Lachlan, as does Clara, and Lachlan is very still, seemingly caught between pride at Amelia's cleverness in noticing these things and regret that she is so aware of all his old hurts.

Amelia wriggles off Jayden's lap and toddles over to Lachlan. He has to manoeuvre a bit to maintain his modesty in the silk robe as she clambers into this lap, stands on his thighs and stares earnestly into this face. He lets her scrutinise him without comment.

She pats the scar at the corner of his mouth. 'Poor ouch.'

'It's nothing, Amelia,' he tells her.

She wetly kisses the side of his mouth anyway.

She peers at him further, then kisses the scar in his hairline. Then she sees something that Clara never knew she could. Amelia squats. Lachlan's hands are on her waist to keep her from falling, and she leans over to peer at the inside of his elbow on his left arm. The track marks are almost invisible.

Almost.

She goes to kiss them and Lachlan flinches, pulls away.

Amelia is immediately full of childish concern. 'Does it still hurt?'

Lachlan swallows.

'No.'

'Was it a big ouch?'

Clara holds her breath, wondering what he's going to say. Her husband, too, she notices has gone very still.

'Not any more,' Lachlan says carefully. 'Your Mummy and Daddy helped to make it better.'

'I want to make it better, too,' Amelia pouts.

'You do.'

'No. I have to kiss it better,' she insists. 'It's the rule.'

Reluctantly, refusing to look at Clara or Jayden, Lachlan holds his arm up. Amelia kisses the inside of his elbow with a loud, wet, noisy smack of her lips. A big kiss for a big ouch.

Then she grins up at him. 'All better?'

His reply is delayed while he clears his throat. 'All better,' he agrees.

Amelia's expression is full of pride – and then she is all giggles and shrieks as Lachlan ducks his head to pretend-bite her fingers. 'Don't, don't, don't!' she shrieks while making no actual effort to escape, 'Don't eat me up!' He manages to get to her belly and blow a raspberry (and narrowly avoid being accidentally kicked in the balls – that's unclehood for you) before letting her squirm free and run across the carpet to Clara

'Mummy, Mummy, don't let Unca Lachie eat me!'

Laughing, Clara drops to her knees and makes zombie-hands and gnashing-teeth motions at her. 'I'll eat you up!'

Jayden jumps to his feet, crouches down and chases Amelia all over the living room, threatening to *eat you all up* until Amelia turns on him, bares her teeth and says 'I'll eat YOU all up!' and chases him in turn.

By evening's end, Lachlan has commandeered a pair of Jayden's track pants and a t-shirt, both too short and too loose on him. He is lying on his back on the sofa, more or less respectable now, and explaining how her Daddy is the most graceless diver the world has ever seen. Amelia, belly-down on the carpet, falls asleep to his voice.

Jayden and Clara are dancing in the kitchen to the radio, kissing, cuddling. *Canoodling*. As date nights go, it hasn't been too bad.

Lachlan is the one who gets the call from the teacher. Clara and Jayden have taken off for a romantic anniversary week in New Zealand and the teenaged Amelia is in Lachlan's care for the duration.

Lachlan is a driving to the school hall as fast as he dare. He wants to go faster, but he can't risk being stopped by the police. He can't risk failing her, though his heart is hammering, because he feels he already has.

How did I miss it? he's thinking. *I didn't. I couldn't have. I would know if Amelia was an addict. If anyone would know that, I would. Therefore, she is not. There has been a mistake. I will fix this. I will fix this. Oh god, what if it's my fault?*

Lachlan doubts himself all the time, but he has never doubted Amelia.

And yet.

He remembers. He remembers choices made because they seemed to be the only ones left. He remembers wanting to calm the storm in his head and his heart, and finding only one way to do it. He remembers defiance and rage and despair and how a simple solution and a simpler needle gave him respite, if only for a while.

Amelia has not done this thing, but if she has, if she has done this unthinkable thing he will...he will...

And Lachlan remembers all the attempts to stop him, to help him, to cure him, to deny him, to fix him and it was all for nothing. Most of it didn't touch him; some of it made everything worse. And then he nearly killed Jayden, and he realised that the simple solution was no longer a solution, that what had helped no longer helped, that he was a danger to the only person who mattered.

So he chose a different path. It took a lot of work, a lot of help, a lot of forgiveness, but he chose it. Sixteen years later, he was still choosing it. Every day.

Lachlan thinks: *if it's true, and I can't work out how to help her, then I will... I'll...*

I will offer her my arm, he decides. *If nothing else will stop her, I will offer her my arm and take the cocaine with her. If I can't save her, I'll go down that path with her. I won't let her be alone. I will not let her walk that path alone. I don't care if I go down with her, as long as she's not alone like I felt I was...*

He stamps on the brake in front of the hall and dismisses that train of thought as destructive and not in the least helpful.

Which isn't to say he won't choose it, if he can't offer Amelia anything else.

He runs to the door, ignoring the loud music and the sound/scent of the close-packed bodies of dancing teenagers. He runs past a clump of kids having a furtive smoke by the bushes. As he bursts into the hall, a teacher is there to intercept him. She grabs Lachlan by the elbow and tugs him aside.

'Mr Carroway, it's Mrs Braithwaite. We've put Amelia in the caretaker's office,' she says.

'Where's Chloe Dyskstra?' Lachlan demands. This is Chloe's school dance. Chloe, 15, had invited Amelia along as her sort-of-date, on the logic that Amelia was a good friend, and good fun, and (Lachlan knew, although Chloe hadn't said as much) Amelia was meant to be the perfect wingman for the evening. 'They were here together.'

'We're looking for her now.'

That's ominous. But first things must come first.

Lachlan follows Mrs Braithwaite down the hall and into the caretaker's office. She lets him in then goes in search of Chloe Dykstra.

Amelia stands in the middle of the room and glares at him. She is furious. He hasn't seen her in such a rage. It stops him like a wall.

'Amelia?'

'If you believe one word of that lie for an instant, I'll never speak to you again.'

The relief that floods through him makes his breath hitch briefly, but immediately he's calm and still and he knows he can and will do anything. Amelia is all right and so nothing bad can happen now. 'Don't be ridiculous. I know you better than that.'

Amelia scowls but nods, satisfied.

'Tell me what happened?'

'Some fart-doodle planted this gear on Chloe. She told me about this guy at school who was stealing from the science lab. She warned him off and said she'd report him if he didn't stop right away. Next thing, I see some dude going to a teacher and pointing at Chloe, and you know, he *looked* like a fart-doodle. So I got to Chloe's bag and grabbed the stuff out first – a needle and a foil. Arsehole. Then that idiot teacher found it on *me* before I could ditch it and wouldn't listen when I tried to explain.'

'Did you see him plant it in Chloe's bag?'

'I didn't have to *see* it, did I?' she says scornfully. Lachlan, in spite of himself, grins. Amelia was always a smart one.

'But he's meant to be a Grade A student, and other people do *love* direct evidence, don't they?' Amelia sighs her bitter disappointment then raises her chin to glare over his shoulder at the sounds coming down the passage.

Mrs Braithwaite brings Chloe into the room. Chloe has been crying.

'Meely!' Chloe pulls away from the teacher's grip on her arm and rushes to her friend, who wraps her in a hug, but does not stop glaring at the teacher.

'You will show some manners, young lady,' the teacher snaps at Amelia.

'I will when you stop being an *idiot*,' ripostes Amelia. Lachlan knows he's not supposed to encourage her in being disrespectful to adults, but honestly, the woman *is* an idiot and Lachlan is not going to berate Amelia for so intelligently noticing this fact.

Mrs Braithwaite takes a breath, no doubt to demand he insist on Amelia exercising manners, but he turns his back on her and faces the girls.

'Now,' he says. 'The facts.'

Mrs Braithwaite, getting angry, starts to tell him about the drug paraphernalia found on Amelia, and possible police charges. Lachlan shushes her. 'Let Chloe tell the story.'

'It's nothing to do with Ms Dykstra.'

'It's everything to do with me,' says Chloe fiercely, and Mrs Braithwaite is forced to silence in the face of the girl's sincerity. Mrs

Braithwaite is unhappy, but she's not an idiot. She folds her arms and waits for the new data.

Between them, Amelia and Chloe tell the story of Jez Palmer's petty larceny and attempted frame-up. Braithwaite's lips are pursed. Lachlan gives the teacher an assessing look.

'I think perhaps I should find young Jez and call his father as well,' she decides. She gives a glare to Amelia. 'You could perhaps have told me this earlier.'

Amelia opens her mouth to snap that she'd *tried*, but she catches the look in her uncle's eye, the one that says *play along now, Amelia, we're starting to win.* She closes her mouth. 'I was upset,' is all she says.

Mrs Braithwaite summons Lachlan to talk with her briefly in the hall. 'Stay with the girls for the moment,' she says. 'I'll see what I can get from Jez. Perhaps we can avoid police involvement.'

'I won't have Amelia suffering because of that vindictive little bastard,' says Lachlan, voice tight with protective indignation.

The teacher raises an eyebrow at him. 'Jez Palmer is certainly not the Golden Child he pretends to be,' she says. 'But Amelia Carroway has her moments too.'

'She's a bit… brash,' he concedes, because right now Mrs Braithwaite has too much power over them. 'But she's also *honest.*'

Mrs Braithwaite gives him a funny sort of knowing smile, and Lachlan thinks maybe she knows a lot more about Jez Palmer's true nature, and Amelia's and Chloe's, than she's letting on.

'Stay with the girls,' she repeats. 'I'll be back shortly.'

When Mrs Braithwaite returns an hour later, it is with the brief news that Jez Palmer has confessed all, that Mr Palmer senior will be handling the discipline for the matter, and that unless they wish to press charges, everyone is free to go home.

Chloe is too embarrassed by her lapse to want anything more to do with it. Amelia seems to feel that justice has been served, because she was looking out the window and she could see how Mr Palmer was berating his son on the way back to the car.

Mrs Dykstra shows up and hugs her daughter while getting the story. Chloe and Amelia hug goodbye and promise to see each other tomorrow. All's well, so they say, that ends well, even though the dance has been spoiled.

Lachlan, with Mrs Dykstra's blessing, says he'll take the girls to a live gig soon, to see a band they both like, to make up for it. Mrs Dykstra, who is single, is promised a ticket too, and she grins like it's Christmas for her as well.

Amelia and Lachlan are silent for a short while in the car ride home. Lachlan is still high on the relief of knowing that Amelia is all right, *she's all right, she's going to be all right...*

He doesn't flinch when Amelia reaches out to rub her hand along his forearm. Under his shirt, the track marks of his past feel the passage of her fingers through the cloth.

'I would never,' she says.

He wants to say 'I know'. What he says is: 'Lives don't always go the way we plan.'

She squeezes the muscle under her hand. 'I'm sorry for whatever made you pick that path.'

Lachlan swallows. 'It was... it made sense at the time.'

'You must have been so lonely.'

Lachlan blinks.

She smiles at him, and he smiles back. She withdraws her hand and folds it with the other one in her lap.

Amelia looks at Lachlan again.

'I know you don't like me noticing them,' she says, and does not need to elaborate. *The needle marks. The scars on his body, the marks of violence.* She has scars too, he knows. For all that he wanted to spare her, he couldn't, and there is a map on her body of mishaps and accidents. Nothing given to her deliberately, though. No harm done to her through malice or anger. He thinks he would destroy anyone who tried.

His silence doesn't faze her. 'Do you know what Mum says about scars?'

Lachlan shakes his head minutely.

'She says that the thing about scars is that you only get them if you survive. Some scars are bad and some of them slow you down a lot, but if you have a scar, life tried to kill you and didn't succeed.'

'Is that what she says?'

'I was asking her about hers, you know, the one from the C-section when she had me. She says she doesn't mind it. She could have died, or I could have died, but we didn't. The scar proves she outlived death, because the dead don't heal.'

Clara, thinks Lachlan, *really is more than good enough for my brother.*

'We talked a lot about scars that day,' Amelia continued. 'Because you and Dad have so many and I wanted to know what it meant.'

Lachlan swallows. 'What else did she say, then?'

'Mum says that some scars are what life gives you for being careless or unlucky, but at least you can learn something from them. Then, she says, some scars you get because you took risks so you could grow. And then, she says, some scars you get because you choose them, so you can protect someone you love or something that matters.'

Lachlan thinks about all of his scars; the ones he got through carelessness and bad luck; the ones he got through risk. The ones he chose.

'Those scars you have, on your head and mouth, the one on your ribs… you got those making sure that drunk old bastard didn't hurt Dad. Mum says those scars are like… sort of like badges that love makes in your skin.'

Lachlan pulls the car to the side of the road, because it's dangerous to drive when you can't see. Tears are sliding out of his eyes, faster now that he's closed them. Amelia undoes her seatbelt and reaches across the seat to wrap him in an awkward sideways hug.

'I know you made mistakes,' she says, her cheek resting on his shoulder, 'but you made up for them, and that's something my grandfather never did. You've got badges, even if you didn't want them, and Dad's scar… I don't think you know. But he and mum, they say that's his badge. Because it helped you to stop. He got his brother back. So he doesn't mind.'

Lachlan's hands are over his eyes and he can't stop crying.

'This thing,' says Amelia, hugging him, 'with the drugs. I promise you. I'd never do that. And if I'm ever that lonely, I promise. I'll come to you. But I never will be.'

Lachlan gathers his girl close, his nose in her hair, revelling in the miracle of her. *No*, he promises her silently, *you never will be.*

CHANGELING

Bloody treacherous faeries.

Faeries get fancies. They see things they like and just take 'em. Pretty, shiny, sparkly things.

And also babies.

Faeries have an unfortunate tradition of taking a shine to some chubby little darling and whisking it away to the Land of Faerie. There they feed it little cakes and sips of flower nectar and generally spoil it rotten.

They're not stupid, though, faeries. Even they have noticed that vanishing infants and toddlers create an awkward kerfuffle amongst those slow-witted and reality-bound humans. Some of those humans are annoyingly attached to their offspring, as well as irritatingly persistent in trying to get them back.

So faeries leave a substitute. A little changeling, very much like the child it's replacing, but quieter. The changeling cries less, fusses less, is more placid and obedient and docile. With this sly bit of subterfuge, the faeries hope that the humans will just be grateful that their infant is suddenly much more pliable and easy to manage. The faeries hope the humans won't pursue the matter. Parents and their attachments to their offspring are just so *pestilential*.

It's not going to work this time though. Do you see that sparkly little jacket? That pink and spangly thing with flowers in it? That belongs to a bright and lively little girl who is always chattering and giggling and, well, yes, also screaming sometimes. She's a kid. She doesn't know all the words yet for what she wants and needs, let alone have oratory skills to help sway her audience to her way of thinking. When she's a teenager, she's going to be absolute hell, in the best possible way. In the meantime she chatters and giggles and screams as occasion demands.

Right now, she is making the Faerie Queen wish heartily she never saw the kid. Right now, she is expressing her opinions rather forcefully, even with her limited vocabulary, about the taste of bleeding *flower nectar* and the use of cobwebs – GODDAMN COBWEBS – as a blanket.

Have these faeries never noticed what kind of spiders live in the Real Plane that is called Australia, that this little girl quite rightly views with concern? It's hard to feel cosy and relaxed sleeping under a little blankie made of the butt-silk of venomous things.

Okay so maybe the kid has a problem and if she just thought about it she'd work it through and think the cobweb blankets were neat.

On the other hand, she's thinking, *you are not my real parents,* who would never make me sleep under poisonous spider butt-silk sheets and wouldn't make me drink bloody flower water and where the absolute hell is my bunny and my ninja and My Little Pony and ***MY MUUUUUUUUUM?***

For their part, her parents are not impressed with the obvious substitute they found in the stroller. This whey-faced, doughy, dull little baby with all the personality of an undercooked bread roll.

Humans are not of themselves magic, but they're not stupid, and they are, as explained, inexplicably attached to their children.

These parents are going back to the gardens with this dull little changeling and they're going to stand under the tree where they last saw their own child and they are going **demand** the return of their daughter. Loudly. Repeatedly. Insistently. With many, many swear words and very little in the way of attempts to bargain with the magic folk. Screw diplomacy.

Give us back our daughter you creepy little winged freaks before we find a way to burn down your fairy fucking halls.

And frankly, the Faerie Queen is going to be much too relieved to be rid of this bold, brave, uncompromising, strong-willed and vocally enhanced human child to worry overmuch about the lack of courtesy.

HOORFROST

Author's note: This is an origin story for *Kitty and Cadaver*, about a rock and roll band that fights monsters with music.

London June 1258

If anyone but Will knew what was causing this snow – that thing in the river – they weren't doing anything about it. Will was, though. He was swearing.

'God's *nails!*' Will swore as he trudged through the fresh fall of snow. He suspected he'd wandered off the road to the Ludgate. Surely this grove of elms was further west than he meant to be? He couldn't see the sun, much less any shadows, to judge the time in this milky light, but it must be no later than the third hour, barely half way to noon.

The air was cold enough that his swarthy skin – heritage of a Spanish mother with Moorish blood – was relatively pale in the frame of his dark hair. His dark eyes ached in the glare of the snow and cloud.

He cursed as his feet crunched down.

God curse this winter and the famine that it brings; God pity the thousands dead for want of food. God curse the frozen Thames and the strange skies of this unspeakable winter. God curse the even stranger thing that lurks in the river's mud.

And triple curse this cocking *snow that will not cease falling.*

When cursing didn't help, Will tried to spell it warmer with a rhyme.

Un-freeze, damn'd-dirt, God's-heart, it's-cold.

His teeth chattered too hard for the chant to be spoken, and numb with cold as he was, it was a poor chant. The result was weak – he never could make much use of water; earth responded best to his call – but the beat of it kept his body moving, less cold than if he stood still. He'd have unslung his tabor, but the drum's skin was brittle with frost. Even encased in fur gloves, his hands were stiff. At least he had boots, and the moss stuffed in the left stopped the snow leeching in through the hole and biting his heel.

Having no lodgings, St Martin's Le Grand's curfew knell last night had forced Will to sleep beyond the city walls or risk prison. He'd sheltered in St Bartholomew's Priory – its founder had been a minstrel, and the brothers there had given him water and a bite of what little bread they had. This morning he'd left, hoping to find some scraps.

But the bells of St Martin's Le Grand hadn't rung to herald the opening of the markets, and that was how William Hawk knew he no longer had a choice in what he did next. Whether the problem was no bell, or no markets, the silence meant this unnatural winter was deepening and a cold and hungry death was coming for them all.

He didn't know what to do about the thing in the river either, but he would make his way back into the city to do it. If the church was wrong and God loved him after all, he would succeed.

A sweet, fluting sound pierced Will's cursing and he halted, listening.

It was the trill of a pipe, played dancingly by a musician of rare skill. Will felt warmer just hearing it. And then his fingers ached less. Will grinned with sudden certainty. He followed the music through the woods and paused when he found its source.

A young man knelt on the ground in a circle of bare earth, playing his pipe. His dark blond hair stood up all over his head, as though he'd spent the morning scratching through it. The cold made his cheeks ruddy, and his grey-blue eyes were dark-rimmed with fatigue.

The melody he played was intricate, dancing swiftly through flurries of notes. The melody line was strong and the notes around it did not rise and fall so much as build and flicker.

In the centre of the ring of earth was a fire, small but bright, fuelled only by air and music. The ground on which the piper sat was dry, but beyond him the snow was pristine, freshly fallen white, marked with the footprints that showed the way by which the piper had come.

Will stepped out of the shelter of the trees.

'God give you good day, friend.'

The music stopped abruptly and the young man rose, his wooden whistle clutched in his left hand, a knife in his right. His stark glare was equal parts anger and fear.

Will held up his hands, palm out.

'Peace, friend. I too am a musician,' he gestured to the drumsticks tucked into his belt. 'Shall I play for you?' He reached slowly for the sticks without waiting for a reply.

The other did not lower his knife, or move, or speak.

Will fetched his sticks but didn't unhitch his tabor. He knelt. With the side of his hand, he pushed aside the snow to reveal the frozen ground. He pulled the gloves off his chapped red hands, took up his sticks, and beat the ground with one stick, then the other.

'Look to your fire, good fellow,' he said, and sang as he played the tattoo.

Slumber not, oh root and seed
for Winter has now overstayed
Earth bring forth thy buried tinder
Let fire feed; the frostbite hinder

The fire feeding on air was fading, but the ground beneath it was heaving, cracking, as the fallen branches of the autumn and early winter broke through, pushed on the backs of shifting roots. The fire licked down towards the dry wood and took hungry hold. It crackled and burned brighter.

The heartbeat drum, the breathing fife
We play to ask you give us life
The strength you had when spring did turn
Release as bones of trees to burn

And flamed higher still.

Will stopped playing and the cosy fire feasted on the fuel that the earth had given them.

'We are brothers,' said Will to the astonished man. 'Fear no harm from me.'

The man considered this, then finally put away his knife. 'Sit by the fire, then. Maybe we'll be friends. My name is Thomas Rowan.'

'And I'm William Hawk. The friends I once had called me Will.' He sat next to Thomas Rowan by the fire.

'You once had?'

'Most are dead now,' Will said. 'Famine and disease, mostly, though sheer cold took its share. My fellows in music. They froze to death on the road a week ago. I dared the charge of heresy and witchcraft to keep us warm and alive, but they fled in terror of me.' Will stared into the fire. 'And therefore are too dead to denounce me a heretic.'

Thomas shifted restlessly. 'My brother had a lovely voice,' he said at last, his own dark with sorrow. 'He tried to sing some safety for us in Lord Hanley's hall, but Hanley hadn't enough to feed us either, so now Dickon is lying with all the others at Spitalfields, waiting for the ground to thaw enough for burials. I hoped to find some other fortune before I joined him as food for worms.'

'I'm sorry for your grief, brother Thomas.'

'And I for yours, brother Will. Where are you going now? Or are you, like me, walking towards death rather than wait for it to come hunting?'

'Walking towards death, I suppose. This winter's taken everything I had, but there's a cause for this bitter season. Something sits in the mud beneath the Thames. I fear it's addled with some ancient, raging sorrow. I feel it when I play the earth. I don't think it means to destroy us, but this strange winter has woken it.'

'You sound sorry for it.' Thomas was not pleased.

'Not really,' said Will. 'The death it brings may not be its intent, but death it brings all the same.'

'You think to kill it?'

'I don't know what it is; still less if it can die. I thought I might try to sing it back to sleep.'

'And if it doesn't want to sleep?'

'I die. But I'll die regardless, in this cold. I'd rather die trying to live.'

Thomas considered this philosophy with a frown.

'How will you make it sleep?'

'I could sing a cradlesong to it. I've sent many to sleep in my time as a minstrel, but that's only ale and my voice.' Will laughed wryly and his breath puffed in cloud. 'I can sing a little magic, but it speaks best through my tabor. Usually I use it to keep bugs from biting, or dry the ground when it rains. Little tricks that hurt none and comfort only me. But I once drummed a stalking wolf into curling like a puppy at my feet, and when I was a boy, a spirit rose from a ruined hall and tried to possess my father. I beat the stones with my hands and sang the ghost to pieces. This thing is doubtless stronger than wolves and ghosts, but I'll die fighting it rather than starve or be frozen blue at the side of the road. What say you?'

'My pipe isn't as clever as Dickon's voice was, but it's yours for this. I've a knife as well.'

'Any tool is useful,' agreed Will.

The city gates were open but untended. Will and Thomas, filled with disquiet, passed through the Ludgate without hindrance. Without fish to sell, the old fish market was silent. Theirs were the only footprints in Thames Street. The only sound was the caw of a raven to the northwest, where Wall Brook was as frozen as the rest.

The quality of the milky light seemed unchanging, but Will thought he felt the dusk descending by the time they reached the place where the riverbanks crackled with wrongness. The Thames was frozen from shore to shore. Spanning the ice was the London Bridge, built in stone under the reign of King Henry's father, King John. The Chapel of St Thomas on the Bridge stood lonely in the centre. The Brethren of the Bridge who prayed there were either all at prayer or huddled before fires in their Bridge House. Or perhaps they were dead like so many others. Will saw none, wherever they were.

Thomas had shoved his gloved hands into his armpits in an attempt to keep warm.

'Where is it then, this angry, grieving monster?' Thomas' scowl suggested he had an angry, grieving monster of his own, furled underneath his heart.

'Somewhere near. I can feel it when I drum.'

Thomas stamped his feet on the snow. Nothing came to the summons. 'You say the strange winter woke it,' said Thomas. 'Didn't the monster cause this hell?'

Will knelt on the ground with his drum. 'That's not what the earth tells me.'

For a man who had woven fire out of air with a fife, Thomas was sceptical. 'You talk to the soil often, do you?'

'The earth's a good listener,' replied Will, unruffled. 'She holds many secrets, and sometimes she shares them with me.'

'What's the secret of this killing winter, then?'

Will pushed the snow aside, took off his glove and placed his hand on the bare ground. 'The earth is round, did you know? Full ripe round like an apple but she has a fire at her heart. Sometimes the fire bursts through her skin. She has burning mountains that birth burning rocks, and the smoke of her womb covers the sky.'

'Mountains have burned and spat rocks and smoke before,' said Thomas, 'but winter has only been winter.'

'This particular mountain burst like nothing before it,' said Will solemnly. 'Do you remember the red sunsets in the spring? Colours as violent as blood, the sun lighting on the smoke from the other side of the world? In that fire's wake, summer never came; then winter came and stayed.'

'I was here for those sunsets too,' said Thomas drily. 'For the failed harvests, the dying cattle, the floods that washed away what little had grown, and then froze the rest.'

'Well, that's what woke the thing that slept in the river's mud. It's been here longer than that, of course. Hundreds of years.'

'Does the mud tell you that?'

'It does.' Will rested his hands on his haunches and cocked an eye at Thomas, who glared at the road of ice where a river once ran. 'Curb your anger, brother Thomas. I didn't make the mountains burn, the skies turn red or the river freeze. I only listen to what the magic tells me.'

Thomas' eyes did not shift from the Thames. 'Shall I tell you what the air says?'

'I'd be most interested to hear.'

'I hear a lament, William. A voice colder than the frozen wastes of the Viking north cries for Baldr, whoever that may be. It begs forgiveness and for punishment for Hoor. For itself.'

Will listened with all his body and thought he heard something of the lament. A cry crackling with cold; the sound of ice breaking like a heart.

'I hear it. It must have done something terrible, to sound so.'

'I'd offer it punishment, if I could,' said Thomas.

'You have no pity for the thing?'

'It killed my sister.'

'Brother, you said.'

'Both,' growled Thomas.

Grief and rage, thought Will, are not the purview of monsters alone.

'What now?' demanded Thomas.

'I never heard this cry before, and I've often passed this way. The ash sky brought winter early and woke the owner of this voice, to cry out. Its lament is what makes the winter last so long. I'll sing a cradlesong, I think.'

'We should kill it.' Thomas' knife was in his hand again.

'Are you very determined to die?' Will asked gently. 'For I think that taking your little blade to this creature will accomplish that nicely. If you're not so very set on dying, though, I thinking putting it back to sleep may give us a better chance of seeing tomorrow.'

'What should we do, then?'

Will wouldn't admit that he didn't know. All his small magics hadn't prepared him for the task he'd taken on. Instinct told him to connect to the earth, however, so he walked to the edge of the frozen Thames and knelt on the ice-hard mud. After a moment, Thomas joined him.

Will began with a tattoo drummed on the ground and Thomas

began to play a warm melody around it, so that the ground softened and steamed.

'Play on,' said Will. He tapped on the ground with one drum stick, tucking the other stick into his belt, and pressed his fingers into the mud to listen to the earth. Will's fingers felt the pulse of the ground, slow and dark and deep. Wet and steady. The Earth was old and patient. The thing waking in it, though much older than London, was still younger than the ground on which London stood, and younger than the river under which it lay.

With the one hand, Will slowed the rhythm of the tune they were making and sang sweetly to the thing under the mud.

> *Hush thy heart, great beast*
> *Let sorrow fly away.*
> *Dwell thee not on life's great hurts*
> *But rest thee while thee may*
> *Softly still thy mind*
> *Let slumber soothe thy pain*
> *Merciful is winter's end*
> *When springtime starts her reign*

Thomas' playing curled around the beat, but his heart was seething. The result was not a lilting cradlesong but something tight and thick; not a letting go but a squeezing of the fist. Will understood too late. Before he could fall silent, or withdraw, he felt it.

Eyes opened deep in mud and *looked right through him.*

Will fell back, a gasp of fear trapping frosty air in his lungs. He tried to cry a warning to the piper and couldn't, so that Thomas' surprise at the abrupt end to their cradlesong was all for Will landing arse-first on the ice.

And then Thomas' eyes grew wide and his mouth opened in horror but no sound came out. The piper's hair stood on end, and so did Will's in sympathy as the ice crackled and cracked and began to heave, and he knew, he knew, he *oh God* he knew that the thing that he'd felt looking through him was rising up behind him through the mud and ice, and he knew he would never see the moon or sun or stars again, he would never know warmth or bread again, he would never know love again…

The piece of the Thames on which he sat cracked, heaved, tilted, and he slid down it. One hand still clutched the drum stick, his tabor banged against his back where it hung, the stick in his belt jammed into his ribs.

He crashed into Thomas who had instinctively opened his arms to receive him, and they fell in a tangle on the snow and lay there, arms about each other in terror, for comfort, and looked at the being which had risen from the frozen river.

It almost looked like a man: tall, broad-shouldered, with arms and legs. But its body was made of mud and chunks of ice, pieces of bone and wood. Its chest was the mouldering portion of the prow of an ancient boat, sunk a thousand years ago. Its hair bristled in shards of weed and pottery: clay-brown, glazed blue, fragments of figures and colours.

It shook its bewildered head, scattering sleet. It raised its chin and opened its mouth and howled at the snow-and-ash laden sky.

Hailstones fell. Will and Thomas flung their arms over their heads and they huddled over each other. Fist-sized chunks of ice glanced off their arms, their bodies, bruising them. One struck Thomas on the forehead, drawing blood. Another crashed into Will's fingers and he felt a bone break.

The man of mud with ice blue eyes roared into the air words they didn't understand. Waves of grief and rage rolled off the sound and from its body and through their flesh and somehow within the waves of sound, Thomas heard meaning.

I am cursed. I am wronged. I am doomed.

Thomas struggled to his feet with his blood frozen in a streak down his face, and he roared back at the creature who hadn't even seen them.

'We are all cursed, all wronged, all doomed! We don't all destroy the world!'

The creature ceased howling and tilted its head down, then moved it slowly left and right, listening. Its ice blue eyes were unseeing, but its face was wrapped with confusion and irritation.

'What are you to speak to me?' it emanated.

'I'm a man you've wronged.'

'I do not know you.'

'Yet you did me harm. You killed my brother.'

'No,' said the giant. 'Not brother. *Sister*.'

'He was my brother and we killed him, you and I.'

The giant was confused again. 'My brother is dead. I slew him by mistake.'

'I killed mine with negligence, selfishness and fear,' said Thomas. He wept and the tears froze on his cheeks.

'I was jealous, I admit,' said the mud-man. 'Baldr was so beloved of our mother, she made all living things swear to never harm him. The other gods threw weapons at my brother to test him, but beautiful Baldr only laughed as all things kept their promise. But Loki tricked me. He gave me mistletoe, which had been too young to swear peace to Baldr, and in my envy I threw it, ignorant of its power. One little dart of mistletoe from my hand and my brother laughs no more. Baldr was slain at my hand.' It howled into the air again then slumped, blind eyes turned towards the musicians. 'Vali killed me in just wrath, but a god never truly dies.'

Will stirred from his watching. He heard Thomas speak to the mud-man, and heard its replies in his blood and bones, through the earth. 'A god, are you? How is it you're here?'

'Loki bound my spirit to an earthen jar. He delivered me to the hands of men to be a talisman. I have travelled far from Asgard on warships, but I never brought those Captains to victory. Another of my brother's tricks. He never tires of them.'

'Baldr?'

'Loki is also my brother.' It frowned. 'He is not always my brother. Perhaps my sister too, sometimes. He takes many shapes.'

'My brother also had other shapes before we killed him.'

'I did not harm your brother.'

'A fire on the other side of the world covered the sun with ash and brought a winter cold enough to wake you,' snarled Thomas. 'Now you're killing the world with ice.'

'I am the god of ice,' it said, as though such deaths couldn't be helped.

'Do you have a name, Loki's brother?' asked Will casually.

'I am Hoor.'

'I think I've heard of you,' said Will. 'By the name of Hod.'

'I have many names.'

Thomas scowled. 'Well, Hoor of Many Names, you killed Dickon with your cruel winter.'

'Not alone,' said the ice god Hoor and his tone wasn't kind. 'Negligence, selfishness and fear, you said.'

'That's right,' said Thomas, just as ruthless. 'We're a pair alike, we two. Just as you killed Baldr with envy, foolishness and spite.'

Will held his breath, sure from the fury on Hoor's face that their luck was done and death was coming.

Instead, Hoor laughed, grimly, without mirth. 'I did.'

'I know what you did to Baldr. Shall I tell you my tale?' asked Thomas.

'Did you kill a god?'

'A god can't die, you said, but my sister-brother died twice, first as maiden then as man.'

Hoor bent his head closely to hear more. Will, likewise, listened. His broken finger throbbed but he gripped his drumstick tight anyway, unsure of what to do, or if anything was possible.

'Lulie was born a rosy lass who could never be a maiden. She never learned the skill of it or to desire that she should,' Thomas said. His voice rose and fell in storytelling cadences, but it was filled with the sharpness of a secret's first telling.

'From youth, my older sister would answer to nothing but Dickon. She was boyish in all things, from her large hands and loud laugh to the careless way she ran and climbed and fought with boys who challenged her wildness. Dickon caused our parents only grief, except for when she sang, for then she sounded like an angel.

'Dickon would not relent in being Dickon, and would not be made to wive, since her body and her heart to womanly virtues would not strive. Dickon grew tall but lean; her menses would not come. At last our parents gave up persuading Dickon to be Lulie and accepted their daughter was a son. As a family, we buried Lulie as a name. Dickon my brother from that day became.'

Will pressed his hands to the earth and ignored the ache of one broken finger while all the rest tapped faintly in the dirt, picking out the uneven rhythm of Thomas' story.

'To me Dickon confessed he'd found a way, a trick of song to make his body obey. To banish his irregular courses and sing his chest flat. I confessed I had my own tricks after that. With my self-made bone and yew pipe I charmed the partridge and the lark to my knife. I fluted fishes to my net, fires to light, clouds to part, warmth to night. We found when I played and Dickon sang, we charmed coins to our purse and our good fortune rang.'

Will felt the dirt under his fingers tremble, though Hoor was, like him, transfixed by the story. Will found in it echoes of a ballad heard last summer. The long tale written by a sarcastic Cornish poet going by Heldris. In the tale, an earl's daughter was raised as a boy named Silence. "The boy who is a girl" – *li vallés qui est mescine* in the poet's hand. What else had the ballad contained? *Jo cuidai Merlin engignier, Si m'ai engignié.* "I thought to deceive Merlin but I have deceived myself".

Will already knew this similar story of Dickon didn't end well. Yet the story compelled, as did Thomas' telling of it.

'We brothers thought it easier to sing for wealth than learn our father's trade, and we did well, until a burning mountain this early winter made. Will says the cold stirred you from your sleep. You brought a bitter cold and we starved, and so my brother's magic grew weak.'

All Thomas' rage seemed now self-directed, the nails of his own curled fists biting into his palm, drawing blood. The vibration in the earth under Will's hands shuddered.

'Dickon dared not carouse with pages and with squires, the body he'd shaped for himself did not hold true. But I was cold and wished for the warmth of other companionship, and the cheerful comradery that ale and wine imbue. I wished to forget, with men like me, that men may die of want. To spend a night without Dickon's fear and rage for his body changing, thin and gaunt. So I went to the woods with other men and wasted life and time, and burned fuel that should have had more prudent use, and fed on Hanley's stolen bread and wine.'

Thomas' chest was heaving as though he had climbed mountains to tell his tale. His body was trembling with the strength of his feeling, which fortunately also masked the insistent tapping of Will's nine healthy fingers on the ground. Will was getting the hang of the rhythm now, thrumming under the surface of the earth, under the surface of Thomas' tale, and under the surface of the ice. A small magic, unheeded as yet by the blind monster.

Will thought he saw something moving in the air, a flap of dark wings. He thought he felt something moving in the sluggish water under the ice, a deep river green. He didn't let himself be distracted, but continued to tap the beat and listen to the words Thomas spoke. There was no spell in them yet, but for all that, they were spellbinding. Hoor, unspeaking, listened hard to every word.

'I returned, drunk, to find Lord Hanley, seeking his unfaithful staff, discovered my poor Dickon whose face and body were womanly round and soft. He could not find the thieves of wine and wood, so he punished the one who had lied to him, though done less harm than good. He locked Dickon in the snow and ice in a pen beside the woodshed, and that's where I found my brother-sister frozen, where he fell and broke his dear head.'

The air almost hummed with the tension of this ending, the death of Dickon.

'Negligence, selfishness and fear,' said Hoor. 'But yours was not the hand that slew your dear.'

Did Hoor know he'd spoken in this land's English tongue, and made a rhyme to add to the magic all around?

'Yet I'm culpable. Dickon died because of me. He also froze to death because of you. The fault is ours to share or refuse equally. You who your brother with envy, foolishness and spite slew.'

Hoor's voice rumbled in its chest of mud and ice and bone, a dark agreement at the remorse.

'What should we do, we guilty brothers?' Thomas asked. 'Would our own deaths make amends for what we've done?'

'I will find redemption or annihilation at prophesied Ragnarok. What fate do I deserve? What should my fate become?'

'Await your final reckoning undisturbed in the mud.'

Will's hands had taken up the rhythm from his aching fingers. His broken finger was swollen but numb. He had begun to hum under his breath.

> *Hush thy heart, great Hoor*

'I am weary with the waiting,' grumbled Hoor. His ramshackle face began to sag.

'Become undone, as was my brother in his blood,' said Thomas, only he was singing now. Will sang softly beneath Thomas' loud, clear voice.

> *Hush thy heart, great Hoor*
> *This body be not thine*

'What are you doing?' demanded Hoor.

> *Dwell thee not on rage and pain*
> *This England is not thine.*

Wet earth and mouldering rubble sloughed away from the body Hoor had made for himself. For a brief moment, he diminished – then, alarmed, enraged, he opened his muddy maw and roared. His body began to form again. Made of mud, stone, ice, slaughterhouse bones and the waterlogged hulls of sunken ships, he reared up three, four, five times as large as before. God-like truly in his fury, yet like a mortal in his desperation.

He raised his arms, as if to bring them smashing down.

Thomas' voice joined with Will's then. Neither had sung this song before, yet the words came to them both, the magic of earth and air combining, and some of water too, where elements of air and earth were entwined in it.

Hoor's arms remained up, his feet melded with the riverbed, straining to move. Unmoving. Arrested by the magic in the music.

A flash of dark feathers caught the periphery of Will's vision again as he drummed the earth, hard now, feeling nothing but the slam of his palms against the cold ground and the slam of his grieving heart against his chest.

A raven's cawing voice suddenly accompanied them, making words in a creaking undertone.

No god may truly perish
Great Hoor, you cannot drown

Hoor's blind-eyed face lifted to the sky, then dropped. A groan vibrated through the air, Hoor's protest against the song-spell that was undoing his Thames-hewn body.

Surrender to the water
Let slumber take thee down

The mud and bones, the ice and rocks and lumber sagged to a sodden mound. In the centre of the mound was a stone jar sealed in silver and amber. The swell of the jar's body was carved with runes and symbols. An archer's bow was etched tightly bound in stylised strands of mistletoe around the centre, spreading up and over the seal.

Wings flapped and a large raven alighted on the ground between Will and Thomas.

'Drum on,' it croaked at Will, then cocked its head at Thomas. 'Your undoing and unwaking song is good. Sing again.'

Thomas sang again. Will beat the rhythm and sang a harmony to make the song stronger.

The raven tapped its beak on the jar, and the amber in it glowed, the silver shone, the stone swelled and thickened, so that the finest crack between seal and jar was rendered seamless.

Then the raven seized the edge of the jar and flapped its wings, tipping the jar over into the turmoil of mud and melting ice. It cawed at the river.

The monstrous shape that Will had earlier sensed roiled strangely under the thinned ice. It heaved, and was gone. Afterwards, Will could not name what he saw. It writhed like a serpent, but was large and thick and scaled, and long ribbons of hair, or weed, had streamed from it. A great, dark maw full of teeth had opened, and shut, and then it was gone. The stone jar, too.

The raven hopped and swept its wings down, rising, then it flew across the frozen Thames, following the shadow of the thing beneath the ice. When it reached London Bridge, the raven came to rest on one of the bridge's great curved starlings – the rubble-filled bulwarks that protected bridge's pillars against the current, wayward boats, sundry debris and other things that lived in the muddy shadows.

The raven clicked its beak and made sounds which Will could hear from the riverbank. Now a more trilling call, now a sharp caw, and then a strange warbling.

'Did that raven truly speak to us?' Will asked Thomas softly.

'We've sung a god into a pot, and you ask about a talking raven?'

'It seems the easier discussion,' confessed Will.

Thomas grinned at him, mad-gleeful. 'Then yes, brother Will. I believe the raven who is singing to the river spoke to us.'

Will nodded. 'And the god?'

'Sung to sleep into a jar, as far as I can tell.'

'Good. Good. And we're still alive?'

'Yes.'

'However did we manage these miracles?'

Thomas looked down at the instrument he held in his hand. 'With a yew pipe.'

'I never even got to use my drum.'

They fell silent again as the raven at the bridge took flight, returning to them. As it approached, Will could already feel the air becoming less cold.

The raven alighted on Will's drum where it lay on the ground.

'Hoor was never very clever. You don't have to be Loki to trick him into his prison,' said the raven.

'What are you?' Will dared to ask.

'I am Heimdal, charged by Odin to watch over his foolish son. I think he meant my name as a joke,' said the raven. It tilted its head to stare at them again. 'Loki's mischief makes trouble for us all. I imagine it will make more trouble for you, as well.'

'What kind of trouble?' Thomas asked, but the bird had launched into the air again.

Above them, the clouds parted and the pale sun gleamed through.

Thomas and Will watched the bird fly east towards the Tower of London keep.

'Should we warn King Henry that a magic raven is living in his tower?' Will asked.

'I think we should leave London, as Heimdal the Raven suggests.'

Will fetched his drum, which he slung awkwardly across his back. The action caused his broken finger to throb painfully, feeling having regrettably returned to it. He cradled his hurt hand. 'I know a place in Cornwall,' he said. 'I don't know how quickly Loki may learn of today, but I think we can put some miles between us.'

'The raven could be lying.'

'It could be trying to help. It helped us once already.'

'You have a point, Will. Come on, then. Cornwall it is.'

'Or Ireland,' said Will, 'Which is across the sea and therefore further away.'

'Dickon always wanted to see Ireland,' said Thomas.

'Then let's see Ireland, for Dickon.'

Thomas and Will fell into step, side by side. By the time London had finally stirred to the thawing day, the minstrels had left the city walls far behind.

A few centuries passed and a raven again perched on the tip of the London Bridge starling, watching the elephant crossing the frozen Thames down by Blackfriar's Bridge.

For over 500 years, the inheritors of Thomas Rowan and William Hawk had come to do this duty – the rebinding of Hoor.

'I thank you for coming,' said the raven to the man and woman behind him.

They were all three watching the fair taking place on the ice. Sheep were roasting with a sign declaring them "Lapland mutton". Two men were charging sightseers to watch the spectacle, plus a shilling for a slice. Elsewhere on the ice, gambling huts and tents for drinking houses were making the most of the novelty. A printing press was turning out terrible poetry on thick paper, boys were playing skittles, and a swing named The Sky Lark was filled with giggling courting couples. The spectacle was new to the eyes of the man and woman with the raven, though they'd read of such things.

The raven had seen it all before.

'You humans can't resist dancing on ice,' it said, ending the pronouncement with a caw made of equal parts admiration and impatience. 'Your Kings and Queens especially. That fat Henry the Eighth, and then his red-headed daughter. And now here is your paunchy Prince Regent, poking at the ice with no care for what's beneath it. Anyone would think Erra Pater's prophecy had never been printed, eh Lily?'

'We were never sure that was a prophecy,' said Lily Thorn, drawing her thick winter coat more closely about her. In her left hand she gripped a bundle wrapped in soft leather. Erra Pater's ridiculous lines of poetry, scribed in 1684, were often analysed in her family's journals, but no conclusion had ever been reached.

Lily's companion, equally snugged against the cold, crouched on the broad base of the starling, which created a bulwark for the pylon and foundation of the bridge. A fiddle and bow were tucked under his arm. 'The lines "and now the struggling sprite is once more come, to visit mortals and foretell their doom" suggests knowledge of the HoorFrost.'

'Not all songs are magic, Guy, and not all doggerel claiming to foresee is a prophecy,' countered Lily.

'Yet here we are again,' said Guy Hawk drily, 'trying to keep an ice god asleep in a jar.'

The raven gave the ice below the starling his full attention.

'Lady Greenteeth doesn't mean to regurgitate the thing,' it said, 'It's not easy to swallow a god and keep it down. And these two bridges' – it meant London Bridge and Blackfriars, where the elephant was stepping back onto the banks – 'slow the river's flow too much in winter, so it freezes, and frost is Hoor's element. Makes the runes burn on the vessel. It's a combination for indigestion.'

There, beneath several feet of ice, was the suggestion of movement.

Scales and a sinuous body. Trailing green weeds. Lily wasn't sure how she could see such a thing, or even if she had. Yet the knowledge was certain. She had inherited more than Thomas Rowan's minstrel voice and his pipe through the preceding generations.

Guy rose to his feet and brought up the fiddle. Not long ago, he and Lily had been playing out there among the Londoners on the Thames, but only in part for the coin. Coin was good for bread, but applause was good for magic.

His bow across the strings asked a question of the creature below. The creature moved, rolled. Granted grudging permission.

Lily had unrolled the package and lifted the pipe to her lips. It was made of yew, a wood said to aid witches to speak with other realms. She'd found it useful in quieting ghosts and banishing demons. Guy's fiddle, birds and vines carved into its body, wasn't made of anything magical, but magic had been played through it for two hundred years. Magic had been sung into it when Gideon Hawk had made it after the 1608 frost fair, replacing the one broken by that year's binding.

Gods were indeed hard to keep bound.

Lily, Guy and the raven all saw then how the creature of the mere rolled under the ice, among its coils a glowing thing. Amber light and silver, and runes pulsing. Hoor was waking up.

Lily played the pipe. The raven called a rhythm with its "tok tok tok". Guy's fiddle sang around Lily's fluting notes, the raven's croaking ones, and he sang.

> *Hush thy heart, Great Hoor*
> *Tis not yet time to wake*
> *The fate of Asgard waits for you*
> *Sleep on, for London's sake.*

The words changed every time the Thames froze, but the melody persisted, and Hoor was bound afresh. They sealed the cracks in the rune-marked jar that held him. The river's guardian grudgingly opened her maw and re-swallowed Hoor's prison, then sank again down through icy waters to burrow into the mud at the foundation of the bridge.

When the verses were sung and the creature with a god in its belly subsided, Lily and Guy put their instruments away. Walking carefully on the ice, they followed the raven back to the banks.

'We should warn these people off the river,' Guy noted. 'The journals say the ice always melts quickly after Hoor's put back to sleep.'

'We should get this bridge knocked down so it doesn't slow the water to ice and keep waking the old bastard,' croaked the raven.

'Can we do that?' Lily asked.

The raven's feathers ruffled in a shrug. 'I heard talk of rebuilding the bridge, last time they were clearing ravens from the Tower.'

'Heard talk or suggested it?'

The raven let loose a sly cackle. 'Perhaps it's as you say. Perhaps I'm suggesting other things too. It's annoying and inconvenient when they clear the ravens out. The Tower is my best view of Hoor's prison, after all. It's not a lie to say England may fall if the ravens are made to leave.'

Lily stamped her feet on the banks to shake the snow off her boots. She didn't look at the raven when she spoke. 'Are you the same raven all our ancestors write about? Are you Heimdal?'

The raven laughed again. 'What makes you think I would be?'

She bravely raised her head to look at it. 'Nothing makes me think you aren't.'

The raven only laughed again and took flight, returning east to the Tower.

Guy stamped his feet too, seeking warmth. 'If it's Heimdal, he's over 550 years old.'

'If it's not Heimdal, it knows a lot about all the other times our family has been called to bind Hoor again.'

'Perhaps ravens have journals, like we do.'

Lily finished wrapping the pipe in the soft leather again then adjusted her bonnet. 'Don't be foolish, Guy.'

Guy only grinned at her. 'It's in my nature to be a jester, Lily Thorn.' He offered her his elbow, though. 'Let's go call to these ice-mad revellers to beware of the thaw, and then find a place for supper, shall we?'

Lily, having pulled her gloves on, slipped a hand into the crook of his elbow. 'Oh God, yes, tea. And then I'll record today's binding in the journal.'

'You're a conscientious minstrel,' said Guy, dropping a light kiss on her gloved hand.

'One of us has to be,' she teased, but her mouth had dimpled in a smile.

> **Author's note:** The poem about 'Silence' that Will reflects on is *Le Roman de Silence*, written in the first half of the 13th century but not rediscovered until the 20th.

RECYCLED WATER
Do Not Drink
WORKS IN
PROGRESS
UPGRADE
OF
FOUNTAIN

LOST AND FOUND:

THE SOLO RAPTURE

When the Rapture came, only Henry Smithfield noticed. Everyone else was too busy just living their flawed lives.

Henry, a paragon of virtue in a tarnished world, heard trumpets and looked to the sky as he walked past the Federal Court of Australia on La Trobe Street. To his left was the court building, all imposing glass and concrete with its brightly coloured entryway, and the rather less glamorous concrete fountain. Over the road to the right was Flagstaff Gardens, filled with morning joggers, tai chi classes, city dwellers taking their city dogs for a run on the green.

To tell the truth, Henry was a bit smug that he was the only one to notice the call of the angelic host. He thought it more than a little ironic, too, that the call had come while he was part way between the halls of justice on one side and a former cemetery on the other. The final judgement was coming at just the right place.

Henry stood on the edge of the non-functioning fountain (nobody seemed to have cared enough to turn it back on again after the easing of a decade of water restrictions) and held his hands to the sky. Waiting.

The heavenly host played a few more notes, allowing stragglers to catch up. But no-one else heard. No-one else stopped to look towards the heavens. Well, one or two people, but they were checking for potential rainclouds. In Melbourne, you could never entirely trust the forecast.

A few people cast a curious glance at Henry, but the daft bugger in his jeans, hoodie and dark sneakers looked more beatific than dangerous. Perhaps his case had been found in his favour. One jogger gave him two thumbs up and a congratulatory grin.

The heavenly host gave a little sigh, looked at their sole audience member, shrugged and figured that maybe Facebook hadn't really been the best way to send invitations to this particular party. Still, there was no need to blame Henry the Pure for being the only one with manners enough to notice the call.

With a beat of their wings, the host created one hell of a downdraft, which collected Henry and then drew him up.

It was startling at first. Henry kicked his feet, trying instinctively to stand on solid ground. His shoes fell into the puddle of water lying on the base of the defunct fountain. He waggled his socked feet, then decided it was quite pleasant, this flying business. Grinning, he let himself be lifted.

Nobody noticed.

Henry got to heaven and found himself the sole occupant of a significantly more dull than expected paradise.

The remaining inhabitants of the Earth didn't notice that Judgement Day had been and gone. They each went on being the embodiment of good and evil, heaven and hell, god and the devil, in their own personal way, as they'd done ever since they'd been given the gift of choice.

Only one person ever missed Henry. Daisy had loved her brother but frankly found him so impossibly perfect that she felt inadequate. Away from his oppressive saintliness, Daisy felt she wasn't such a bad old stick. She was kind to animals and the elderly and bought *The Big Issue.* She was good and supportive friend, and though not perfect, she made an effort to be kind. If heaven had been less rigid in its spiritual dress code, she might have heard the call.

But rigid it was, and most people are flawed, and really, the vagaries of heaven and hell had never really had that much impact on daily life on Earth, the in-between place where devils and angels were part of the same clay that made everyone else.

In the end, the heavenly host withdrew entirely from earthly affairs, and valiantly tried to hide their disappointment from Henry that Judgement Day had been such a fizzer. Words were definitely going to be had with the marketing people.

And the world? It went on, being good, bad and indifferent, depending on the predilections of its individual inhabitants, as it always had.

Lost and Found:

Wanderlust

He assumes it was an accident. He assumes it was drunken forgetfulness, or frustration with a blister, or something to spite the original owner of the shoe.

He tells himself it was not knowingly cruel.

It's cruel, all the same. Somehow it's worse that it's only one shoe. One garish purple boot, made for striding confidently in the world. A statement of sorts. *I wear sturdy footwear, for the road I walk is long and hard; but I wear my footwear purple because fuck you, that's why.*

The shoe rests against his own feet. He sees it in his peripheral vision, stuck as he is with his gaze forever drawn upward, his mouth in that *moue* of astonishment.

When he first reached this town, with his two equally gormless, equally impressed bronze friends, he was astonished. He was impressed. Now he's just here. All the time. Every day. Staring at the roofscape and wondering what else he's missing. The people who pass him talk of other things. A river nearby. A tall gilded tower from which they can see way out to the ocean. (What is an ocean, he wonders? The closest he can understand is that it's vast like the sky and wet like the clouds: the moon on storm clouds is his understanding of ships and seas).

Other people speak of even stranger places. Sand and forests and cities with great bridges and snowfall. He doesn't know what those words mean, but they sound *wonderful*.

He longs to go. To bend and snap his metal feet from the concrete and take a step. Take two. Three and four and to see a new angle of those rooftops, a new street, who knows, maybe that river (a ribbon of dense cloud on the ground, he wonders, is that what it looks like?).

He longs to move and to *discover*.

Instead, one purple shoe leans against his own cold feet and reminds him that his wanderlust is futile. All he can do is stand and gawp and wait for the world to come to him, and hope that their exotic words like *pyramid* and *bridge* and *mountain* and *free* will one day make sense.

WORDS FAIL

For my nanna, Bessy Harris

The collected words
Of all the languages in all the world
Can't capture you
A few can describe the way you smiled
And the scent of your skin
Nouns and adjectives may collide
To approximate your voice in all its moods
Or the picture of you
Standing at the crest of your back yard
Feeding the crows

But these are merely sketches
The outline of a woman

But hearts speak another language
and have a vocabulary of laughter
patience, joy, humour, tears and endless comfort
Not limited by mere words
Our hearts are fluent in you.

Lost and Found:
Plot Bunny

She is small, to hold so much rage in her. Small and ferocious and so, so tired. She had to dig her way out, and her with no bones, no muscles, just cotton and stuffing, weeping all the while.

Dig she did, though, and she found the sky again, and now she seeks something more. It will take a long time to find it (to take it) she has no doubt.

But revenge is patient, yes it is. Revenge has time enough. A dish best served cold, they say. Has no use-by date, they say.

It's a long way home, but that's all right. That will give her time to think, to plan, to plot.

The days and weeks and months she'll spend wending homeward will provide so much careful, burning time to decide which of them to punish – or punish first, at least – and how best to share with her enemies how it felt.

How it felt to be seized in hot, hard jaws and taken away.

How it felt to realise that Beloved Little One didn't raise a squeak of protest, being too enamoured of the splash of low-breaking waves on the sand to notice or care that the Beast was in motion, Bunny in its mouth.

How it felt to hear Uncaring Adult say in a bored, peeved tone, 'No, Cheezle, put Bunny back; bloody dog,' as ineffectively as a cat protesting, with no real interest, the closing of a door.

How it felt that no-one came to her rescue.

How it felt that nobody cared, and that Older Bully only laughed when she saw Cheezle carrying Bunny away on the beach.

A heart of cotton and stuffing (but a heart all the same) can still break when it understands the words: 'I'm not digging my way up and down the beach to find that bloody rabbit. Amelia has plenty of toys at home. Forget it. It's starting to rain. Let's leave.'

Bunny, down in her damp and sandy grave, buried there by Cheezle (jealous Cheezle, vicious Beast) was afraid, and then bereft, and then forlorn, and then *outraged*, and then **enraged,** and then, oh then, so full of fury and fire and hatred that despite the softness of her unboned limbs, the tatters of her stuffing heart, she began to dig.

Rabbits dig, you know. Even the soft ones. Even the ones made of cotton and polyester and tagged with washing instructions, they can dig, if properly motivated. Usually they burrow into little hearts, making a kindly warren of comfort and safety; days of play and nights of comfort, and those tunnels and dens make memories that keep old hearts gentle down the long, long years.

Bunny's burrows of love and comfort have been blasted and filled with stones, this day. Instead, Bunny dug up, up, up from the pit where Cheezle (filthy Cheezle, the Beast who will know what it is to be sorry) buried her.

A moment's pause by the sea, by the vast desert made of millions of pulverised bones and stones and dead things, and then Bunny will be off to fulfil her purpose.

Bunny will take whatever time and effort it takes to retrace her steps; to follow the path that the Metal Toybox on Wheels followed to bring her to this cold and loveless shore. She will return to the home she knew and lay waste to Older Bully and Uncaring Adult and Cheezle the foul Beast and even Beloved Little One, faithless tiny bitch that she is, and Bunny will know what it is to be drenched in blood as well as sea and sand.

And they, the family that spurned her, will know what it is to be mauled and buried and left unmourned to be swallowed by the sea.

Oh yes, they will.

FAITHFUL

'**M**ust you make such a godawful stench in the living room, Holmes? I can hardly breathe!'

I paused in my work – burning precisely measured squares of fabrics and recording the properties of the resulting ash – to glance at John Watson. He sat scowling behind his newspaper.

I dismissed several sharp retorts as unhelpful. A rebuke to open the window would avail us nothing, with a nasty pea-souper curling past the glass; suggesting he retire upstairs would be churlish; and pointing out that he was usually perfectly sanguine about my tabletop laboratory would have been deliberately obtuse.

I knew why he was in such a mood. John's old wounds were troubling him, and no response of mine would do anything but make his irritability worse.

'I'm done,' I said briskly, dousing the flames. Kinder comments were as useless as sharpness. He takes any sign of conciliation at these times poorly, just as these times make him quarrelsome. I understand that he suffers, and I make allowances. He's made enough of those for my own moods over our years together.

Truly, my John is the best of men; and, though he's the only one of my acquaintance, I've no doubt he's the best of werewolves too.

On that thought, I quietly made my final notes on ashes and their odours, labelled the samples in their jars and placed those in the specimen box I kept for the purpose.

'Sorry, my dear chap,' John mumbled, as I knew he would. John's ire is rare and his control is exemplary, however those injuries plague him. He is at heart a patient soul.

Neither of us mentioned the obvious cause of his mood. He loathed the reminder and I detest repetition. October's morning sun was hidden beyond the fog, and the moon was itself hours beyond the horizon. That by no means meant its influence couldn't be felt.

No wonder John's list of my limitations had included astronomy, given its critical role in his life. When we met, I'd little care for the movement of the spheres, and even less for the notion of ghosts and monsters. The presence or not of moonlight might at least affect a case. That was a trifle compared to how it affected him.

Ghosts and monsters turned out to be far more relevant than I'd ever allowed as well. Since John confessed his altered nature to me (or rather, since I was convinced to believe it by irrefutable evidence), I've kept a strict familiarity with the moon's cycles. John, of course, can never escape his own lunar awareness. It's in his blood and he has no need of an almanac.

I drew my dressing gown closed and walked to my chair, squeezing his shoulder as I passed him. He was adamant, always, that no more intimate forms of affection were permitted in the days around the full moon. John feared that his condition could be transmitted to me if we even but kissed, let alone indulged in more carnal exchanges. His medical training insisted that, as he'd been both clawed and bitten, saliva or sweat might expose me to it. I'd argued that surely those fluids would need to come into contact with my blood through an open wound, but he refused to risk it.

It troubled me that the time he seemed most in need of comfort was the period where his care and concern for me simply would not allow it. Thus I, in my own unromantic fashion, gave comfort where I could, by bearing his difficult moods with calmness and adhering to the limits he laid down for his peace of mind.

Once in my chair, I stretched out, nonchalant, and stared into the fire. John sat hunched in his own chair, moodily glaring at the unanswered mail I had most recently knifed into the mantel.

'Do you have a case to occupy you this evening?' he asked.

'My commonplace books need attention,' I said. Last night he'd been complaining about the untidy pile of clippings on the bedroom floor.

John grunted and fell to glaring at the fire. He has in the past urged me to attend concerts during his exile on the full moon. I don't know the extent of his suffering during his change, but I know he does suffer. I may not be welcome to comment on or to ease that suffering, but I'll be damned if I spend that night entertaining myself while he hurts.

John heard the hansom draw up in Baker Street before I did. His transformation takes place only after sunset at the height of the full moon, but on that day, and for a day either side of it, his senses are more acute. He lifted his head to sniff the air, then realised he was doing so and, shamed by these animal instincts, resumed scowling at the fire.

I rose to open the door to Inspector Lestrade, whose tread I heard upon the stairs.

'Inspector! What brings you to our door on such an inhospitable morning?'

Startled to be greeted before he'd even raised his hand to knock, Lestrade shook his head with a rueful smile, too used to such surprises to even ask how I'd known it was he.

'Good evening Holmes, Dr Watson,' he said, holding his hat and shifting anxiously from foot to foot. 'I'm sorry to bother you in such foul weather, as you say, but the thing is a boy has been kidnapped and I daren't wait till the fog clears.'

John's funk evaporated and he rose at once, concerned and alert. 'A child?'

'You'd best explain,' I said.

Lestrade laudably leapt straight to the business at hand.

'One Mr Emery Leggett raised an alarm at six o'clock this morning that an intruder had broken into his house in Wapping High Street and made off with his only child. A splash of blood at the window through which the boy was apparently taken made him certain of it. A constable on the beat arrived within minutes of the outrage and determined Solly Leggett was indeed taken and wasn't simply making mischief by hiding in the attic or the cellar…'

'An egregious waste of time,' I snapped. Lestrade's sour expression agreed with me, even if he couldn't bring himself to disparage his subordinates to civilians. I strode to the door as I spoke, fetching up coat and hat. 'Tell me the rest on the way.'

John was by my side, also reaching for his coat and hat. I cast him an enquiring glance. He met it with a determined look. 'I have until sunset,' he muttered to me, 'and this cursed heightened sensitivity may be of some use in the fog.'

I couldn't argue the truth of that, and trusted John to know his limits.

During the hansom ride, Lestrade completed his tale. Solomon Leggett, six years old, had been taken with barely a cry, though the blood on the window suggested the little lad had struggled against his abductor. Mrs Leggett had fallen in a faint, but not before crying out to her husband, 'This is your fault!'

'Mr Leggett claims he'd heard of kidnappers in the area intending to steal children for ransom and should have nailed the window shut. He's lying, obviously, and yet in earnest dread for his boy. What he finds more fearful than the child's abduction, that he won't tell us the truth, is more than I can fathom. But in the end, a little boy is in danger, his parents are of no use and I know no man better than you, Mr Holmes, for winkling out the facts when a case is tight as an oyster.'

Wapping High Street was even denser with discoloured fog than the rest of London. Being unable to see much made external deductions difficult. I left John and his heightened senses to walk a circuit of the house while I accompanied Lestrade within.

The Leggett home showed at once that Emery had been a prosperous boat builder whose fortunes had fallen dramatically. Good pieces of furniture, pictures and ornaments had been sold and the room rearranged to mask their loss, but patterns on the carpet, walls and cupboards betrayed how recently this had been. More tellingly, two Gladstone bags by a shabby cupboard were stuffed full, suggesting imminent flight from this house.

Leggett's wife had recovered from her swoon, and lay across a green baize sofa glaring accusingly at her husband.

Emery Leggett stood at the fireplace, fists clenched so hard his knuckles were white. He countered his wife's glare with one that was so perfectly balanced between fury and despair it might only take a nudge to send him in either direction. Most satisfying. It really couldn't have been more fortuitous.

'You know who took your son, Mr Leggett,' I stated immediately. 'Is it worth his life to keep the reason to yourself?'

Leggett started and turned white beneath his unshaven jaw and unkempt hair.

'Or do you assume little Solly is already dead?'

He teetered on the brink of attack or collapse. His wild eyes darted towards the poker by the unlit fire, but the door opened and John joined us. He was instantly at my side, ready to stand between this anguished father and me. Leggett immediately abandoned any thought of attack. Outwardly, John seemed still to be a perfect English gentleman, but he subtly carried himself with a predator's tread. Even Lestrade stepped away from him, unconsciously wary.

'You must save him,' cried Leggett, burying his face in his hands. 'Dear God, oh my God, if it's not too late, please save my boy.'

'Who took him?'

'That brute Samuel Whitehead, I'm certain of it!' he said, tearing at his hair and sobbing. His remorse was wasted on me. I had nothing but contempt for the man; my concern was all for his son.

'Samuel Whitehead,' I said, recalling one of the clippings awaiting inclusion in my files. 'Of the Liverpool Whitehead clan. Recently released after serving ten years for his involvement in The High Rip gang murders.'

'Why wouldn't you tell us this before?' Lestrade was disgusted, and missing the point.

Leggett was motivated by more than fear of a gang. His shifting glance, even now, and the way his wife snarled 'Tell them why!' told me that guilt had kept him silent.

'Whatever you did to prompt this vile act,' I snapped, 'is less important than finding the boy.'

'I don't know where Solly's been taken! I swear! I only heard that

Whitehead and his son were asking for me last night, and that some fool told him where we live. We were to leave this morning, but he came in the night! Oh god, oh god, Solly!'

I was thoroughly tired of his wailing by now. He'd have done better to confess all at the start. I turned to John for his report instead.

'I think the boy was only slightly scratched by a wooden splinter. The blood trail's very faint and stops by Black Eagle Wharf,' he said grimly. 'The lad must have been taken on a boat from there. I found no other sign of him between here and the Thames.'

Lestrade was startled at John's pronouncement, and John started with an unfortunately guilty twitch.

'I'm gratified you've been paying closer attention to my methods, Watson,' I asserted to deflect attention, then carried on without giving Lestrade time to question him further. 'If they've taken Solly with them we may have more time. I doubt they've gone into the Wapping Basin: the docks would trap them. Rowing upriver against the tide at this time would be a challenge – collision with any vessel brave enough to travel in this fog would be a risk. It's a brazen crime. I suspect Whitehead could well have the boldness to sail downriver past the Thames police station. What's downriver, Leggett, that it's where Whitehead would take your son?'

The boat builder blanched further and gasped: 'My boatyard. Where the accident happened.'

'Accident?' demanded Lestrade, but I was already striding for the door, buttoning my coat. The details of this precipitating accident, which surely coincided with the downturn in Leggett's fortunes, could wait.

'Leggett's Boatyard, I take it?' I demanded. I recalled my memorised map of London, 'That's a little beyond New Crane Stairs.'

John at my heels, we ignored the hansom, which couldn't hope to navigate at the speed required in the fog, and ran eastward.

A hundred yards from Leggett's Boatyard I was feeling the evil effect of the foul fog in my lungs, but John was barely breathing heavily. It was left to him, therefore, to intercept the young street Arab darting towards us.

'Tom Raker, is that you?' I heard John exclaim, seizing the boy by the shoulder. The boy tugged down the scarf concealing his nose and mouth in surprise.

'Doctor Watson? How'd you know it wuz me? Izzat Mister Holmes wiv you?'

'We're looking for a man who perhaps docked a boat at Leggett's,' John told him, 'and a little boy who may have been hurt.'

'Two men,' I corrected and then coughed till my eyes watered. Leggett said that Whitehead and his son had been asking after him.

'We seen two blokes carrying a bundle,' Tom said firmly. 'Wiggins an' I bin mudlarking, lookin' for pennies, an' we saw 'em land. Bloody dodgy, says Wiggins. He got a nose for dodgy, see. Bin paying note to Mister Holmes' methods.'

'Where's Wiggins?'

'Keepin' watch while I come lookin' for a peeler to help, but you're better.'

Tom guided us quietly into the boatyard. We were almost upon him when the vapours swirled away and the chief of my Baker Street Irregulars beamed at us. Wiggins, clearly expecting praise for his quick thinking.

'The young cove left a few minutes ago, arguin' wiv the old one. Fair threw the old bugger out of this shed an' wouldn't let 'im back in.' Wiggins nodded at a dark rectangle just visible through the swirling yellow eddies. 'Dragged him orf to the pub to cool down. I wuz about to take a gander at the swag they left behind.'

John lifted his head again. His nose wrinkled at all the scents that assaulted it and he shook his head ruefully. I was myself so overwhelmed with the odour of the fog, with old fish, wet timbers, creosote and the mud at low tide that I could hardly chide him for failure to detect any useful scent in the air.

Asking the lads to keep watch, John and I crept towards the shed. I picked the lock on it easily and we entered cautiously.

A whimper in the darkness was a great relief. John dashed to a mound of sailcloth and parted it to reveal a small boy shivering in a dirty nightshirt. His hands and feet were bound and a rag was tied over his mouth. The child stared at John with terrified eyes and gave a sharp squeal of fear, swallowed up by the gag.

'Hush Solly,' John said, his voice radiating reassurance. 'Your father sent us to fetch you home. Don't be scared.'

John first untied the boy's feet, and then his hands, leaving the gag until last, just as I would have done, to minimise the likelihood of shouting or flailing about. Good man.

'I'm a doctor,' John said as he worked. 'Are you hurt, Solly?'

Solly, who was tiny, even for a six year old, had calmed admirably. John, even with the pull of the moon, has that effect on the frightened and the ill; another reason why I value him so much. Solly sniffed. 'I scratched my arm on the window, sir,' he said with a hiccup, showing the wound to John.

Poor John recoiled suddenly from the dried blood. I moved rapidly to sit with Solly, hushing him as I did.

'There's a good lad,' I said. Solly was less convinced by my bedside manner.

'He seems well enough,' said John brusquely. 'The scratch is nothing, and a return to his mother's care is the best treatment for the fright.'

'Zat Leggett's kiddy?' asked Wiggins from the door of the shed. 'I wuz hoping for gold.'

'Here you are then,' I said, putting a sovereign into his grubby hand, and one for Tom as well. 'Can I trust you to take this boy to his home on Wapping High Street, Wiggins? Number 24. Inspector Lestrade is there.'

'Ol' Rat-face Lestrade?' Wiggins grimaced but pocketed the sovereign. 'Orright. He won't try to nick me, will he?'

'Not if you show better manners than to call him names,' I said sternly, but I couldn't argue that it wasn't fitting. I addressed Solly then. 'Solomon, Wiggins here and young Raker will take you home to your mother. Do as they tell you and you'll be safe very soon.'

He nodded solemnly and wiped his sticky nose on the sleeve of his nightshirt. Raker held out his hand for the boy to take and Wiggins grudgingly did the same. Then he squeezed the boy's hand.

'Come on Solomon Leggett,' Wiggins said impudently. 'If I take you home your mum might gimme a nice cuppa tea wiv a biscuit.'

'I'd rather cake,' said the little boy tremulously.

'Cake's a hunnert times better than biscuits, for sure,' Wiggins conceded. 'Come on Tom, let's go have cake an' tea.'

I watched them leave, confident that Wiggins would see him home. They left the boatyard unmolested.

'I take it we're to wait here for the Whiteheads' return,' said John.

We were within the shed, which stank strongly of fish and creosote. 'You should be away,' I said.

'I've a few hours, and I'm not leaving you alone to face the Whiteheads. I… *Holmes*!'

Too late, the sound of footsteps muffled by the fog came to my ears. Too late I realised the enemy was right behind me. Distracted by the danger to John, when I should have known better. He knows the time to sunset within the minute and without the aid of a timepiece, of course he does.

These thoughts came later. At that moment there was only the sudden pain of a blow to my head and John, my love, the fool, leapt to aid me rather than at the men who attacked us. A sack went over my head and I heard the sound of a beating. He wasn't fighting back, that much I knew. He was more frightened of passing on his curse than he was of them.

Before I could struggle out of the bag, another blow took me in the forehead. Disoriented, I inhaled too sharply, filling my already abused lungs with fibres and dust.

A body fell hard against me, slumped with the undirected weight of unconsciousness.

The blow to my head made it difficult to track our progress. I was hauled towards the river's edge and could hear another labouring beside me, dragging John's unconscious form. I calculated odds and options on the chance we were to be dumped in the Thames.

'Not the river,' said the younger of the two men.

'They'll be found too soon,' agreed the older, his accent straight from Liverpool. Whitehead, then.

I was tumbled over a wooden rim and into a boat. The graceless thump beside me reassured me that John was with me still.

'You can't be thinking of snuffin' these two, Pa.'

'Don't tell me what I can't be thinkin'.'

'Only, if the Leggett brat's gone, ain't sure of the point.'

'And whose fault is that?'

'He's just a nipper, Pa. Ain't his fault what happened to Albie.'

'That bastard Leggett killed your little brother, and I won't rest till I've an eye for my eye.'

'But Pa…'

'You cost us our revenge, you milk-livered wretch. But I'll have recompense. Now shut it and row.'

The sway of the boat indicated one of them had risen to his feet. There was no reason to rise except to do us harm. I lurched to my knees, every nerve extended to judge from where the danger would fall, thinking that if I could not protect my own skull I might at least protect John's.

Another sudden, swift blow hit me on the head. I heard the elder mutter something self-satisfied, but the words were lost as I lay dazed and nauseated.

But at least John, motionless beside me but breathing, was spared further abuse.

I learned what Dr John Watson had become only by chance, during the Stoner case on the grounds of Stoke Moran. A monstrous wolf leapt from the darkness to slaughter Grimsby Roylott's prowling cheetah (and so saved my life). I'd have dismissed it as a rare but natural beast, were it not for the fact that I tracked it in the morning to a tangle of brambles by the estate's river, only to find John Watson, naked, distressed and bearing the scars of his curse.

John Watson had returned from Afghanistan a truly altered man. His wounds were twofold: the bullet that had almost shattered his leg at Maiwand was the first. His orderly Murray had brought him safely from that field of slaughter, but John's long and slow recovery almost ended in death again at Peshawar base hospital.

He'd recovered to the point of limping about the wards. He tells people that enteric fever brought him low, but I know now that it was a fellow Englishman, his doctor, who became responsible for John's fate.

Doctor Gould had told John tales of werewolves at which John understandably scoffed. Yet this man was insistent, claiming to have himself been bitten at the last full moon and fearing the one to come. 'The locals tell me werewolves are susceptible to silver,' Gould told him. 'I should inject myself with silver nitrate if I begin to change, but I fear I lack the courage.'

He should have been braver.

As it was, the moon took Gould at sunset while on the ward, and he had torn the throat out of one recovering soldier and the stalwart nurse who tried to protect him before John could act.

It's a testament to John's spirit that he took on the curse while protecting the other patients, armed with nothing but a scalpel and a syringe of silver nitrate drawn in full concentration from the medical cabinet. My brave boy was facing the monster when it savaged him – those claws raked John from shoulder to sternum and its ferocious bite tore into his trapezius front and back. Gripped in its jaws, he injected the beast's heart with silver and cut its throat with a silver blade.

At Stoke Moran, wrapped in my overcoat, John reluctantly confessed his affliction to me. He related the events as calmly as though it were not the bravest thing he's ever done.

Every faculty at my disposal deduced the unbelievable truth of his words. The cheetah's fur still in his nails, its blood in his teeth, told their own tale, though John remembered not a moment of the deed.

It turns out that the improbable has more scope in it than I ever imagined.

The appalling truth of it explained why John had prevaricated so bitterly before joining me in Sussex for the case. We knew Roylott had killed and planned to again, though we didn't know then his weapon was a venomous snake. John's solution to the dangers he saw to me from both Roylott and his moon-changed self was to lock himself in an outbuilding on the Roylott estate for this one night, but the bolted wooden door was no barrier at all. He'd transformed, broken out, and roamed the grounds with the wild animals until the cheetah's snarl brought him to my defence.

In the dawn, his dreadful secret revealed, John was full of shame and ready to leave me forever. I forbade him, of course. I'd known he kept a secret which was one of many things preventing us from the deeper friendship and attraction we'd felt.

At least he could be sure that, with precautions, he wouldn't transmit his condition to me. He'd stayed at Peshawar, recovering, long enough to learn that Dr Gould's wife and son, who'd worked with him at the hospital, were not cursed, despite the month he'd spent with them while infected. This knowledge gave us confidence that in ordinary days we were safe to live in similar intimacy.

With this new honesty between us, we embarked on a life together as partners in every sense. From that time we've shared every aspect of our lives, except for this. For one night each month he takes himself away, as he'd done in the first years of our friendship, to endure this change alone and in safety. I've located the vault he rents near Tilbury Fort to lock himself into, but I've never broached it.

In all our years together, I'd never witnessed his transformation.

I knew he suffered. Until this awful night in fogbound London, I never knew how much.

I won't say my worst fears were realised when I regained consciousness. John wasn't dead. But for that, the situation was the very worst it could have been.

John sat stiffly against a wall opposite me, dishevelled, bruised and bleeding from the beating he'd taken at Leggett's Boatyard. He was pressed hard to the mildewed stones as he stared at me in the utmost despair.

'John?' My voice rasped.

'I'm sorry,' he said in a hollow voice that filled me with dread. My John is usually fearless as a lion.

'It's my own fault,' I said, brushing aside my uncharacteristic fancies of doom. 'We'll find our way out of here soon enough. I see we're being held in an unused cellar.' The old stone room afforded a little light from a tiny window at the ceiling and smelled mainly of the river, a little coal, and a little ale. 'An old storage facility near the docks.'

'It's too late.'

'Nonsense. If Whitehead didn't murder us outright, there's something he wants. We can buy a little time.'

'No. Sherlock.' He took in a shuddering breath and released it again. 'Sunset is almost on us.'

Oh.

'I've searched and searched this prison, and I can't find any way out. The gate is locked, the chains are too solid to break. The window's too high, and too small.'

'John…'

'We only have a few minutes.' He rose and swayed on his feet. So did I. We stepped towards each other, but I could tell that this wasn't to be a fond embrace farewell. A ridiculous notion in any case. The full moon change wouldn't kill him tonight, any more than it had these last eight years.

My John stood tall before me, suddenly calm, though his eyes were full of sorrow. He reached out for me, which he never does on the full moon night, and he took me by the hands.

He raised them as he spoke.

'There's only one way to keep you safe, my dearest. I tried to find a way to do it while you were recovering your wits, but I can find nothing.'

He placed my hands against his own throat.

'You must,' he said, as I read his intention.

'No.'

'The curse will come on me in minutes and it'll be too late. Please. If you love me.'

'You know I do.'

'Then don't let me murder you. Don't let me wake in the morning with your blood in my mouth and your torn body on the floor.'

'John.'

'The wolf will have his way, Sherlock. And if I kill you, be sure that I'll follow you into death before the day's end. Do this now. For me.'

He held my hands against his throat and I could feel his pulse thundering, and feel his body trembling in grief and terror for me.

'I give my life willingly for you,' he said, his beautiful brown eyes bright and looking deeply into mine. All the love of his noble heart was in that gaze. 'Please, Sherlock. Don't let me be the instrument of your murder. Please, my love. Live.'

Almost without volition, my thumbs stroked the skin on either side of his Adam's apple. With a slight shift, I could press upon the hyoid bone in his throat and break it. I could crush his windpipe, end his suffering and save myself from the fate he foresaw for me.

I stroked his throat, as I have done when his body was beneath me, arching in pleasure. I have kissed him often then, his throat and jaw and cheeks and mouth, owning the taste of him. My one true love. My best and most wonderful puzzle. My heart's delight.

John closed his eyes. A terrible calm came over him as he accepted his fate.

I pressed my cheek to his brow, adhering still to his edicts that we must not risk the transmission of the werewolf curse to me.

My dear boy, who bent his care and mind to the protection of others, myself most especially, let his arms fall to his sides and tilted back his head, eyes closed.

'Hurry,' he said softly. 'The moon's rising in my veins.'

He needn't have told me. Beneath my hands, his skin grew notably rougher. The change was coming.

But I had already made my decision. I remembered that night at Stoke Moran, when his transformed self stalked the darkness and saved my life as the wild cat sprang at me from the brambles.

Hands pressed still to his throat, I leaned close and whispered into his ear.

'I have faith in you. You won't harm me.'

I stepped away, letting my hands fall.

His last look to me was of despair.

And then the change took him.

Oh God.

Oh my God.

God in heaven, how he suffered.

John's flesh rippled, stretched and altered before my eyes. I could hear the wet sound of his soft tissues tearing, the hard crack of his bones, as his body bent and changed shape, shrinking and growing. His face grew long, thick hair forced itself from his skin.

His cries, *oh God,* of agony, of despair, as this horrific curse and the moon took my darling, tore him apart and reassembled him as this creature, this wolf, this beast.

I lost my faith in a merciful God that night, because He had allowed this grotesque and wicked fate to happen to so good a man.

When the ghastly transformation was complete, a creature stood among the shreds of John's clothes, and it turned its great, shaggy head towards me.

At Stoke Moran I'd only seen a glimpse of the werewolf, hurtling past me in its attack upon the cheetah. Here I saw him unhindered and whole.

He was terrible and beautiful. The beast stood on his wolf-like hind legs, as natural as a man would and so an outrage to all that was natural. His human-like arms ended in clawed hands, the talons sharp and black. His legs ended in paws, the claws no less black and cruel. His noble head, magnificent and inhuman, was golden-furred, ears alert, fangs bared. His snout wrinkled as he sniffed the air.

His eyes. My dear boy's eyes were still his, still human in that lupine face, though he seemed not to know me. Every line of those bestial features was savage and without human compunction.

Slowly his head turned towards me.

I admit that my courage failed me. My faith failed me. For just that moment.

'Forgive me, love,' I whispered. John would wake in the morning with my blood in his mouth and my death on his soul. Yet I couldn't for an instant regret my decision. I could no more kill him than he could prevent his transformation.

The snarl disappeared from his features. He took a step towards me, and another, and I held my ground. If I was to die, I wouldn't do it running from the man I loved, whatever he'd become.

He leaned towards me, and I held my breath.

The cursed wolf that was my John sniffed at my face. His snout roamed over my cheek and to my throat. He snuffled against the thundering pulse of my carotid artery. I held still, wondering if he would tear my throat out.

He did not. He snuffled from one side of my throat to the other, nudged his snout into my hair, and huffed a sound that seemed like satisfaction.

'Sherlock,' said the snout that should not have been able to speak a human language. But what was one more impossible thing?

'Mine,' he said in the same low, gruff voice. He snuffled from my throat to my armpits to my stomach then back again, as though the scent of me filled him and brought him peace.

'John,' I began, but then behind us came the sound of scraping metal. He whirled, dropping to a crouch.

'What's goin' on in there?' demanded the elder Whitehead.

'You'd best stand clear,' I said.

'You're in no position to make threats,' he said, mistaking my attempt to keep him safe. 'Leggett let a boat fall on my youngest in the boatyard and dumped his body in the river instead of owning to his carelessness. If I can't take his youngest in payment, then I'll cut the throat of the men who kept me from my vengeance.'

'Wait!' I cried as he pulled on the chains of the gate. Maybe in the darkness he didn't see the wolf crouching, or hear the low growl. Perhaps Whitehead could see nothing but the revenge he sought.

'I've waited long enough,' he said, 'arguing with Will. He hasn't the stomach for this work, which is a disappointment to a father, but I've dealt with him and now I'll deal with you.'

He raised a pistol between the bars he'd never intended to open, and pointed the barrel at me.

'I can see the whites of your eyes,' said Whitehead. 'And those of your busybody mate. Now hold still and make this easy on yourselves.'

The spit of flame and smoke showed his aim was true, but even as he fired, the wolf with John's voice snarled and leapt in front of me.

The bullet struck him mid-leap, and he twisted with a strange, guttural yelp.

Whitehead fired again, but John had regained his feet and stood in front of me, arms and claws spread, to catch the bullet with his body. I tried to push him aside but in this form he was taller than me, stronger, and absolutely terrifying, if only Whitehead would have the sense to be afraid.

As I thought it, Whitehead seemed to suddenly realise that something wild and savage was regarding him from the shadows as a predator regards the prey. 'God defend me!' he shouted. He fired his Bulldog revolver in blind panic.

John's upright wolf body jerked with the impact of the remaining shots, and then he stalked towards the gate. In the darkness I could see pools of blood glistening in his wake.

With a bowel watering howl, the wolf hurled himself at the gate, seized the chains in his monstrous hands and tore them from the bars as though they were mere wire.

Whitehead screamed and ran.

The wolf bayed and gave chase.

I ran after them, with no notion how I might stop John from slaughtering this villain but certain I should try, for John's sake.

None of us got far. Whitehead, shrieking, fled from the vault onto the dock and flung himself into the Thames. He thrashed in the water, clearly no swimmer, but panic had made the choice for him.

John paced the wharf, snarling and snapping. He limped too, and wiped at his matted fur where the bullet holes gaped and bled.

'Hell take you!' the wolf snarled in a rough and feral version of his human voice as the thrashing Whitehead was carried downstream. Then John swayed on his erect hind paws and dropped to all fours.

I tried to help him back into the shelter of the cellar, but he recalled himself enough to pull away. He growled in warning when I tried to come closer, so I made do with holding his arm and guiding him back to our former prison.

Once inside, I could do nothing to help. I could hardly call out for the police or other aid. I had no idea what the wolf might do. Perhaps all he'd do was die, and I was wracked with despair.

In the cellar I avoided the pool of his blood and sat with my back to the wall. The beast dropped at my feet, lying on his side like any injured animal. His eyes were sheened with silver, but they were undoubtedly John's eyes.

'What must I do?' I asked.

'Be safe,' said the wolf.

For a time he lay there in the dark, panting, but after a short time I noticed his breaths were less harsh. The pool of blood didn't grow. The wounds in his chest and abdomen bled more slowly. Then, as I watched, a misshapen piece of lead oozed out of a bloody crater in his belly and fell to the ground with a faint clink. He grunted and panted as his battered body ejected the bullet.

'You're in terrible pain,' I said, a far cry from my usual aloof observations. My voice cracked with my helplessness.

'Silver kills,' he said, with a sound like a laugh. 'Lead…' He winced and hissed as another bullet was forced out of his body. 'Hurts.'

I took off my coat and crept forward. He could glare a warning as much as he liked. I knew I was safe from him. I folded my coat and placed it on my lap and then, gently, lifted his tawny head and rested it on my thigh.

Slowly, marvelling as I did so, I stroked the fingers of one hand through the golden fur of his neck and then held them there against his pulse. Just as it had before the moon took him, his pulse was racing, his skin trembling under my touch.

So we stayed through the long night, John's wolf body shivering as it mended itself, pushing the lead backward through torn muscle, and slowly healing. From the angle at which he lay, I could make out the scar of the bullet wound that had nearly cost him his leg and his life at Maiwand, a furrow in the skin and fur of his wolfish pelt.

Despite the horrors of the night, I stayed awake and alert, but neither Whitehead nor his son Will returned. Towards dawn, John's eyes closed and he seemed to sleep.

It was some measure of mercy that this time, as the sun rose and claimed him back, John's wolf body twisted and shrank without his consciousness feeling every warp and shift. I had to relinquish my touch from his throat as he convulsed on the floor. Finally, however, he was naked and shivering but human. The bullets he had taken in my defence were bloodied on the ground, but those wounds had healed completely. Only the older scars remained. The dent of the bullet wound and subsequent surgery scar in his thigh stood out against his pale skin; the four raking lines of the claws on his upper body, punctuated by the bite mark on his shoulder, were a sin against his broad chest.

I was about to throw my coat over him to keep him warm when his eyes fluttered open and he stared at me in anguish and bewilderment.

'You're alive,' he gasped.

'Evidently.' I smiled, reassuringly I thought, but his expression didn't change.

'God. Oh God. Sherlock.' He lurched to his hands and knees then reached for me, kneeling at my feet. His fingers barely brushed my cheek. 'How did you survive? Are you real?'

He clearly held no memory of the past night. I pressed my hand to his and then pressed his hand to my cheek so he could feel the unshaven bristles and the heat of my skin and know I was no illusion.

'You're no danger to me, my dear.'

Of all the things that had shocked me in this terrible affair, John's sudden sob was the greatest. His eyes brimmed with tears and he shook, his fingers caressing my skin.

'I was certain the wolf would butcher you,' he said, voice breaking, and he wept. Ashamed of his tears, he dropped his hand and looked away, but I'd have none of that.

I put my arms around my darling and pulled him close. I draped my coat over his shivering shoulders. After a moment's resistance, John took the comfort I offered. He wept against my chest as I held him close and pressed my cheek to his hair.

'A werewolf protects its mate, it seems,' I murmured to him. 'You knew me and you spoke my name. Even if you don't remember by the morning, you are still some form of yourself. My darling. My dearest. I will never get your limits.' And I said the thing I rarely say, though I feel it down to my bones. Not sentiment, but an immutable truth. 'I love you.'

John's shuddering subsided and when he looked to me again, his tears had dried. A new strength was in his eyes. 'I still have a soul,' he said, full of hope. 'And with my heart and my strength, it's yours, Sherlock.'

He still wouldn't let me kiss him.

The remainder of this sorry tale required deftness and discretion. John's clothes were in shreds and so I gave him my underthings and my coat, while I wore my trousers and shirt, and we made our way back to Baker Street in the back of a costermonger's cart.

Will Whitehead's father had tied him up and left him in the rowboat after their argument. Who knows what he'd planned for his eldest, but Will had managed to free himself. His attempt to flee London ended ignominiously when the police arrested him returning to his lodgings for funds.

The whole story came out of course. The blocks on a boat being repaired had slipped in Leggett's boatyard and the eleven year old Albie Leggett, caulking the seams, was crushed under the hull. Leggett had panicked and conspired with the chief builder to weight the lad's body and sink it in the Thames.

But truths, like the drowned, tend to bob up. Rumours spread and both work and labourers for Leggett dried up. He'd begun selling his finer household goods to meet his debts.

Whitehead Senior, who'd recently been released from prison for the Liverpool assaults, had come to find his sons and found this great loss instead. A decade behind bars had not softened his temperament, and his enquiries, made with word and fist, taught him the truth of his son's fate.

Fortunately for Solomon Leggett, Will Whitehead had no stomach for child murder. He interfered and delayed, allowing the boy to be rescued and, in due course, delaying his father's intention to shoot John and me during the daylight hours.

The delay cost his father his life, however. Whitehead Senior's drowned body washed up some days later at Gravesend. I can't say that I'm sorry for it.

Will Whitehead was freed with a judicial warning, and Leggett was brought up on charges, so there was justice of a kind at least.

The following night, as John scrubbed himself clean of full moon sweat in a tub in Mrs Hudson's kitchen, I sat by the fire musing on my own shaming scars. The needle tracks were old. I haven't been bored in a long time. I live with and love a werewolf. There is always something new for me to learn. For John, too.

The full moon is different for us now. Ever cautious, John still forbids too much intimacy, but I'm allowed to hold him and offer what comfort I can. My faith in him is absolute.

I go with him to Tilbury now, and sit outside the reinforced vault he made for himself. He takes a slaughtered sheep with him to appease his wolfish appetite.

It's appalling to hear what the moon does to him, but I won't abandon him to the suffering that afflicts his body as much as his spirit. When he is that terrible, beautiful, golden man-wolf, I sit by the triple-chained gate and speak with him. If he is calm, I put my hand between the bars and rest my fingers on his throat.

'Mine,' he tells me in that feral voice. John the wolf is a beast of few words.

'Yes,' I agree. 'As you are mine,' which makes him huff a laugh that is almost like my daylight John.

When I tell him I love him, his wolf-laugh is even more like himself. 'Tell me tomorrow.'

Wolf John doesn't remember, but I do tell John this, every tomorrow. Every day.

For everything we've learned, one solid, dependable truth is unchanged. My John is the best of men, and the best of werewolves too.

Lost and Found:

Peaceful

In late December, while the world carried on in its usual mad dance, peace came to Altona.

It didn't look much. Mistaken for a pendant, peace manifested itself as a small brass symbol, tiny and easily overlooked. A glint on the concrete, a shape made of lines and spaces.

A modest peace, its effect was localised and felt in tiny ways along the beachfront and in the park, along the streets and among the trees.

This little peace made the sound of gulls less of a strident, frustrated demand and more a cry of endless, beckoning horizons. The cry of a gull, for a time, was a response from the great blue sky that answered isolation and made the world less lonely.

It made the cold, rough waters invigorating rather than daunting. It made the child gaping wide-eyed at the never-ending sea wonder at adventures on other shores instead of fearing the waves, and she body-surfed back to the beach with the feeling that she could fling herself at the motion of the world and never be afraid.

The people who stepped over this unseen symbol on the footpath felt for a moment that all was if not currently well, that it soon would be. Some of those whose feet hovered above it for that moment felt the urge to forgive a wrong, to take a kinder view, to judge less harshly.

Some of them forgave their own guilty selves for frailty and perceived failure. They realised that it was in the striving to improve rather than in failing at perfection that their better selves could be brought to light.

In the park, a grandfather, ill-tempered with aches and

disappointments, halted an impatient snarl and instead looked at the leaf presented by a small grandchild, and recognised the leaf as an offering and a request, even if the child didn't know it. *The world is huge and fascinating, Grandpa, and it's so so new to me, show me, show me, show me how to grow in it.*

This modest peace was not a place of stillness. All the world is ceaseless change, much of it unconsidered and reactive, at the whim of chance and resistance, violence and cacophony. But some change happens in the quiet, in the momentary peace, in the pause between breaths.

The change of peace is gentle, like rain on stone, like roots in the soil. It is a way to tilt the world, to see old facets anew; it is the contemplative moment in which the familiar is rearranged and new patterns bloom with potential.

Nobody knows how many little peaces exist in the world. Nobody knows if they bring the peace with them or manifest it spontaneously in hushed moments. This tiny symbol is no longer in Altona. Perhaps it was seized upon by a child, or a magpie, or a street sweeper. Perhaps it dissolved on the sea air.

Perhaps in a warm and silent moment, someone will manifest it out of their own brain, and like rain on stone, like roots in soil, a small but significant change will bloom.

LOST AND FOUND:

JOURNEY

Everyone thinks Journey is a bit dizzy, a bit flaky, a bit of a hippy. (Her name doesn't really help.) They think this almost like it's a bad thing.

People like her, it's true – in that abstract way that most of them like summer, or a glass of water when they're thirsty, or a starlit night sky, which they only look at once in a while and think it's pretty but then go on with whatever they were doing.

People like Journey almost like it's a habit, and one that refreshes, but doesn't linger for long. She seems apart from them somehow. It's like she knows something that they don't. She acts like she has the key to uncomplicated happiness.

Maybe the people who like her are a bit jealous. They don't know how to let go of worry. They're never content with who they are and where they are; all too busy being distracted by the concern of *what now? what next*?

It's not like Journey radiates an over-the-top, sing-in-the-street, look-mum-I'm-dancing joy. She's just content with her lot, though distracted, not with *what next?* but with *this right here right now is lovely*.

Journey likes natural fabrics and fresh, organic food and jewellery of pure silver that jangles when she walks. She likes the way cats purr and the vibration travels from their tiny bodies right into her hands when she strokes them and calls them *sweet little kitty*. She likes how bees are fuzzy and how oranges sometimes squirt you in

the eye when you bite into them and the sound of horse hooves on the tarmac of the city street and the ding of the tram bell and the squeal of kids running through the fountain in front of the casino in summer.

She likes rain on her arms and wind in her dark hair. She likes the sun on her face, and that her dark brown skin doesn't burn.

Journey likes walking everywhere. She likes stopping to smell the flowers in a very literal sense. She's been known to stop and smell *grass*.

She likes all these things in a low-key way. She's not all manic-pixie-dreamgirl about them, despite her name and the tinkling silver jewellery. It all simply makes her calm and mindful and content.

Here's a secret.

It's *true*. Journey *does* know something that other people don't know.

She knows what comes next. Came next. Will be next.

Grammar is difficult when you are living in your own past; when you're a grain of the future stranded back in the time Before (but you are still the Yet To Be for the environment you inhabit, for the acquaintances who like you but don't know anything about you).

Journey knows a lot about quantum physics and the machine powered by an entire sun that sent her back to gather data. Her understanding of climate change is very good too – all the survivors have a belatedly good understanding of the stupidity humanity did to itself.

The machines in Journey's head and skeleton interact with the ones she wears on her body to send vital data through space and also time. Earrings and bracelets of silver (and many other things) make her whole body a transmitter to her lost future as they try to work out how to save the little of the world they still have. (In the meantime, the survivors have transplanted to the moon, a staging place before they take themselves to other barren landscapes further from the sun if they can't work out how to get the drowned Earth back.)

Six years after arriving through a tunnel of improbability and bent light, the transmitter is still transmitting.

The receiver broke, though, six months after her arrival. A man wanted to take something she wasn't interested in giving, and he grabbed her and insisted on having what he wanted.

Journey broke his arm in three places, four of his ribs, and his neck. The parts of his body were weighed down and went into the river. Journey feels a little bad about the death, but where she comes from, he and everyone around her died hundreds of years ago, so it doesn't bother her *too* much.

Journey is surrounded by ghosts, in many ways. Some of these fleshly ghosts are awful, frightening things. Some are sweet or kind or funny. None of them know their fate, but Journey does, so mostly she is willing to offer the benefit of the doubt. She'll live and let live because they're all dead, but they don't know it yet.

Journey didn't realise the receiver had been snapped from her ear in the struggle until later, and then she couldn't find the missing piece. Perhaps she could have repaired it, but she decided not to. It was so much more peaceful not to listen to the commands, the directions, the directives. To the envy and the anger and the railing against the people who appeared all so unwittingly in her transmissions, who were partly at fault for the Death of the Earth by Flood and Fire.

Journey knows that each individual couldn't do much to stop it, and she knows that collectively, humans are a bit thick.

She's been inhabiting her past, creeping towards a future she won't live to see again, and she likes it here.

Journey *likes* that she can't go home. She likes that she'll never hear those strident voices through the receiver again. She likes that she still sends them data – it's a relief that it was not the transmitter that was lost – but she *loves* that they cannot summon her home.

Good luck to them, if they think the data will save them. She's sad for the future, of course – for what they've lost and what they'll never have, living on their island of rock, gazing down at the blue ball that used to be humanity's home.

She used to be like them, salvaging hope from the away teams that go (went, will go) to salvage scraps from the ball of water and wasteland that once housed a trillion life forms. The fraction that remain are all caged in some way. Animals and insects in the great Moon Zoo – too many slowly dying off because the gravity and the air are all wrong. Plants in greenhouses, and no-one can predict yet which will thrive and which will fail.

Not to mention the people. In their domes and in their environment suits that don't always work. Humanity is ingenious at survival but also at self-immolation. The individual will to live is nothing like the collective lunacy that convinces people that *someone else will fix it*.

But here, in the past full of ghosts, Journey already knows that no-one fixed it. She already knows the limited life that awaits the survivors.

So Journey goes through her ghost life, enjoying every simple pleasure before it's burned or drowned, and she breathes the open air and is content to just be in the moment.

After all – what could she possible do? She's just one woman. She can't change the future alone, and collective humanity won't listen to her if she tries.

Because if it were possible, surely she'd have done it.

Bad Night at Bite Club

Author's note: This story is set after the events of my Vampires of Melbourne novel, *Walking Shadows*.

Everything changed for Nathan when his father Evan came back from Australia. For a start, he returned without the family vampire, Abe.

Abe, the vampire who killed other vampires, was no more; staked-and-cremated dead. Evan wouldn't explain who had done the deed, or the circumstances leading to it. Whatever had occurred, without Abe, the Cobb family's 400 year old vampire slaying business was at an end.

Suddenly, Nathan's future was open and free of the weight of terrible expectation. He really, truly could be anything.

'Will you be my date to senior prom?' Jackson didn't look up from the biology textbook as he asked, but he caught Nathan's dazzled, dazzling grin from the corner of his eye.

'Course I will,' Nathan replied, badly feigning nonchalance.

'Good.' Jackson pretended to read a little longer, while Nathan practically vibrated beside him.

'I'm tired of reading about biology,' said Nathan after a minute. 'Want to do some prac?'

Jackson had his shirt off half a second before Nathan, which is how their study dates always ended. Kissing and touching and being delighted as only two 18 year olds can be when they're in love and left alone together. Only the sound of the rest of the Cobb family downstairs kept the boys from stripping off entirely.

Nathan settled for lying in Jackson's arms, admiring the contrast of Jackson's dark hand against his own pale chest.

'The school won't buck, will they?' asked Jackson.

'It's 2010. A gay prom date won't kill anyone. Besides, we're a power couple.' Nathan waggled his eyebrows for emphasis. 'They won't dare pick on us.'

Jackson flexed a bicep. 'They better not.'

Nathan, laughing, swung himself on top of Jackson to sit across his thighs and shadow-box an imaginary enemy above the bed-head.

'Let 'em try.'

Jackson reached up, wrapped his arms around Nathan's shoulders and pulled him down for more kissing.

Jackson was big; Nathan, more lithe, had boxing and fencing trophies to go with the ones for his speed and agility. If the school's wrestling champion and its star triathlete wanted to dance together, they would.

Nathan and Jackson arrived at the senior prom wearing matching white rose *boutonnieres* in their lapels and matching "luckiest guy in Boston" grins. Some classmates applauded them. They bowed, cocky and stupidly pleased with themselves.

Kelly Clarkson sang about how her life would suck without her prevaricating boyfriend, and they danced, foreheads pressed together, arms around each other. No kissing. Mr Vance the geography teacher was a No-Public-Displays-of-Frenching vigilante, but he was even-handed, not allowing the guy-girl or girl-girl couples lock lips under his watch either.

'Let's go to the lake, after,' murmured Jackson in Nathan's ear as they swayed together.

Just his voice was enough to make Nathan half hard. 'We could go now,' he said, holding Jackson closer.

'After this song,' agreed Jack with a wicked laugh. *My First Kiss* was playing.

'Okay.' They both knew what they planned at the lake would be a different first.

They held hands on the way to the lake; bumped hips, shoulders, thighs, as they walked. Each touch was a sip of what they'd planned, when they could lie down in the grass together and taste each other's mouths, skin, bodies by moonlight. They laughed, high on happiness and anticipation. They were young and in love. Their future was sunshine and blue skies, theirs for the taking.

Three hours later Nathan was staggering along the turnpike, sobbing, a ragged but healing bite mark on his throat. His phone, spattered in blood, was clutched in one hand.

He fell to his knees as his father and his Aunt Lori drew up in the car. Evan raced to his son, desperately checking the wound then crushing Nathan fiercely in his arms.

'You'll live. Thank God.' Nathan had never heard his dad sound so horrified and relieved all at once. 'Where's Jackson?'

'I couldn't help him,' Nathan gasped, in shock from blood loss and grief. 'I tried. I tried. Everything you taught me, everything I knew. It didn't help. I wasn't strong enough. I staked that bastard vampire and I *missed*. Jack told me to run. So I ran. Oh god. Oh god, I ran.' Shame overwhelmed him.

Lori looked after Nathan while Evan searched the shores of the lake, then deeper into the woods. He found nothing.

The police found blood, but never Jackson. They assumed Jackson's body had been weighted and trapped somewhere under the lake, or perhaps that the killer had disposed of his body in the Bay.

A month later, Nathan went alone to Crystal Lake to lay flowers and a mix-tape CD for Jackson.

Jackson's death was the worst thing that had ever happened to Nathan, in a life that had contained some pretty bad things.

No scars marred Nathan's throat where the vampire had tried to kill him. His skin still tingled anyway, with the memory of nearly dying.

The flowers first. The CD he'd meant to give Jackson before losing the chance went beside them. He didn't hear the movement in the trees.

'Nate.'

Nathan's hand flew instinctively to protect his healed throat, then fell away as he saw Jackson emerge from the woods.

He wanted to run to Jackson. He wanted to run away.

He did neither.

'I thought he'd killed you,' Nathan said, more steadily than he felt.

His heart double-timed. Jackson-Jackson-Jackson. Not-dead, not-dead. Even though he knew. He'd grown up with Cousin Abe in the house. Jackson was unmistakably not alive. His dark skin was tinged with a peculiar bloodless grey; his once expressive face now mostly a blank. Even his beautiful brown eyes were dulled.

'He did kill me.'

'You know what I mean.'

'He bit me and drank. It stopped hurting after a while. I'm glad you ran like I told you to, though. I want you to know I'm glad he didn't get you.'

'I'm not glad,' said Nathan, the guilt and grief written wetly down his face. He recalled Jackson pulling him along as they ran, the blood streaming down Nathan's throat, palm pressed to the wound; Jackson behind him, pushing, saying *run;* and then realising Jackson wasn't behind him anymore. He'd never before regretted being the faster of them. 'I went back for you.'

'I remember.'

'I was too late.'

'It's not your fault,' said Jackson. 'You always said old vampires were hard to kill.'

'I should have known what to do. I was raised to be a hunter. I should have known how to stake him right.'

'I don't think I ever believed all your stories about your family,' Jackson said. 'I suppose I should apologise for that.'

'I'm so sorry.' Nathan's voice cracked in anguish and a sensible amount of fear. He shuddered from head to foot and didn't even look for an escape route.

'I'm not going to hurt you,' said Jackson suddenly.

'Why not?'

'Don't be an asshole, Nate.'

'You're a vampire now.'

'Yeah. Turns out, it's really not cool, like it is in the movies. I've only been undead a month and it's pretty fucked up. I thought I'd want to be drinking blood all the time, but mostly I feel. Far away.'

'Dad says they. You. They drink blood to feel alive again.'

'I'd have thought if you wanted to feel alive you wouldn't become a vampire. It was hard work, dying and coming back, just to have to drink blood to feel like I'm not dead.' Jackson pulled a sour face. 'He said his name was Edward Bennett, by the way. He said your Dad knew who he was.'

'I think Dad and Abe hunted in his neck of the woods when I was in junior high.'

'Cousin Abe. The tame family vampire.'

'Dad used to call him our family heirloom.'

'I told Bennett that your heirloom was dead. He didn't care. He said he wanted to turn you as a punishment for your family, but I'd do as a warning for starters.'

Nathan stood at the edge of the lake and felt his heart hollowing out to make more room for all the hurting, all the guilt, all the shame.

'He said he was going to get you next. He said it while he was pulling your stake out of his back, the one you missed with.'

'I'm sorry.'

'He acted like I was nothing. Collateral damage, maybe a tool he could use to damage your father. He thought I was ignorant and expendable. So when he was ditching that broken branch you'd used in the woods, I pulled up a road sign and stuck it right through his chest.'

'Jackson…'

'I pulled his heart out, so I could burn it, like you said hunters are supposed to do to make sure he stayed staked. He shrivelled up like a raisin, and all this dark goo came out of him and sank into the ground.'

Nathan was dumb with misery and horror.

'That's the stuff in me now. He made me drink it out of him, and I could feel it taking over my body. I can't feel my heart beating any more, Nate. I just feel this stuff moving inside me.'

Nathan swallowed and held out his hand. 'I still love you. It's okay. What you have to do, it's okay.'

'Thirty nights ago I was in love with you. All those nights, all those feelings, feel so far away. Being horny and in love with you is a long time ago.'

Nathan let his hand drop when it was clear Jackson wasn't taking it. Eyes shut, he turned his head to offer his throat to him instead.

'Aw, Nate,' said Jackson at last. 'You know I hated *Romeo and Juliet*, right? Stupid kids in that stupid play dying for stupid reasons. I'm not going to hurt you.'

Nathan had been taught that all vampires – even the family heirloom – were dangerous. A family tree full of bloodily truncated branches didn't count for anything at all this afternoon.

Nathan walked up to Jackson, put his arms around him, held on tight and cried.

Jackson didn't cry. He didn't breathe. He was cold to the touch and seemed like he hardly knew how to work the body he inhabited, but he put his arms around Nathan and held him, too.

Nathan had been keeping Jackson a secret from everyone he knew for more than a year now. Part of him knew that was stupid. Vampires were deadly.

Except the ones that weren't. Abe had never been a threat to him, only a melancholy and unsettling presence in their house.

Like Abe, Jackson had never drunk a drop of human blood, but he was saner than Abe had ever been. Jackson wasn't a monster, and he wasn't human. He camped in the woods, read books, listened to music, talked with his old boyfriend whenever Nathan could come to him, and made no plans for an endless future that wasn't really his anymore.

Jackson wasn't a threat, but Nathan felt like the horrible suspension of nothing-ever-changing might kill him.

'I'm going to find out what happened in Australia,' Nathan promised Jackson one chill afternoon.

'What good will that do?'

'I don't know, but my dad is hiding something. I'm going to find out what.'

It took a few days, but Nathan finally found his father's Australian journals in the attic. He read them over and over, forgetting to come down to dinner in his frustration as he went through them yet again, making notes in a separate book.

A rap on the door was followed so swiftly by the door swinging open, Nathan didn't have time to hide the notebooks.

'What have you got there, son?' Despite the question, it was clear that Evan Cobb knew exactly what his son had there.

Nathan slammed the journal shut and failed to look innocent. The urge to lie collided with the knowing arch of his father's eyebrow, and wilted.

'What happened in Australia?' he asked instead.

'You've read my journal,' was his father's dry response.

'It doesn't really say anything though, does it?'

'The facts are all there, Nathan.'

'Facts. Right. Two years ago, you and Abe went to Melbourne to kill some vampires. You met a girl and her weird-ass vampire friend who convinced you not to hunt any more. Cousin Abe died, though you won't say who staked him. You wrote down all the big events and none of the why.'

'The why is complicated.'

'So after four hundred years of vampire slaying, it's just no more hunting for the Cobbs, no explanation.'

'I thought you were pleased about that.'

'I am.' Nathan's gaze dropped to the cover of the journal. *Evan Cobb. Australia. 2009.* 'I can do anything I want to, now. I don't have to be a hunter. I wasn't going to have any more vampires in my life, was I?'

Nathan didn't look up when Evan squeezed his shoulder. 'No. You weren't.'

'We'd have finished our first year of college together, this week,' said Nathan bleakly.

'I know. I'm so sorry. I should have been more-'

'It wasn't your fault,' snapped Nathan. 'Jackson's death is the fault of the vampire that killed him.'

Nathan flattened his palm over the journal that gave him more questions than answers. Angry tears made the ink of the title run. *I have secrets too, Dad.*

'I know you miss him,' said Evan, full of kindness and regret.

'I love him.'

'He was wonderful person.' At least his father didn't try to give him the "there'll be other boys" speech.

'Wonderful' was a pitiful description. It captured nothing of the way Jackson smiled whenever he saw Nathan, like happiness came Nathan-shaped. It said nothing about the breadth of his shoulders and chest or the strength in his arms that made him the star of the school's wrestling team but only ever made Nathan, strong but slender, feel protected.

Wonderful was the very least to be said about the fire in Jackson's eyes on the sports podium or arguing in English that Romeo was an idiot and Friar Laurence a criminal lunatic, or looking into Nathan's eyes between soft and then eager kisses.

'We were going to do everything together,' Nathan said. 'Go to college and change the world. Get married in New York or London. We were supposed to have a *life. Together.*'

'I know. It would have been a good life.'

'He was supposed to come skiing with me at Castle Mountain this year.'

'Do you want stay home? I can cancel the-'

'I want him back.'

Evan kissed the top of Nathan's bowed head. He didn't say the obvious.

Nathan was beyond grateful that the conversation ended there. He hated lying to his father.

That journal didn't give him any answers, but it told him where he might find them.

He just had to tell Jackson what he planned.

'Don't go.' Jackson's low, even voice didn't betray the slightest worry, unless you knew him well.

'I'll find out whatever I can and be back before you know it, Jack,' said Nathan, who knew him better than anyone.

'Something could happen to you. Australia's a long way away. You're trying to meet a strange vampire, and I won't be there.'

'I'm gathering *intel*,' insisted Nathan. 'And Dad's journal says this Gary Hooper's different. Like *you're* different.'

'Your dad doesn't even know me.' Jackson delivered this in the same almost-neutral tone, but Nathan knew every tiny flicker of his face. Jackson's dark brown eyes were never fully blank to him. His face so often seemed on the verge of fuller expression. Nathan felt like it was a secret language only he could understand. Jackson's eyes were full of clues, as was his mouth, which moved into wry near-smiles, thoughtful almost-pouts, flat lines of disapproval. Like now.

'He knows you.'

'He *knew* me when I was your boyfriend. He thinks I'm dead. Properly dead, I mean. He doesn't know I'm a vampire.'

'Aren't you still my boyfriend?' Jackson frowned instead of answering, so Nathan added, 'And anyway, he's retired.'

Jackson shrugged at the technicality. 'Once a vampire hunter, always-' he began.

Nathan cut him off. 'You didn't see his face when he finally got home. He's done with all that.'

That didn't mean Evan would be thrilled that his son was still in love with the Technically Late Jackson Kimball, and still seeing him. Nathan knew better than to let that secret out, but he still thought it was stupid. You couldn't suddenly stop loving someone just because they were undead now. It's not like Jackson had ever tried to hurt him; the opposite, in fact.

Nevertheless, Nathan had organised this trip without telling his father or aunt. Better they think he was going skiing in Canada for the winter break than know he was flying off to find this mysterious, atypical Melbourne vampire.

An announcement blared through the departures hall. 'Would Mr Nathan Cobb please report to Gate 12 for Cathay Pacific flight 811 to Hong Kong. Your plane is now ready for departure.'

Nathan congratulated himself on sending his father off with a hug two hours ago, having convinced Evan that he needed to leave on his

Big Adventure to Canada on his grown-up, independent ownsome. Hong Kong was definitely not on the way to Canada.

Jackson tucked his hands in his pockets. 'You have to go.'

'I do. But I'm going to find out what this Hooper guy can tell me, and be right back. I promise.'

'It may be nothing. It may not even apply to me. Maybe he hasn't got anything to teach us.' Jackson tilted his head back and stared at the ceiling. The tips of his fangs showed. Nathan remembered Jackson doing the head tilt thing in the days when he breathed and was trying to hide his feelings.

With Jackson's hands in his pockets, Nathan couldn't grab hold of them. Instead, he leaned in to kiss Jackson's cheek.

'And maybe he does. I won't know till I've asked,' Nathan said. 'You'll be okay without me; just don't get staked while I'm gone.' He tried to make it a joke, but it really wasn't funny.

Jackson shrugged, but he'd lowered his chin to meet Nathan's gaze again.

The overhead announcement called for Nathan Cobb again.

'I'll miss you,' said Nathan.

Jackson relented. He pressed his forehead to Nathan's.

'I promise not to get staked if you promise to come back.'

'I promise.'

Nathan took up his bag and ran to his gate.

Nathan toyed with leaving his phone off during the transfer at Hong Kong, long after he was supposed to have arrived in Canada. Then he thought about the days and nights he'd waited for word while his father and Abe travelled the world, slaying vampires, wondering if this time the vampires had done the killing.

Forty messages pinged on the screen, mostly from his dad but Aunt Lori hadn't been slack either. He didn't want to talk to either of them, so he texted them both at once.

> Something important for me to do.
> Don't worry. I'm fine.
> I'll be home before term starts.

Then he turned the phone off again so he didn't have to deal with the replies.

The very first message had been from Jackson.

My (un)life would suck without you.

Nathan foolishly cradled the phone in his hands, held against his diaphragm because holding it over his heart would have been really not cool. Especially if it made him cry. Bloody Kelly Clarkson.

On arrival at Melbourne Airport, Nathan took the transfer bus into the city and asked for directions until he was helped by friendly locals onto a streetcar to the bayside suburb of St Kilda. There he paid cash for a private room in the backpackers' hostel where his dad had stayed in 2009.

He knew he was snatching at the thinnest of hopes by sneaking off to Australia – to find the vampire from his father's Australian journals; and this Gary Hooper, who apparently did things other vampires couldn't and had a deep friendship with a human that wasn't about the biting.

It all seemed so far-fetched, but who was he to judge? Nathan had his own complicated relationship with vampires. He knew them mainly as bloodless, bloody, stone cold killers.

Yet he'd grown up with a 400 year old teen vampire mooching around his home, more victim than villain, created as a tool of revenge. Abe had never killed living people. Convinced he was on a holy mission, he'd only helped his family's descendants to kill other vampires.

And now he was in love with a boy who had become a vampire – but the boy he loved was still there. Jack had never killed anyone but another vampire either.

Evan's dry account of his mission hadn't given Nathan any idea what St Kilda would be like. From the sparse, functional prose Nathan had assumed it was a dull, underpopulated suburb full of light industry and the kind of low-rise office blocks used by cold-calling telemarketers.

Ha.

Nathan couldn't think of any place in Boston that was like it.

Shabby-hip, rowdy-sassy, half upmarket, half seedy. He'd walked past luxury car rooms and flash restaurants. Behind the shopfronts hid 19th century apartments with gates and faded Victorian grandeur, but the street itself bustled with workers, day-trippers and wastrels.

Sex workers beckoning from side alleys were no temptation. The tourists stopped at teeming bars and cafes on their way to Luna Park. The amusement park with the wide open mouth at the entrance wasn't a temptation either to a boy who'd grown up on vampire lore and its attendant caution about big teeth.

The cafes of Jewish and Italian origin were another matter. He watched the people gathered in cluttered groups around tiny tables, eating cake and drinking foam-topped coffees and regretted his very tiny budget, which went on accommodation and fries.

Streetcars – the locals called them trams – rumbled up and down the main street leading to the esplanade that followed the curving bay. Nathan could hear them from his room, along with the rise and fall of other voices, raised in laughter or in strident dispute.

St Kilda had an undeniable energy, though, grubby and grand in turns. Nathan was sorry that he'd never be able to bring Jackson here.

Evan's journal had failed in other, more important ways too. Such as really useful information on how to find Gary Hooper and his human friend, Lissa.

Leafing through the photocopies he'd made, Nathan frowned again at the material his father had blacked out with too much ink, obliterating the references to Gary Hooper's residential address.

One intact address was for The Gold Bug, a bar in the centre of Melbourne's downtown. Evan had summarised it as a Bite Club (surely not his father's phrase) where humans willingly offered their throats to vampires, exchanging a little blood for a gothic thrill. The humans enjoyed their dance at the precipice, the vampires drank without having to deal with the consequent and tedious 21st century drama of hiding the bodies.

Under this precis were further notations about the club: *Cleansed with fire* was written in Abe's curious 18th century handwriting. *Burned down*, his father had written in his economic style. *Escaped:*

Magdalene (Proprietor) and a number of other names, with cross references.

As vampire hotbeds went, the Cobbs had considered Melbourne and its lack of a body count as under control. A vampiric murder spree in 2007 ended all that. Uncle Miles was supposed to have seen to it, but then he'd been butchered by vampires, and the slayer mantle passed to his studious younger brother, Evan..

Evan, a chemist by trade, had made a dog's breakfast of the whole Melbourne thing, then wisely took the scenic route home while Aunt Lori nursed Grandpa through a series of ailments of the angry and elderly, the last of which was a stroke.

Nathan had been giddy with relief to not have to follow in his father's footsteps. Then came prom night, and the world Nathan thought he'd escaped closed in on him again, stealing Jackson from him. Stealing their future.

Well, Nathan was damn well going to steal it back, if he could only figure out how. Evan had written about this vampire who was almost human; who'd managed some horrifying miracle without describing it. Whatever Hooper had done, Abe had wigged out about it. Next thing, Abe was dead and Evan was slinking home in disgrace and relief.

Nathan tapped his finger on the only other useful potential address in the notebook. A library in a suburb called Fitzroy, on the other side of the city, according to his map. The margin note read only *Lissa W.* In the original notebook, that notation was cross indexed with an earlier entry that had been so heavily crossed out it was impossible to read. Nathan only knew she was the human who'd made friends with Gary.

Tomorrow, Nathan would ask for Lissa at the library and see where it led him.

Nathan glared through the window into the street, his teeth clenched against the welling frustration. To have come all this way to find help, only to find his first, best clue was on *vacation*. As he'd suspected from the margin note, Lissa Wilson worked at the library. Her colleague at the helpdesk had said at once she was "on leave". She'd also been really skilful about not telling him when Wilson would be back without actually saying she thought Nathan was creepy and suspicious.

That was thousands of dollars and three weeks wasted, unless maybe that Gold Bug place was operating again. He'd really, really hoped not to have to go to a nest of vampires, no matter how civilised and non-lethal they were reputed to be. Not with a family history like his. But fine. Fine. He'd go, if that was how to find this Gary.

'Why do you want Lissa?'

Nathan almost jumped out of his skin at the soft voice directly behind him. He hadn't heard anyone approach, though now he looked he could see the reflection of a chubby white dude in a luridly coloured shirt behind him.

Light refracted off vampires like it refracted from everything else, of course, but it was no wonder vampires avoided their own reflections. They always looked so… Dead. This one was chubby, pasty, and unnaturally still. The tiniest hint of fang pressed at the edges of his mouth.

Nathan's human instincts reacted in suppressed panic to other things about that human-looking thing that didn't breathe, had no heartbeat, and was full of hunger.

But he hadn't come all this way for nothing. 'I. I'm. I need to,' he addressed the reflection. This was not how he'd rehearsed it in his head. He took a sharp breath. 'I'm looking for a guy named Gary,' he said at last and in a rush.

The vampire reflection regarded him with an unfriendly frown. Or maybe it was a puzzled frown. Hard to tell unless he looked right at him, and Nathan didn't want to do that. But then, he also didn't want fangs in his jugular. The hairs on his neck prickled with the proximity of that undead thing.

Nathan turned very slowly. The vampire's expression was perplexed. That was more disconcerting than the skin-crawling sense of being prey.

'Why are you so scared?' it asked.

That was too much. 'You're a goddamned–'

He realised he'd raised his voice in a public library and ended in a fierce whisper. '*Vampire*. Scared is an autonomic response.'

The vampire's mouth twisted in annoyed exasperation, as if to say *here we go again*. Then it scrutinised him more closely. 'Who are you, though? You look familiar, but you're not from around here.' The vampire tilted its head and inhaled, and his expression resolved into pure irritation. 'Oh. You look like that American bastard who hurt Lissa a few years ago. And he tried to kill me.'

Nathan swallowed.

'You smell like him. Maybe it's the aftershave.'

Nathan decided then and there that if he survived this encounter, he was changing brands.

'He's my dad. And he wouldn't hurt a human.' Nathan skated on past the disgusted expression on the vampire's face. 'He doesn't hunt vampires any more, either.'

'Well, he couldn't, could he?' the vampire said. 'Not after he killed Abe and burnt his heart.'

Nathan blinked rapidly, letting that sink in. *Dad killed Abe*. Hell. No wonder he'd never told the whole story.

'Are you Gary Hooper?' Nathan asked.

'Yeah.' Gary Hooper the Vampire gave him another puzzled frown. 'Your heart's going like the clappers, and you've got that weird smell. Shit. Sorry. Lissa's always ticking me off for mentioning that. But. You know. Fear does whiff. The hormones, I think.'

'Elevated cortisol and adrenalin under stress create pheromones.' Adrenalin made him babble.

Gary seemed genuinely interested, 'How do you know all that?'

'I study biomedical engineering.'

'I was going to be an engineer, once. Not that kind.'

'Oh. So. Yeah. That's. Probably what you. Smell.'

'You look like you think I'm going to eat you.' He paused. 'I'm not. I don't eat people. Not even a little bit. Didn't Evan tell you?'

Nathan started breathing more deeply. 'He said you weren't like other vampires.'

Gary scoffed at that. 'I suppose Lissa will want to talk with you.

She's got a funny thing about your dad. I'll get her.' Gary started off towards the counter.

'She's not here,' said Nathan. 'The librarian said she's on vacation.'

The vampire, puzzled again, took a phone out of his pocket, and stuck his tongue out one side of his mouth in deep concentration as he slowly recalled how to check his messages. His shoulders sagged in disappointment.

'She's gone away for the week with her boyfriend. *Bugger.*' He stuffed the phone back in his pocket and scowled at the floor. 'His name's Chase. *Chase.* What kind of a name is *Chase*?'

Gary the vampire sounded like nothing so much as Nathan's Grandpa. Any moment he was going to start complaining about Young People Today and shaking his fist at clouds.

'It's you I wanted, anyway,' admitted Nathan.

'Me?'

'I've got… a friend. He needs help.'

'Pretty sure I'm not the bloke you hunters ask for help,' said Gary. His glare was resentful again and he headed for the exit.

'I'm not a hunter,' said Nathan, dashing after him. 'Best day of my life was when Dad said the family business was kaput.'

Gary kept walking, down the library path and onto the sidewalk. Cars and then a streetcar – *tram* – rumbled past.

Nathan caught up with Gary's determined pace. 'But he said you're the most human vampire he'd ever met. In his journal he wrote that you did something weird, and amazing, and I need to…' He walked faster to keep up. 'I need to know!' Nathan said, grabbing for Gary's elbow.

'It's private,' snapped Gary. 'And I don't know what use it is to any friend of Evan's.'

'Dad doesn't know about Jackson,' Nathan snapped back. 'A vampire turned him but he refuses to go bad. He won't drink blood, he says he doesn't have to be a monster. I have to help him come back to me, but he's, he can't, he…' Nathan stopped, gulping back tears, shocked at the shock on Gary's face. 'I love him and I don't know how to help him.'

'You… love… Jackson. He's. A bloke?'

'Yeah, I love a dude.' Nathan was defiant. Screw homophobic vampires anyway.

'And he loves you?'

'You don't have to sound so surprised. Guys love guys sometimes. Get over it.'

Another tram rumbled by, pausing at the stop further down the street then trundling off again.

That puzzled expression crossed Gary's face again, then cleared. 'My friend Drew's gay. His last boyfriend was a dipshit. Mez and Tina let him win at pool all that night so he'd feel better. I didn't know I was supposed to, so I beat him. I usually do, though.'

'Ah...'

'Has Jackson tried to bite you?'

'No. He hasn't and he won't.'

'Not even a bit?'

'He won't even kiss me anymore.'

Gary blinked again at that. 'Why do you think I can help?'

The question was left hanging as Gary's phone rang – *Bad Moon Rising*, which displayed either a terrible or an excellent sense of humour – and he eagerly answered it. 'Lissa?'

Nathan heard an angry gabble. Gary winced and jerked the earpiece further away. Nobody needed acute vampire senses to hear that enraged voice.

'...and so I chucked him out of the hotel and he can sleep in the street for all I care!'

'He'll probably go to her place,' Gary said, reasonably, holding the phone in front of him, like it might bite.

'Yes, fine, all right, that's probably what he did. Thanks for pointing out the bloody obvious. Like I didn't feel stupid enough.'

Nathan was captivated by how humanly crestfallen Gary became.

'Sorry. Sorry, Lissa. You're not stupid. He's stupid. His name's *Chase*, for crying out loud.'

'Chase by name, Chase by nature, huh?'

'It's a really stupid name.'

'It is.' Nathan could hear a bubble of rueful laughter in the woman's tone now. 'You're right. I'm sorry I snapped. It's not your fault, and you're right. He has gone to her place.'

'I could go shred the tyres on his motorbike if you like.'

'Thank you but no. It's fine. Better I know what he's like now, than two years down the track.' A sigh emanated from the phone. 'How is it that all the men in my life are creeps?'

Nathan watched Gary blink at that pronouncement.

'Except you. Obviously not you. Gary, you are the one shining light of the menfolk in my life. One day I will find a man as good and decent as you.'

'So I'm still your worst best friend?'

Laughter. 'You are the *best* worst best friend a girl could ask for. I'm giving up on boyfriends. Only mates from now on. You and me, yeah?'

'All right.' Gary relaxed, obviously pleased. 'I went by the library to see if you wanted a movie night. I forgot to check my messages again.'

'Movie night would be awesome. Head for my place; I'll meet you there in thirty.'

'In thirty,' Gary agreed. He waved absently to Nathan, then dashed to the tram that was just coming into the stop.

'Wait!' Nathan shouted after him. 'We need to talk!'

Gary smooshed himself up to the window of the departing tram and shouted something almost unintelligible.

'You want me to go to the Gold Bug?' Nathan shouted back, incredulous. '*When*?' but the tram, and Gary, had gone out of earshot.

Nathan didn't know what he'd expected from Gary Hooper, but this wasn't it. He was nothing like Abe. He was much more like Jackson, while also being nothing like him.

Gary was friends with a human. They bantered, with mutual affection; though that didn't mean much. Humans could get attached to all kinds of things. Pets. Cars. Songs. Vampires only got attached to blood.

Except that Gary was clearly very much attached to Lissa, the way that friends were. Cousin Abe had never been like that with any of the family; certainly never with him. Abe had been the kind of family you couldn't get rid of, and he'd never been *attached*.

The shouted suggestion to go to Gold Bug was a bad idea. It was all the bad ideas rolled up into one Super Bad Idea.

But right now it was Nathan's best hope of finding Gary again – of learning his secret, and teaching it to Jackson.

It was no comfort at all that he'd been right. Coming to the Gold Bug had been a super, super, *super* bad idea.

Nathan was bleeding. A lot. Blood oozed from his throat, through his fingers pressed against the wound and it wouldn't stop.

Nathan knew how it went from here. He'd done Grandpa's training and read four hundred years of journals. A vampire bite normally stopped bleeding after a few minutes. Vampire saliva had healing properties. Unless the bite was ragged; unless the vampire had torn the artery. Unless the vampire meant you to die.

Oh god.

Nathan wished this awful bar had still been charred walls and ashes when he arrived. But the vampires who ran it had rebuilt their damned Bite Club and even called it by the same pre-inferno name, the Gold Bug. Vampires, being unchanging, hated change.

He more deeply wished he'd given up on trying to find the damned place at the end of this long, dog-legged and ill-lit city alley. The half dozen narrow alleys and laneways he'd tried first, attempting to follow the journal's unclear directions, had led him to numerous innocently cool and atmospheric bars, all theatrical élan and enticing atmosphere. Melbourne's love affair with semi-secret enclaves had lulled him into dangerous complacency. He'd found the heavy black door with the golden beetle painted in its centre and knocked.

All he'd had to say was that he was looking for Gary, and they had let him in.

So stupid.

And then he'd encountered that tall and severe vampire at the bar, looking like someone in charge.

'Looking for Gary, are you?' she'd asked, voice chilly and amused. 'He's out the back, in the booths.'

Gary had not been out the back. Instead, the severe woman had shoved Nathan into a booth veiled by heavy curtains and lunged at his throat. She'd bitten and torn him, and now Nathan was here, fingers pressed firmly into the pulse point, calculating how long it would take him to bleed to death.

Nathan gasped against the pain and tried to think what Uncle Miles would have done. Mind you, Uncle Miles had been murdered by vampires, so it wasn't like he'd had all the answers. 'Isn't this… bad for business?'

'It's not my business, darling,' said the vampire. 'I'm not Magdalene. I have a score to settle with that bitch. You'll do nicely. She does hate to waste blood, and you dead boys are so inconvenient.'

With that, she was gone. And here he was, surrounded by heavy curtains, plush furniture, mellow music and soft lighting, the smell of his own blood leaking down his throat, soaking his shirt.

The curtain moved but Nathan didn't look up. He was afraid it would make the blood spurt.

'Ha. Lissa was right.' The speaker sounded vaguely impressed with the prediction. 'She worried you'd misheard me. She doesn't have a high opinion of hunters. She thinks you only hear what you want to hear.'

Nathan looked, then. The blood pulsed over his fingers and he whimpered. He couldn't think of anything to say beyond 'I was looking for you', which seemed a singular waste of breath when he had so few of them left.

Gary crouched down, eye to eye with Nathan. 'I said "don't go to the Gold Bug".'

Nathan squeezed his eyes shut. He really couldn't bear to look at the clueless dead guy pointing out the obvious, just before he died.

Cool fingers overlaid his own and pulled them firmly back. Nathan fought that, because he knew it would only make the end come sooner, but even at the best of times his strength was no match for a vampire's.

When Nathan felt Gary's mouth on his throat, his eyes flew open, disbelief, terror, and a kind of grief overwhelming even the knowledge that it was finally going to happen. For a short, glorious time he'd thought he would avoid this fate and have a life.

You said you weren't into this, he wanted to say. Or he wanted to bury a stake in Gary Fucking Hooper's lying vampire heart. If it had to end this way, he was only glad it wasn't Jackson drinking him dry. His gorgeous, lost Jack.

Only…

Only Gary wasn't biting. He wasn't sucking. He was… *licking.*

Nathan drew a shuddering breath, woozy from blood loss, which really didn't explain why a vampire licking his throat was making him inappropriately emotional.

The strange intimacy paused, then resumed, the cool mouth on his skin growing warm on his blood, sliding over the torn flesh and pulsing artery.

Nathan groaned as he realised that maybe he wasn't going to die, and his inappropriate emotional response became an even less appropriate physical one. Not quite arousal, but an intense surge of something like it.

He's saving my life. I'm going to live.

Nathan tilted his chin up to give Gary's mouth better access. He raised his hand to the tousled head nestled in his throat.

Nathan had a sudden, powerful memory of making out with Jackson in his own bedroom instead of studying chemistry. Jackson nuzzling into his throat; kissing and licking him, sucking on his throat to leave a hickey.

Nathan's fingers flexed against Gary's scalp. He encountered the line of an old scar hidden there and traced it with his fingertips. Vampires didn't scar. This must have been from before Gary became one. Nathan – lightheaded with blood loss and relief, soothed by the sensuous lapping at his throat and all its yearning reminder of Jackson – ran his fingers through Gary's hair.

The firm-but-gentle motion of tongue on skin ceased. Nathan blinked into Gary's face, meeting his ubiquitous, slightly puzzled expression.

'Sorry,' said Gary, with an air of incipient embarrassment. 'I thought I should stop the bleeding.'

Nathan couldn't take his eyes off the blood-smeared mouth. He forced his gaze up, to the hazel eyes, shining almost green with the pseudo-life of Nathan's blood, and that was better. Sort of. Only not.

This is what he looked like before he died. Kind of clueless, but kind of cute. I kind of want to kiss him.

Shit.

Gary, oblivious to the reason for the staring, self-consciously rubbed the back of his hand across his reddened lips, wiping away the traces of blood. 'Sorry,' he said again.

''S okay,' Nathan mumbled, embarrassed. 'Thanks.'

That brought a tilted smile to Gary's mouth, which Nathan was watching again, damn it.

'Beryl is going to be so in the shit with Magdalene,' said Gary, apparently with approval. 'She said if Beryl damaged another volunteer like this she'd make her cut off a finger in penance. I reckon she might do it too.' And then Gary frowned again, like he didn't approve so much after all.

Nathan let Gary pull him to his feet, then he wobbled right into Gary's solid form. The vampire extended an arm to steady him and Nathan considered sagging against him and staying there for a few hours. Safe. Relatively speaking.

Or how about not being stupid again for a very long time?

Nathan kept a hand on Gary's arm so the wobble didn't show too badly as Gary guided him out of the club into the shabby, graffiti-splashed alley.

At the door, Gary peeled off his eye-achingly bright Hawaiian shirt, leaving on the faded T-shirt underneath, and handed it to Nathan. Nathan blinked at it.

'You look terrible and you're covered in blood,' Gary said, gesturing at Nathan's clothes, 'But I figured you'd rather not clean up in the loos here, with vampires hanging about.'

So Nathan dragged off his hoodie and his shirt, scrubbed at the blood on his throat and chest, then left the ruined gear in a stiffening pile by the entrance. The collar of the vivid replacement shirt was rough against the sealed bite in his throat, but he could pass for respectable.

If the vertigo would go away, that would also be good.

'How do I look?'

Gary regarded him earnestly. 'Less shit.' He seemed to realise that this lacked tact. 'My shirt suits you.'

'Your shirt doesn't suit anybody. It looks like a kaleidoscope exploded in a rainbow factory and they wove this shirt out of the wreckage.'

Gary grinned. 'Yeah.'

That made Nathan laugh. 'You're a weird fucking vampire, you know that?'

'So I gather. Mostly from comments like that.'

Was that a wounded feeling Nathan detected faintly there? He patted Gary on the shoulder. 'I didn't say you weren't… kind of cool. In your way.'

Gary blinked owlishly and hesitantly ran his fingers through his hair. 'Why did you do that, before?'

You were saving my life when I thought I was dying; and you seemed nice. 'Do what?'

A frown, and then. 'Never mind. Where to now?'

'Can you help me back to my hostel? Maybe you'll let me talk this time.'

'All right.'

That was slightly more easily said than done, with Nathan listing into the dirty brickwork on one side. He thought it might help prop him up and shouldered into it as he stumbled a few more steps.

'Here,' said Gary, suddenly at his side again. Nathan yelped as the vampire scooped him up into his arms.

Gary was comfortably plump, without Jackson's wrestler build, but his easy strength reminded Nathan of Jackson anyway. He thought of those times that Jackson had laughingly lifted him up to show off his strength. They'd wrestle then, nobody trying to win and everybody winning when the muscular flirting resolved into making out on whatever surface was handiest.

'I can walk,' Nathan muttered, not enough blood left in him to blush. He stumbled again when Gary set him down. 'Maybe a little help,' he conceded. Gary put an arm around him and kept him upright on the way to get the last night tram to St Kilda.

Once on board, Nathan, exhausted, sagged against Gary and dozed fitfully. Gary's arm around his shoulders kept him steady. Nathan pretended it was because Gary liked him, though he thought it was probably so Nathan wouldn't fall onto the floor every time the tram rounded a bend.

'How was it you were even at the Gold Bug?' Nathan asked during one more clear-headed bout, trying to distract himself from the sense of solidity and reassurance he got from Gary's arm across his back.

'When I told Lissa about you, she was pretty pissed off. The last time someone came looking for me it was Evan and Abe, wanting to kill me. Then she decided she wanted to meet you. I didn't know where you were, only that I told you to steer clear of the Gold Bug, and she got it into her head that that's probably exactly where you'd gone. I thought I'd better see if you'd been daft enough to come. And there you were.'

'She didn't come with you.'

'Nah. Only an idiot goes to the Gold Bug.' But Gary smiled at him, like they were sharing a private joke. *Banter.* Gary was still flushed pink with Nathan's blood, of which there'd been too much. The vampire looked almost human, and Nathan was struggling with a lot of feelings that should have been complicated but weren't.

I think I like you. You saved my life. You're trying to banter with me. You're a dorky kind of cute.

Nathan was fairly convinced that inviting Gary back to his hostel room was another Bad Idea, but he did it anyway, partly because his vertigo was still so bad he needed the help to get there, and partly because he was lonely and far from home, and an hour ago he would have died except for Gary.

It was a Particularly Bad Idea because Nathan kept wanting to kiss the vampire: a simultaneously wonderful and terrible idea. He wanted to surprise Gary and thank him with the kiss, and see whether it was anything like kissing Jackson used to be. Mostly he wanted to see what awkward-shy, perpetually puzzled, adorkable, unlikely saviour Gary would do.

Nathan half-on-purpose collided with Gary as they entered the lift. Gary put an arm around him and gave him a sideways glance of mild curiosity. Nathan put his cheek on Gary's shoulder, and gazed up at him while the lift music played.

'You're nice,' said Nathan, before he realised he'd said it out loud.

Nathan couldn't help thinking that if Gary could still blush, he'd be blushing now. His eyes averted from the way Nathan was gazing at him.

Nathan's skin tingled with a memory of Gary's mouth on his throat, the unconscious eroticism and, with it, Gary's utter cluelessness.

Nathan straightened as the lift opened, and Gary followed him out into the hushed corridor. It was the slightly tinny silence of cheap accommodation after even the heavily partying Scandinavian backpackers had given up for the night.

This was so dumb and dangerous. He should go to bed, arrange to meet Gary tomorrow, in the daylight, in the company of his salty librarian friend. That would be sensible and safe.

Nathan fumbled his door open and stepped over the threshold. Gary stood in the corridor, waiting, seeming friendly, polite. Hopeful.

He's trying to be friends with me. He's a vampire with friends. *Lissa. Drew with the lousy ex-boyfriend. Tina and Mez who played pool with them.*

He saved your life, you dick. Invite him into the fucking room.

'Hang on,' said Gary as Nathan opened his mouth to do the friendly thing. 'I want to try something.'

'It's fine, Gary, I'll just…'

'Don't say anything,' said Gary, unexpectedly, unnaturally sharp.

Nathan snapped his teeth shut on the unspoken invitation.

'I wouldn't normally…' began Gary, then he faltered. 'But you seem. I don't know.'

'Normally what? Jeez, Gary, can you just…'

'**Sshhh!**'

Nathan shushed, startled by the ferocity of the hushing.

'I can do this *thing*,' said Gary. 'I don't tell people about it. Especially not other vampires. I don't think they'd like it. But I wonder sometimes, if I'm the only one who can.'

'I don't understand.'

'Let's see if I can do it, and I'll explain after.'

'Do what?'

Gary poised on the threshold, body held rigid, face tense with concentration.

And then the vampire stepped, uninvited, into Nathan's hostel room.

Nathan's jaw dropped, and he was too shocked to be afraid.

Holy. Fucking. Hell. In a fucked up undead world where Nathan thought he knew all the rules, this… was ***new.***

Nathan couldn't help himself – he reached out to place his fingers over Gary's chest, only to feel the last of the body-wracking shudder that shivered through the vampire's body, like the act had scraped his nerve endings and cost him something in pain. When it passed, Gary wore a shyly proud half smile.

'Whaddyaknow?'

Nathan stared. 'Are you okay, man? I mean, did that hurt?'

'Not how you'd measure pain, I think, but it feels horrible. In my head mostly, but my blood doesn't like it, either. The vampire stuff, I mean. It tries to stop me. I have to make my brain win the argument to let me cross the threshold.'

'Shit. Have you always been able to do that?'

'I only tried the first time when Lissa and I became friends. I do it at her place, mainly. She's never had to invite me in.

Nathan stared hard at Gary, trying to see if this Melbourne vampire carried some mark that set him apart as different, as able to do this impossible thing. The flush of Nathan's blood from earlier might still fizz in his body somewhere, but the sudden sense of animation in him was fresh.

'Who else knows you can do this? Does my dad know?'

'Lissa and her sister, Kate. Your father and Abe. They were there the time it nearly killed me.'

A door closing down the corridor brought them back to the fact that Nathan's door was wide open. Nathan pushed it shut and ushered Gary further inside. Then Nathan sat on the bed because he didn't think his legs were going to keep holding him up.

He had so many questions.

'Are you all right, Nathan?'

'I don't know. Are you? You look different.'

Gary shrugged but seemed secretly pleased. 'Doing that makes me feel like I've drunk blood when I haven't. I did tonight, to fix you, but I don't usually. But being with Lissa and coming into places uninvited makes me feel like… like all the living is spilling into me.'

'Could any vampire do that?'

'I honestly don't know. Technically, I guess, if they really, really wanted to. The wanting is hard, though. It's hard to make your brain win the argument to choose being part of something. That's not what vampires are. Being dead but not dead is all about choosing to be outside of all that. I don't know what it does to me, long term. I don't care. I don't know how to be human again, but I'm trying.'

'Why are you showing me this?'

'I want you to find out if your boyfriend can do it.'

'You do?'

'Maybe if someone else can do it too, it means there's more I could try. I can't quantify it with a data point of one. If it's replicable, then…' Gary looked at his clenching fingers then up again. 'If it isn't just me, it'd be less. Scary.'

Nathan continued to stare, and started to wish he had a bottle of Grandpa's best scotch because right now he could use it.

Gary's smile faltered. 'Do you mind?' he asked.

'Mind?'

'You look kind of freaked out.'

'Fr… oh, man, you walked into my room!' Nathan leapt up from the bed, flung his arms around the vampire and hugged him fiercely.

All kinds of hope had just been born inside him, springing up in sunny patches of burning colour that matched the ridiculous shirt of Gary's he was wearing. Rays of optimism burst all over the place in his brain and his skin and his heart. He knew it was far too soon for optimism where Jackson was concerned, but god*damn*.

And Nathan finally gave into the impulse that had been making his lips twitch all night, and he kissed Gary, hard, full on the mouth.

The sharp teeth pressed against his lower lip and it wasn't a dissuasion at all.

Gary didn't react with either disgust or interest, but he went suddenly still. Nathan drew back, enthusiasm quashed.

'Sorry.'

'It's fine.' Gary was biting his lip, tasting the kiss still. That made Nathan think of Jackson and that song they used to like. *Tastes like you but sweeter.*

'What was that for?' Gary asked, in a slow and (of course) puzzled drawl. He acted like someone had spoken to him in Latin.

'I like you.' It was the simplest of the true answers.

'Oh.'

'I should have asked. Sorry. I don't know if you've ever kissed a guy before…' and technically he still hadn't, only been kissed *by* a guy.

'It's… um. Fine. I've never kissed *anyone* much. Being the class square and, you know, brain tumours and surgery and shaved head and dying and stuff. They weren't exactly lining up.'

The scar in his hairline, Nathan realised. Gary must have seen the penny drop, because he said, 'That's why, you know, I chose this. It seemed the best option at the time.'

'Shit.'

'I suppose that might be my first kiss ever, really. The other one I don't think counted.'

'Why not?' he asked faintly. Nathan's brain reeled with the shocking notion that this was Gary's *first ever* kiss.

'She did it for a bet.' Gary's resigned/hurt expression said that debacle had been par for the course, and that's what decided Nathan on his next fantastically Bad Idea.

'That definitely doesn't count. So we should kiss again, then. Make sure we get it right. If it's the first.'

'Second, that would be now.'

'Second. Right. If you're okay with being kissed by a guy.'

'I'm okay with it.' Gary wore a bemused, intrigued smile now. 'I had a stupid crush on the school footy team's centre half forward, but it was the 50s. He'd have beaten the shit of me if I'd tried. I had a crush on the girl who kissed me for a bet, too. I wasn't very bright about my crushes.'

'Don't think about them,' said Nathan, suddenly and unreasonably angry that this dorky kid had died and woken undead without anyone ever kissing him properly. 'Think about me.' Then he pressed against Gary's cool, still body and kissed the vampire a second time.

Gary held very still and let himself be kissed.

'You're supposed to kiss back,' Nathan muttered, starting to feel very foolish.

'Oh. Sorry. Ah… How–?'

'Follow my lead.'

Nathan showed him, and Gary followed, and it was okay, it was more than okay, it was good, it was great, it was amazing, it was a truckload of turn-on as Gary shifted from clueless-to-curious, uncertain to sure.

Gary made a small noise, a *hmm* of curiosity satisfied, and drew away. 'Was that all right? Did I do it right?'

'You did it perfectly,' Nathan said. 'We can do it again. A proper boyfriend kiss.'

'You've got a boyfriend.' Gary was matter-of-fact rather than accusatory.

'And I'll go home to him, and tell him about this incredible vampire guy I met, who makes himself cross thresholds without invitation, and wants to know if he's the only one who can. And I'll tell him I kissed you, and maybe he'll stop being too scared to kiss me in case he hurts me.'

'I won't hurt you,' said Gary.

'I know.'

Nathan kissed Gary again, and Gary cautiously reciprocated. Then Nathan pressed a line of kisses along his cheek. Gary was so alertly still that Nathan fancied he could feel the vampire vibrating under his hands. He slid his arms around Gary's cuddly body, then continued dotting kisses over Gary's face and jaw before he nuzzled a line down to mouth and kiss Gary's throat.

Gary went suddenly utterly still again – a strange, poised-on-thebrinkness. Nathan raised his head from the soft point of Gary's throat, where a human pulse would have thudded under his tongue. Gary was staring at him, and Nathan could have sworn that had Gary been capable of tears, his eyes would have been wet.

'What is it?'

'That's where… where Gunther. The vampire that turned me. That's where he… bit me. Nobody has ever…' Words dried up.

Oh. *Oh.*

No first kiss. No sex. No tenderness. The only physical intimacy Gary had ever experienced was also an act of murder.

'I'm sorry,' said Nathan softly.

Gary shrugged one-shouldered. 'It's fine. I chose it. I'd be dead otherwise.' His mouth tilted up in a half smile. 'And I'd have missed my first kiss.'

'Well, that's something, then,' said Nathan. He pressed another light kiss to Gary's throat, and another to his lips. Gary, eyes closed, expression shyly pleased, put his arms around Nathan and gave him a very careful hug.

'I don't know why you're doing this,' Gary said quietly. 'But it's nice. Thanks.'

Nathan didn't know why either, except that Gary seemed sweet, and gave him hope. 'It's a thank-you kiss,' he said at last.

Gary nodded and stepped out of Nathan's embrace. 'I suppose I'd better be going. It's a long walk home.'

'No trains?'

'Not since 1987 in St Kilda. But the trams don't run this late either.'

'You could bunk here tonight, if you like.' Finally an idea that felt more Good than Bad. It's the sort of offer friends made. 'You don't sleep, right?' He glanced at the uncomfortable looking chair.

Gary looked too. 'I can sit on the floor and read. I do that when I stay with Lissa.'

Nathan really had to meet this Lissa person, who had vampire sleepovers.

'I don't have much to read. I brought a copy of *Jekyll and Hyde.* I've got a Stephen King. Oh, and a biochem textbook.'

Gary's face lit up with curiosity at the latter, so Nathan brought all three out for him. Without more discussion, Gary sat on the floor, back against the side of the bed, and started on the biochemistry text's introduction. It was like they hadn't spent the last ten minutes making out.

Nathan kicked off his shoes, stripped to his T-shirt and underpants and crawled into bed.

'G'night.'

Gary, not looking up from the book, raised a hand and waved his fingers.

My life was bizarre before I got to this point, and now it's just plain surreal.

The mysterious Lissa was there at the hostel in the morning, joining them for breakfast. She was not a sun-kissed Australian, her pale skin indicating she was very much an indoors kind of librarian.

She hello-kissed Gary on the cheek and sat beside him while Nathan stabbed at a plate of watery scrambled eggs.

'Hi.' Nathan was nervous, and mad at himself for it. Damn. It felt like meeting the parents. 'How was your night?' *You massive dork.*

'Gary texted me in the middle of it,' she said drily.

'Sorry,' said Gary. 'I forgot you'd be asleep. I meant to send a message earlier.'

Lissa patted Gary's hand. 'All good. I'm always happy if you let me know what's going on. So I know you're not being staked by anybody.' She cast a judgemental eye over Nathan.

Gary put his elbows on the table. 'He's okay, Lissa. He's trying to help his boyfriend.'

'Boyfriend?'

'Jackson got turned into a vampire.'

Lissa's face fell, all coolness fled. 'Shit. I'm sorry.'

She clearly knew first-hand about this kind off loss, and she was still friends with a vampire. No wonder his dad had been intrigued by her.

'It's okay,' said Nathan. 'Well. It's not okay, but Jackson's going to. Not be fine. But better. Maybe. Maybe he can do what Gary does. The.' He dropped his voice. 'The not invited thing.'

'You told him about that?' She arched surprised eyebrows at Gary.

'I *did* it.' Gary was pleased. 'It's not as easy as visiting you, but a lot easier than getting into that house after Evan kidnapped you.'

Nathan's eyes widened. 'My dad kidnapped you?'

Lissa scowled. 'He did.'

'He still liked you though,' said Gary, trying to smooth over this awkward patch.

'Hmm.'

'I know he did. Especially since you and he-' Gary stopped abruptly and gave Lissa a startled look. She looked just as startled back at him.

'…went…' Gary was searching desperately for how to end this sentence he never should have started. '…to a… bookshop?'

Lissa folded up into sudden laughter, then caught his hapless expression as she was sobering up and dissolved again.

'Your face!'

Instead of being offended, Gary looked smug that he'd made her laugh. 'See, I do listen. I'm learning.'

She leaned against Gary's arm, still giggling fitfully. 'You do, and you are.' She grinned at Nathan. 'And no, you don't want to know.'

Nathan remembered a line from his father's journal, describing in terse words his shock at discovering this wonderful woman he'd met was colluding with vampires. (*That night was a mistake*, he'd also written, and underlined.) Nathan put two and two together and came up with seven, and decided that no, he really didn't want to know any details.

The two of them were colluding away right now, laughing, Gary not quite human but not aloof. He was engaged, and fond, and *attached*.

A waiter arrived with coffee for the three of them, which Nathan found strange – vampires could ingest only blood – until Gary lifted his coffee to inhale the scent deeply and wistfully.

'It always smells better than it tastes,' Lissa offered.

'Liar,' said Gary, but he smiled.

'If you play your cards right, I'll let you get a whiff of my bacon when breakfast comes.'

'That smells better than it tastes, too.'

'You keep telling yourself that, Gary.'

'At least I don't have to pretend I like your sister's cupcakes.'

'Don't remind me. How does she manage to make them look great and taste like nothing?'

Then they put their heads together, and whispered 'sugar-free!' in dire tones.

'If you tell her they're awful, you're banned from the house,' Lissa mock-threatened.

'I can't eat them, so how would I know?' Gary demanded with deadpan dignity, but then he grinned, and his fangs were showing. 'I tell her they smell great.'

'Do they?'

'No.'

'Good man.'

Nathan sipped his own coffee, watching them being playful together.

After breakfast, they returned to Nathan's room. Lissa asked a lot of questions, first about Evan, then about why Nathan had come all the way to Melbourne, and finally all about Jackson.

She sat on the floor with her back against the wall. Gary sat beside her, his shoulder pressed to hers.

'You really didn't tell Evan you were coming to Australia?' Lissa asked. 'How pissed off is he going to be with you?'

'I don't know. Aunt Lori's furious, but I can handle her. Dad emails every day to see if I'm okay, and I tell him I'm fine. He's always been weird about the time he spent here. He hardly talks about it, even though it was the biggest thing to ever happen to this family since that lunatic ancestor made Abe into a vampire in the first place.' He nodded at Gary. 'And that uninvited thing? That's *epic*.'

Lissa placed her hand over Gary's, where it rested on the floor between them, proud and proprietorial. 'Gary is pretty epic.'

'You know what you do is revolutionary, don't you?' Nathan asked Gary, drawing Gary's gaze up from Lissa's hand on his. 'You're right to keep it secret from other vampires. Dad says vampires are like those super-conservatives who hate anything that makes them feel like their way isn't the only way. Mostly, vampires hate change.'

'Ironic,' said Gary, 'Given we outlive everything else. The world's nothing *but* change, and there we are, staying the same forever.'

'Not you, though.'

'Not me,' Gary agreed. He considered. 'Maybe not your boyfriend, either.'

Nathan drew in his breath, but it didn't calm the hope much. 'Maybe. I love him. I'm not scared of him. He saved my life.'

'Do you think he can…*evolve*, the way Gary has?' Lissa asked.

'It's worth finding out if he can.'

'You can boyfriend-kiss him when he does,' said Gary.

'I hope so.'

Nathan was aware that Lissa was glowering at him. 'How do you know we-?' he began.

'Gary texts me everything,' said Lissa darkly.

'Wasn't I supposed to tell her? And why are you angry?' This to Lissa.

'I'm not angry.'

Gary cocked an eyebrow at her.

'All right. I'm a little bit angry. He boyfriend-kissed you and now he's going back to his actual boyfriend. He's as bad as bloody Chase.'

'No he's not.'

'He's as bad as Evan, then. If he hurts you,' declared Lissa with an evil sideways look at Nathan, 'I will make him sorry.'

Nathan didn't know what making him sorry would look like, and he was almost certain that Lissa didn't know either, but those thoughts were less distracting than how odd and charming it was that she had made herself a vampire's champion and was looking out for him.

'You're treating me like I'm an idiot again, Lissa,' said Gary evenly. 'It was a nice first kiss, but he doesn't love me, and I don't love him. You're making a fuss over nothing.'

Lissa subsided. 'I don't think you're an idiot,' she muttered.

'You think I'm naïve.'

A pause and then: 'A bit. I don't want you to be hurt. And it hurts when people you like use you.'

'I wasn't…!' Nathan began to protest.

'He didn't,' said Gary, and folded his arms. 'It's not like I can love him anyway. I haven't got the chemical responses for it. Sorry Nathan.'

Nathan appreciated the deeply sceptical look Lissa gave Gary. He'd been watching Gary interact with and talk about Lissa since the library, and thought that if the vampire didn't think he had strong feelings for his friend, he was very, very self-deluded.

Gary seemed sincere in his belief, though. He was like Jackson that way, too. 'Vampires can't love!' Just because they didn't produce the dopamine, serotonin or the norepinephrine, their hearts didn't quicken and oxytocin was not a thing.

Right. And vampires didn't get attached.

'Can we just agree that it was a nice kiss and nobody's upset and everything's cool?' asked Nathan, 'Because this is *really* awkward.'

Everyone fell silent, and then Gary said in a low voice, 'I can still go shred Chase's tyres if you want.'

Lissa laughed shakily. 'I want to say yes but I think the answer's still no.' To Nathan she said, 'I'm done with my questions if you are.'

'All done.'

'By the way, Gary, Drew called and asked about meeting up tonight. We decided to form a Broken Hearts Club, play pool and drink beer. I know you're heart's not broken but you'll come, yeah?'

'Yeah.'

'Ah… you're welcome too, Nathan. If you want…'

'Not tonight. I'd better change my flights and make some calls.'

Despite the occasional awkwardness, Nathan enjoyed their company. He imagined briefly staying here, being friends with people who understood at least a little about his weird life. But watching them, he also realised how much he wanted to go home. Hanging around with these two, if they'd let him, had its appeal, but it would only ever be a temporary solution.

You don't save what you love by running away from it.

Nathan still had no idea what the future held for him and Jackson, but he was sure now it could still hold both of them. He wanted to be with Jackson so they could find out their future together.

'Okay. Well. Bye. Say hi to Evan from me, I guess. Tell him we're still working through all that source material he left for us.'

So that's what had happened to his father's mysteriously missing laptop.

'I'll say hi.'

'And good luck with Jackson.'

Nathan went to hug Gary goodbye just as Gary reached out to shake his hand. So then Gary went to hug as Nathan stuck his hand out. Finally they managed a hug.

'Thanks,' said Gary, 'for… you know.'

'Thank you too,' said Nathan. 'For everything.'

Aunt Lori was still furious with him, but Evan calmly paid the airline fees to let Nathan change the dates of his flight home, and he was back in Boston before the end of the week. Aunt Lori's lecture was all about how anything could have happened, and how irresponsible he was, and how he'd upset his grandfather. When she finally wound down, she wrapped him in a fierce hug and cried.

'I've been so happy you were out of this vampire bullshit. Don't take off like this again, okay? I love you and I can't stand the thought of anything happening to you.'

Nathan made promises to Aunt Lori, and made some more to his grandfather, who glared grumpily at him while grabbing onto Nathan's hand and squeezing it.

Nathan kissed the old man's head. 'Sorry I scared you, Grandpa. I think I made some friends, though.'

Later, in Evan's study, Nathan waited for a lecture from his father.

'How's Lissa?'

'Good. She says hi.'

'Gary?'

'Good. He. Ah.' Nathan decided not to talk about Bite Club. 'He helped me out, and he. Walked into my hostel room without an invitation.'

'You got to know him well, then.'

I was his first kiss. 'Yeah. I like him.'

'I always said he was an unusual vampire.'

'He is astonishing; almost unprecedented.'

'I don't know I'd go that far.'

'I was quoting your journal.'

Evan only laughed ruefully. 'Damn.' Then straight out of the clear blue sky, he said, 'Do you think Jackson will be able to do it, too? I think he's willing to try.'

Nathan blanched, staggered backwards into the chair, fell heavily into it and hyperventilated.

'Nathan! Nathan, breathe. I'm sorry, son, I didn't mean to give you such a fright. Head between your knees. That's it.'

Nathan breathed raggedly, with his father's comforting hand stroking his head, over his neck, down his back.

'Y-you know ab-bout Jackson. H-how long ha-?'

'I finally found him last week, and we had a chat. I knew he had to be out there. His body was never found, and *somebody* staked Bennett in the woods. I found the fire and the ashes of Bennett's heart, and I found what was left of his body. Wild animals won't touch vampire corpses, no matter how withered they are.'

'B-but…'

'What I didn't know was that you were still seeing him. I've been looking for him on the quiet for the last year. I couldn't see how it would help you, to know he'd been turned, especially if I ended up having to stake and burn him to keep you safe.'

Nathan surged angrily out of the chair. 'If you've hurt him, I'll…!'

'He's fine. Sick of living in your ratty tent, I think.'

'Jackson wouldn't hurt me.'

'I believe you. He wouldn't even hurt *me*, and he thought I'd shown up to kill him.'

'Had you?'

'No, son. When I found out you'd snuck off to find Gary Hooper, I realised you had to have been seeing Jackson for a while. What other motivation could there be? How long?'

'Since a month after Bennett attacked us.'

'That's an impressive time to keep a secret.'

'I thought you'd try to stake and burn him if I told you.'

Evan didn't respond to that, which made Nathan suspect he was right.

'He's still a nice boy,' said his father at last. 'There's something about him that's very like Gary. He has that same yearning to stay part of the world, that vampires don't usually have. I think, like Gary, he didn't survive the turning because he didn't want to die. I think it's because he wanted to live.'

'That's the same thing.'

'I don't think so. Being a vampire is as much metaphysics and psychology as it is altered biology, and there's a shade of difference in motivation that counts. Newly woken vampires aren't usually strong enough to kill their makers, but your fresh-undead Jackson staked a 200 year old vampire because Edward Bennett threatened you. I know we always used to say that vampires don't get attached to people, but I think he's already proving us wrong.'

'Does this mean you'll help?'

Evan sat on the edge of his desk and kneaded his forehead with fingers and thumb. 'I'm not happy that you've been seeing Jackson, or that you have this idea you can save him. He's a vampire. He may not mean to hurt you, but even without all that inherent threat, you have no future with him.'

'You don't know that.'

'I know that even if you live to be an old, old man, he'll outlive you and without ever looking older than he is right now. That's not the only problem you'll face, and not even the worst, but it's a start. And your mother and I always wanted a happy life for you. I can't see you having one with him.'

'That's your problem, and I can do this without you.'

'Nathan, you're only nineteen. You're so young.'

'How old was Lissa when you slept with her?' snarled Nathan. 'She's not much older than me. Is that why sleeping with her was a mistake?

If he hoped to shame his father he failed. Evan only looked sad.

'We met before I knew she was friendly with the vampire community.'

'She's friendly with *Gary*. She thinks the rest of them are assholes.'

'I didn't realise that when I made the journal entry. My own actions afterwards made it impossible for Lissa and I to become anything else. I regret how it ended much more than how it began.'

'I don't see how I can screw up any worse than you did. Let me make my own mistakes. Jackson isn't one.'

Evan abandoned the argument. 'You're legally an adult. I can't stop you seeing him. But promise me you'll be careful. Come to me if you need to talk.'

'Because our family is so good at the talking.'

But his father looked heavy with regret.

'Are you going to help me and Jackson or not?'

'I'll help. But for God's sake, don't tell Lori or your Grandpa.'

Nathan figured his father had agreed mostly so he could keep a cautious hunter's eye on Jackson. Yet he'd found Jackson, spoken with him, and not staked him right off, the way Grandpa might have done.

'Your dad's right,' Jackson said when Nathan got to his campsite the next day. 'I'm going to outlive you.'

'Don't you start. That's not only a vampire thing. My mum died when I was still a kid. Grandma died when I was in Junior High. Dad's brother, Uncle Miles, was murdered a few years ago. Then there was Abe, even if I wasn't sad about him. Grandpa's going soon, I think. Most of us live on after the people that we love.'

'But I'll be doing it after *every single person* I love has gone.'

The present tense didn't escape Nathan. 'Do you still love me, then?'

'Can I? I'm a vampire. I haven't got a working heart anymore.'

'Love doesn't happen in the heart, Jack. We feel it there maybe, but it's more than hormones and chemistry, isn't it? Love is things like talking shit all night because you like the sound of their voice. It's wanting to know what you think, and laughing at the same stuff.' He thought of Gary and Lissa. 'It's teasing each other and liking it, because it isn't mean. It's feeling safe and strong when you're together, and wanting the other person to be happy, and being happy when you're with them.'

Jackson rested his fingers on Nathan's cheek.

'You're in my head,' Jackson said. 'Everything about you is in my head, and when I think about you, it feels like the world still matters, even if I can't feel my heart beating any more. If that's still love then I guess I love you.'

Nathan leaned towards him and Jackson gravitated towards him too, and their mouths met in a gentle kiss. Then a less gentle one. Nathan could feel Jackson's fangs against his lips, but Jackson was careful: slow and deliberate, his stillness so concentrated that Nathan's heartbeat quickened.

Nathan smeared kisses down Jackson's jaw and to his throat, and Jackson clutched him, not too tight. Just like Gary, Jackson had died with that appalling intimacy. He kissed the place tenderly, then cupped Jackson's face in his hands and dotted little kisses over his cheeks and nose.

Jackson's eyes were not quite dulled. His face was not quite blank. His Jackson was still there, and still loved him, and maybe he could, like Gary, evolve.

'Dad's given me the keys to the family's old cabin on the other side of the lake,' he said. 'I'm not going to invite you in.'

Jackson pressed his forehead to Nathan's and breathed, even though he didn't have to, so he could inhale Nathan's scent.

Nathan pulled Jackson close. He wrapped his arms around him and Jackson lay his head on Nathan's chest to listen to his heartbeat.

In companionable silence, they watched the water. The future may not turn out to be everything they hoped, but at least they had one now.

6
6
BOOTS
COUCH
BALSAM HOREHOUND
USE

Lost and Found:

Horehound and Flour

The quaint sign appeared on the two-storey, double brick house one sunny afternoon. In faded lettering, the advertisement said:

STOP THAT COUGH! DR SCOTT'S BALSAM HOREHOUND 6D.

The washed out sign that appeared alongside it

USE J KING GROWN BRAND SELF-RAISING FLOUR

was superficially much less alarming than the Horehound, though that depended on how alarmed you were about flour raising its own self.

The general feeling among the public was that the owners of the house had discovered the old shop signs while renovating and had decided to go for that retro-distressed look. How charming, the passers-by thought. How delightful and hipster-chic. How handsome and Victorian Medicinal Gothic.

They, of course, did not have to live with the Horehound. Or the Flour.

The Flour self-raised itself with very little fuss, really. Small clouds of flour swirled and formed a little ghost girl who ran through the house leaving white powdery handprints on all the darkest surfaces. Sometimes she laughed a wheezy, floury giggle. All the exorcists, priests and witches who examined the house swore that yes, this ghost had raised itself from the flour, no external magic necessary. None of them were able to make the little girl leave. The sprite had decided to

"

manifest and played on weekdays and Sundays. Nobody knew what she did with herself on Saturdays, and decided it best not to enquire.

The Horehound was something else entirely. Woven from musky weeds, it sat in the entrance to the parlour, long forepaws of tangled green crossed, its large head uplifted and alert. It huffed puffs of downy white flowers that drifted up into its ears shaped like mint leaves and stuck there, like dandelion confetti on a curtain of green.

Eleanor, who owned the house, read about the horehound plant and had tried giving this dog-shaped horehound a throat lozenge in the misguided belief it might rid her of the herbal beast.

The hound lifted one ear, cocked a crinkled green eyebrow and made her feel so inept that she apologised three times and brought a bone for it in apology.

The Horehound wasn't interested in the bone either, but otherwise seemed pleased enough with the peace offering. It showed this by thumping its twiggy green tail on the carpet, which sent puffs of Flour and accompanying wheezy giggles into the air.

The assorted exorcists, priests, witches etcetera had no more luck in banishing the herb-made hound than they had the Flour. This might have had as much to do with Horehound's spell-repelling properties as it was to do with the general incompetence of the specialists.

The housing market being what it was, Eleanor thought a quick sale would help, but it didn't. Flour running through the house in a white puff of glee every day but Saturday was hard enough, but on Saturdays Horehound took up the slack by flumping its sturdy weed-built self in the entrance and giving that accusing green eyebrow to everyone who looked inside. Nobody would buy and eventually the real estate agents refused to visit. Perhaps repelling them was another of the Horehound's medicinal properties.

Eleanor has learned to live with Flour, who these days never does anything worse than leave a giddy pattern of handprints on the polished marble around the fireplace.

'Yes, Flour, yes, I see you,' says Eleanor now, and Flour eddies in delighted flurries before settling back into the kitchen cupboard.

The guardian Horehound still makes her feel inept with a well-timed cock of the green eyebrow. Eleanor has left bones, chew toys and an old slipper in tribute, and these things are piled up underneath the hound's chest and paws of woven stems and oval leaves. He's a bit of a nuisance but, on the plus side, and true to the nature of the herbs it used to make itself a body, Eleanor hasn't had a sore throat since it appeared on the same day as the painted signs. Menstrual cramps are a thing of the past. Not a single wound has become infected since he took up residence 97 years ago.

Eleanor also hasn't aged a day in all that time.

On the whole, Eleanor would very much like to have a strong word with Dr Scott and J King, wherever the bastards are hiding.

THE PATH

For my mother

The days since the call
Are a series of short, sharp shocks.
I see a photo:
> *Our family pulling faces*
> *You, young, in curlers on a boat*
> *Triumphant owner of a sausage roll*

I read a message:
> *Those who knew you, or us*
> *Taking the time for kindness.*

A memory steals in:
> *The story of the Bill Haley movie, and dancing home with grandma*
> *That time the cat swallowed my pendant and you followed her all day to...*
>> *retrieve and clean it*
> *The way you danced with us, cheeky, happy.*

And there it is again.
The sudden knowledge,
> *New again*

I won't see you any more.
For a moment it feels like the ground beneath me

tilts.

A paving stone on which I've always stood has crumbled.
My gaze drops down to seek the gap

But it's all right.
    It's all right.
The part of you that built my path is not gone.
That stone – made of everything you were and what we were
together
    Good and bad
Is still there.
However rough it was at times,
It has worn smooth with use,
With the footsteps of our lives.
You loved me; I loved you.
    The rest is detail.
The ground is firm beneath my feet
You are still part of the path I walk;
That holds me up and guides me.
I won't see you any more,
But you're still here.
In my path,
    In my feet,
        In my head,
            In my heart.

Lost and Found:

Bouquet

The wedding between the mermaid and the maiden was a small affair. Members of both families gathered by the shore to wish them well.

Or to hope for the best, because, to listen to some of the guests, theirs was not the most auspicious of pairings. The maiden's family feared Tia would follow her mermaid wife into the sea and drown. The mermaid's family, that Merleine would give up her voice for a pair of legs only to be spurned on land.

(It had happened before. Great-great-grandma's sister's tragedy was a cautionary tale – or tail – for them all.)

That's without even getting into the "how" of pleasure for a mermaid and a maiden.

Tia and Merleine naturally ignored their family's fears. They were in starry-eyed, forever kind of love, but not an all-or-nothing love. And the biology of pleasure was simple when you combined imagination and the will to use it. Mermaids and maidens both had hands and mouths and the giddy will to use them for desire. This they'd shown each other in words sweet and lewd, in the arch of back and fin, the gasp of air and swirl of water, in deep and wanton cries and after-sighs.

(To be fair to the families, nobody wanted much to think of their maiden and their mermaid in the throes of passion with each other. Uncomfortably arousing meets but-this-is-my-relative! was the general import of that kind of visualisation.)

Tia and Merleine were not to be put off by the doubters, accepting that the reservations were meant with love even while they spoke of mistrust. 'They'll learn to see us,' they said to each other. 'Our life together will teach them better.'

On their wedding day, Tia and Merleine sat together in a little boat just off the pier. Tia's red hair was woven and coiled high and circled with a crown of white roses, and Merleine's wet, black ringlets curled around her face, one side held back with a little comb of pink coral. They smiled at each other, Tia's eyes sparkling like sunshine on wavelets, Merleine's like moonlight on sand.

Tia and Merleine spoke their vows and the landed priest blessed them, and the merfolk elder blessed them, and the families threw petals and prayed that their daughters would not break each other's hearts.

Tia and Merleine kissed, soft-sweet, and held each other's hands and shone happiness on each other.

Then Merleine took her bouquet of shells and seaweed and threw it over her shoulder into the sea, where her sister Yara leapt from the water to catch it, then gazed shyly from under her long, damp lashes at a pretty merman she longed to hold.

Tia took up her bouquet of blue hydrangeas and white peonies bound in a ribbon of white silk and she threw it over her shoulder onto the pier.

Tia's little nephew stretched out to catch the bouquet. Six years old, milk white skin, hair of flaming red, sea-green eyes, he stretched and jumped and missed and fell.

Off the pier, into the green sea, a shout, a splash, and then down down down into the deep.

Merfolk are prone to seeing portents in every little thing. Landfolk are little better. The moment he fell, people from both families saw it as a sign of impending doom.

'Gannet!' cried Tia, almost falling from the little boat in her urgency to save her favourite. Merleine was faster, diving overboard, her dry land-legs fusing at once at the touch of salt water (going knickerless was a safety measure, not a statement of ribaldry).

In moments Merleine had her arms around the little boy. She placed her mouth over his, she took the water he'd inhaled from his lungs into her own; she fed him oxygen back, filtered through her gills. A powerful flex of her rainbow-scaled tail brought them both back to the air.

Gannet coughed and gulped in air. Merleine rocked him in her arms then flexed her mermaid body to rise up in the water and hand the boy back to his parents.

'Where're my flowers?' asked Gannet, as though his bouquet were more important than the drowning he'd just avoided.

Tia's bouquet had floated away, land flowers drowning in the salty sea. Two days later they were found, beached at last, bedraggled.

But a drowned bouquet is not a portent. The flowers weren't waterlogged with a surfeit of tears. Hydrangeas and peonies were washed to shore and were forgotten.

Gannet, on the other hand, was chided for carelessness, then fussed and coddled and given extra cake. His Auntie Tia gave him the white rose crown to wear, and he liked it better than the bouquet. His new Auntie Merleine taught him a merfolk song which sounded a bit like gargling and a bit like splashing and it made him laugh.

Ten years have passed since the wedding by the sea. Tia and Merleine are still starry-eyed forever in love. It's still not an-all-or-nothing love. Like all the best kinds of love, it is full of balance. They have worked together to find the compromises that keep them both happy and keep them both safe.

Tia and Merleine live in a cabin built over the sea. They catch and sell fish at the markets. Merleine finds shells and treasures in the sea and she and Tia make them into rare and beautiful jewellery to sell at craft fairs. They have a happy life.

Mermaids and maidens lack the biology to make babies. Given their preferences, that would be just as true if they'd fallen in love with a woman of their own kind. Maternal love has been lavished anyway, upon Gannet who visits with his family often, and doesn't realise his ability to hold his breath for ever-so-long is the sea-magic gift that Auntie Merleine sang to him on her wedding day. Merleine's sister Yara brings her own baby girl to visit too, and Gannet is teaching tiny Pearl how to catch.

In the centre of the cabin, a hole cut in the floor is Merleine's own door where she comes and goes. Some days she walks about on dry land-legs and on others she sits in the circle of sea, her rainbow scaled tail wafting in the water with her darling Tia splashing in the sea beside her. Sometimes Tia lies along the wooden floor and combs her seabound wife's black, curling locks with a comb made of coral, and they kiss and caress here where their two worlds meet.

In the cabin, in the sea, in both worlds by the mermaid's door, they love each other with voices, hands, mouths, hearts. They give each other pleasure and joy. Neither keeps the other prisoner and neither is alone.

Tia sleeps on the floor, her hands in the water. Merleine sleeps on the tide, Tia's hands in her hair.

Landfolk and Merfolk are both 60 per cent water anyway. It's enough affinity to make a beginning and the rest, like all love that lasts, is in making the most of where their differences meet.

The Beekeeper's Children

Author's note: This story is set in 1916, but in the same universe as *The Adventure of the Colonial Boy*.

The emptiness alongside John Watson as he woke had the quality of bad dreams: *not right* and yet *accepted*.

A marginally more wakeful thought then occurred to John: *he'll be in the kitchen or out with the bees.*

At last, memory caught up with consciousness, and John's next thought was once again and always, *Please, God, keep Sherlock safe.*

John lay lonely in their bed, still suspended between *not right* and *accepted*, while the rest of his daily litany unspooled in his thoughts.

Is Sherlock's mission over? Is he on a ship home yet? Is he in London, debriefing with Mycroft? He is coming home to me, surely, if all has gone to plan. Unless, God, dear God, he is d...

Through the bedroom wall, in Sherlock's former study, John heard a frightened, wailing cry and then another voice, a soothing murmur. The pain in both moved him, but he was selfishly grateful for their disruption too. It kept him from following the awful direction of his own thoughts.

'Shush now, Davy. Shush.'

'I can hear the bombs, Bobby.' Davy's voice was a fragile sob.

'It's just a bad dream, Davy. See? Here we are in Sussex, safe and sound.' Bobby Wiggins' tone was softly encouraging, sunny and kind as always.

Davy's panicked panting breaths quietened.

Poor lads, John thought, glad again he had been able to offer them a billet – two narrow beds in place of Sherlock's desk and cabinets and laboratory equipment. Those things were packed away Sherlock's upstairs bedroom now, rarely used even when Sherlock was at home. Neither of the men next door could have managed the stairs.

(John often sat upstairs now, holding Sherlock's pipe or his magnifying glass, or clutching his coat and breathing in the fading scent, aware that he was trying to wish Sherlock home by force of will.)

Bobby spoke again, sadly this time. 'Won't you look at me, at least?'

Soon after, John heard Bobby's halting steps to the doorway of the billet, and down to the bathroom. Minutes later came the heavy clump of Davy MacKee's foot and the scrape of his crutches; the clatter of the crutches tangling with a chair. The creak of Davy sitting back down on the bed. The sound of the young man weeping.

With a sigh, John swung his feet out of bed, reached for his cane and prepared for another day of waiting with the bees.

'Tea for you, Doc.'

The cup clattered onto the table, sloshing tea, but John only nodded thanks. Bobby eased himself onto the seat opposite and reached for a slice of bread and the honeypot. He found spreading the honey awkward and switched the knife to his more flexible but non-dominant left hand. He screwed his mouth into a determined pout and made the best job of it he could.

'It'll get better,' said John quietly.

'Me or him?'

'Both of you.'

'Not the eye, though.' Bobby bit into his breakfast, chewed, and met John's gaze with defiant cheer.

One of the young man's eyes was as bright and clear as ever. The other was murky within the scarred socket, and saw only shadows now.

'No, not the eye,' John replied. 'But your coordination will improve.'

Bobby flexed the fingers of his right hand, likewise scarred. The damage all down the right side was awkward, but no longer painful.

'Reckon it will,' agreed Bobby, 'I'm not a looker like before, but then, my brother Will says I didn't have many looks to lose.' He grinned, irrepressible even in the face of injury. He was like his father, Bill, that way.

'Well, looks aren't everything. I've managed perfectly well without them all my life.'

Bobby laughed out loud. 'You're too modest, Doc Watson. There's some consider you right handsome, I bet.'

'I doubt it.' *And the only man who would agree with you is not here to defend me against myself.* But John smiled. Sherlock would only have berated him about false modesty in any case. 'Still willing to help me with the bees again today?'

'Why not? Can't see they can do worse to me than the Boche, eh?'

'Holmes insists that treated correctly, bees are better company than most people.'

'Yeah, but most people, treated correctly, as he says, are all right too.'

John and Bobby wore bulky white beekeeping suits into the meadow, too cautious to emulate Sherlock's bare-handed inspections. Bobby wore Sherlock's own rarely-used suit and smoke scented veil. He walked without Sherlock's grace, especially with the way his now-healed injuries truncated his movement, but his slowness seemed to suit the bees.

They carefully smoked the bees calm and checked the progress of the hive. To keep Sherlock's records up-to-date, John noted the colours of the pollen, from which Sherlock would know where the bees had foraged, and checked the queen's laying pattern to make sure it was even.

Bobby was conscientious about brushing bees away from the box edges while John replaced the inner cover and lid. The boy's care made John think of Sherlock, which made his heart clench and his eyes prickle, so he made a joke.

'I knew I would get on well with the bees when I discovered we have something in common.'

'You're both uncommonly fond of Mr Holmes?' offered Bobby with a wealth of affection.

John was more surprised by Bobby's unaffected warmth than his knowledge, but he huffed amusement. 'Two things in common, I suppose, then. The bees and I all find tranquillity in a good smoke.'

Bobby was kind enough to laugh. 'Now I see all those little bees puffing on tiny pipes,' said the lad, 'and looking around with wee magnifying glasses to pronounce on the habits and histories of the flowers!'

John laughed too, but the heart-hurt closed his throat suddenly.

Bobby's gloved hand patted John's white-shrouded shoulder. 'He'll be home soon, Doctor Watson, right as rain, you know what he's like. And he always comes home to you.'

John mastered himself. 'Well, there are times when I have to go and fetch him,' he said.

Sherlock spent the weeks before he left England training John how to look after the bees and keep the records on their behaviour, marking up books and leaving him notes. John still found notes randomly, in cupboards, in books, tucked into the pockets of his coats or the heels of his boots.

Some of the notes didn't strictly relate to the bees.

Some bees forage very far from the nest in search of necessary pollen, yet the bee will return to the hive and its Queen. Always.

John wasn't as easy with the bees as Sherlock, but he took his commission seriously. He used his best bedside manner with them, speaking encouragingly, kindly and gently to them, making no sudden movements. John was clever enough to learn quickly, brave enough to not be cowed by the threat of stings, and sentimental enough to be soothed by the tasks of beekeeping. He felt that by taking care of them, he was caring for Sherlock, too.

He thought the bees knew he, and now Bobby, weren't Sherlock. It gave him a feeling of solidarity with the hive, to feel that the bees missed Sherlock. He became superstitious, though. He felt he mustn't let anything happen to the colony; these bees that Sherlock had raised.

If anything happened to them, it would be a harbinger of Sherlock's fate.

Sherlock would have scoffed at the notion. John knew it was ridiculous. Illogical, unreasonable, even damaging, to think of them that way. It didn't stop the thought, or keep him from tending them as perfectly as he knew how.

Davy MacKee was at the kitchen table, fixing the clock, when John and Bobby returned from the meadow. Davy's crutches rested at an angle against the wall. The stump of his left leg swung in time with the tock of the timepiece as he tested the mechanism.

'Post's come,' he said, pointing with the delicate screwdriver but not looking up. 'Tea's brewing.' The pot sat on the end of the table, steaming fragrantly, the cups arranged about it, along with the jar of last harvest's honey. Davy's shirt was more rumpled under one arm and his hand was reddened where he'd had to grip the crutch tight in the effort to manoeuvre cups and pot to the table over numerous trips. John didn't comment on it. Davy wouldn't thank him for noticing the effort it had taken to do something so normal.

Bobby poured tea while John took up the letters addressed to Dr. J.H. Watson. He put aside the ones addressed to S. Holmes; pleas for help with strange puzzles, most of them. *The Strand Magazine* readers didn't know Sherlock was away applying his gifts to a larger good.

Davy glanced up at Bobby. 'There's a letter from your Ma,' he said. His gaze fixed briefly on Bobby's ruined eye then returned to the clock.

Bobby sighed and opened the envelope.

'Ma says she's heard from Will,' he said with brittle cheerfulness. 'He's coming home on leave, all in one piece too, which is a relief. Don't know as Doc Watson has got room for another recuperating soldier, though the bee shed's warm enough to doss in at a pinch. At least it's dry and nobody's shelling it.'

At the table, Davy MacKee finished screwing the back of the clock into place. 'I don't reckon the bees'd take to William like Dr Watson says they've taken to you. He's all fidgety.'

Bobby grinned. 'He's got ants in his pants, Ma says. And anyway, I'm sure the two of us is enough to be getting on with, eh Doc?'

'I'm very glad to have you both here,' said John. It had been lonely in Sherlock's absence, until Bill Wiggins wrote to ask if Dr Watson knew where his Bobby and Bobby's friend Davy could get out of the noise of London to recover their nerves. The quiet here did both boys good. Not enough good yet, mind. Some things, as John knew to his chagrin, could take years to sort out, if the men involved were fools enough.

He had no notion how to remedy that, however, so he leafed through his correspondence. The first letter was from Stamford, the next a missive from the British Medical Association. The third…

John abandoned his tea and tucked the third letter into his coat pocket.

'Hand me the wool and needle, Bobby,' John heard Davy say as he headed for his room. 'Might as well make myself useful with some darning.'

John sat on the side of his bed, put on his reading glasses, then slipped his thumb under the flap of the envelope, tore it carefully open and shook out its contents.

The grubby slip of paper bore a sketch in fine black ink, of John Watson's own eyes, rendered perfectly, down to every line of his 64 years – minus the ones he'd developed since Sherlock had been summoned to a mission for His Majesty.

Fingers trembling, John lifted the paper and inhaled its scent. It smelled of soot and ink. He couldn't discern anything of Sherlock's scent on it: but he had touched this paper. Within the last week, Sherlock had drawn this image, sent it with his dispatches to Mycroft to forward onto John. He had sent the only message he could.

I live, said the message, and *I remember you in every detail; you are always with me.*

It said other things too.

John brushed his fingers over the ink. He folded the paper in two again, to protect the drawing, pressed the back of it reverently to his lips, then set it onto the bedside table. He opened the top drawer and withdrew his old cigarette case: that once heartbreaking memento that Sherlock had left for him on a mountainside in Switzerland.

The cigarette case contained precious things – the letter Sherlock had written to him, believing he was to die at Moriarty's hand. An 1893 telegram summoning John to Australia, which had caused so much anger and led to so much joy. Now it also contained the series of Sherlock's sketches, the only communication he could safely make to John, keeping his patient vigil in their Sussex cottage.

John took the drawings out. He had nearly wept ten weeks ago on receiving the first confirmation that Sherlock was at least recently well – a carnation etched in faint green ink – and then laughed. Green carnations, indeed.

The second, a month later, was a delicate rendering of a willow tree. *Their* willow tree, its sheltering branches sweeping over the creek, where springs and summers and even warm autumn days, they stretched out together, to talk, to kiss, to give and enjoy pleasure.

Two weeks ago, John had added a simple sketch of the Southern Cross constellation, under which they had first declared their love and first consummated it.

John placed the new drawing with the others into the cigarette case, and placed the case back into the drawer. It was no good sitting here pining. There was work to be done.

John sat by the front door to pull off his muddy Wellington boots. Beside him was a basket of beans, marrows, a few tomatoes, from their garden. He'd enjoyed the last hour there, weeding, pruning and picking ripe produce for their dinner. He had worked surrounded by the scent of the soil and the hum of the bees, thinking about the day Sherlock had knelt beside him in the garden and found a golden Roman coin in the dirt. Sherlock had kissed his cheek. 'Ah, my Boswell, always at hand for the great discoveries!'

Now, as he tugged at the boots, John thought he might go upstairs and look for the coin. He'd meant to drill a hole in it for Sherlock to wear on his watch chain.

A voice rose, anguished, from beyond the door that stood ajar.

'Why won't you look at me, Davy? Do I horrify you that much?'

John listened. (A terrible habit, this eavesdropping, developed over years of working with Sherlock Holmes. He shouldn't listen. Or he should make a noise. But he listened.)

'Don't, Bobby. Please.' Gruff. Terse.

'It's not so bad, you know,' said Bobby, the cheerfulness a thin, cracking veneer over pain. 'It still works a little, and the other's as fit as a fiddle.'

'Don't, Bobby.'

'Look at me, Davy. Please. Don't take on, so. Open your eyes, now. Unless you just can't bear to look at me anymore.'

'And what of me?' Davy's stricken voice was a match for a broken spirit. 'How can you bear to look at *me*? I don't want to see how you'll look at me, Bobby. I'm a cripple.'

John remembered his own return from Afghanistan, long ago: coming home broken and full of grief, lost in spirit and mind, his nerves shattered and his health ruined. Not forever, it turned out, but when you are young and have been stripped by the battlefield, you can't know that.

'Oh, love,' Bobby said, softly, so softly, so softly and sweetly. 'I see my Davy MacKee. Even with one leg, you're still my Davy-boy. My beautiful boy. And it's awful, but it could've been worse. You might be dead, and then where would I be? How would I live? Look at me. Please, Davy. Please. I won't pity you, I promise. How could I? You saved me.'

'No. No. You saved me.' A gasping breath, tearful.

'Of course I did.' Bobby's voiced hitched in a kind of laugh. 'I'd have marched into hell to take you from the devil himself, and plugged him in the eye while I was at it for hurting you.'

John knew the story, from their old Baker Street Irregular, Bill Wiggins. At the battle of Festubert, May 1915, Private David MacKee had thrown his childhood friend clear from an exploding bomb. Private Robert Wiggins, despite the burns to the right side of his body, dragged his badly wounded friend off the battleground to aid, and refused aid himself until Davy was seen to.

Their bodies now as healed as they would ever be, these young men had found living in London too wracking to their nerves to bear, especially during the Zeppelin bombing raids. Bill Wiggins had written to John, asking for advice, and John had said, *send them to me, your son and his friend. It's quiet here, with Sherlock away for the war. I could use some friendly faces. Send the boys to me.*

John had no children of his own, but his heart hurt as a father's might for those boys, as it did for Wiggin's grief for his sons. Bobby so grievously injured, Will recently enlisted, and George, the eldest, killed in action on the Somme.

'That's it, my lad, my boy.' Bobby's choking voice was flooding again with that irrepressible good cheer. 'Look at me. See? I love you, Davy. I'd have died for you out there, and you for me, I know it…'

'I would have, Bobby.'

'And now we have to be alive for each other, and not give up.'

'It's hard, Bobby. It's *harder*.'

'That it is, my sweetheart. But we've courage enough together, don't we? I'll help you walk, and you'll help me see, and we'll get through this world side by side, like we always did.' Bobby made a self-deprecating sound, half a laugh, half grief. 'Even though my looks could curdle milk, now.'

'Shh, no, no, Bobby. You're my best boy. You're still beautiful to me. You've got a beautiful soul and there it is, right in your eyes. Yes, that one too, don't hide. If I can't hide my face, neither can you.'

Tearful breathing for a moment and then Bobby said, 'Good. Right. So you and me, Davy. Like always, like it should be. How about we show those German sons of whisky-faced eel pies we're not done for, not by a long chalk.'

A stifled giggle was his reply. 'Whisky-faced eel pies? Good God, Bobby, you can't just swear like the rest of us, can you?'

'You know my mum doesn't hold with swearing.' Bobby's tone was brighter under the mock-seriousness.

'Tell me another and make me laugh.'

'Old General Haig is a rabbit-tailed cheese wheel and a cloth-eared fathead to boot.'

Davy snort-giggled, and then their laughter turned to a promising not-silence. A rustling kind of quiet. A sighing, murmuring kind of hush.

Smiling, John pulled his Wellingtons back on, took up his cane and decided to say a long good evening to the bees.

John woke to that *not-right*-yet-*accepted* emptiness in their bed. He looked through his cigarette case and, like a sentimental old fool, gazed on each of the drawings. He pressed them, and the old letter and the telegram, to his cheek and pretended that each transferred the touch of Sherlock's fingers to his skin. *Soon, please God. Soon.* Then he put them all away and rose for the day's chores.

The boys were still abed. Not separate beds either, judging from the sounds during the night. John hummed Sarasate as he made tea and set out bread, butter, and condiments for the morning repast.

He went out to see to the bees, alone but gladdened. Perhaps only a touch envious. No need to open the boxes today; record-keeping was the morning's agenda. Date, time, temperature. Were the bees gathering pollen or nectar? Any sign of propolis?

In the bee shed, John found one of Sherlock's bee notes tucked under an empty jar.

Buzz pollination is the process wherein a bee vibrates its flight muscles rapidly, causing the flowers and anthers to vibrate. This releases the pollen for the bee to gather. Solanum lycopersicum *, for example, requires this type of pollination.*

John flushed, remembering, as Sherlock had meant him to. A warm, lazy day, and Sherlock lying between his thighs under the willow tree. Moving languidly, the scent of lavender oil, his hands on Sherlock's backside, caressing, kneading, pulling him closer. Warm breaths and murmured endearments, then languid became urgent. *Vibrating. Releasing pollen.*

'If I were a bee,' Sherlock murmured afterward, his head on John's chest, indulging in a whimsical mood, 'I should prefer your stamen to all others.'

'If I were a flower,' John had replied, his expression wreathed in merry contentment, 'I would bloom only for you.'

John folded the note to place in the cigarette case later.

A half hour later Bobby joined him, relaxed and pink-cheeked and singing '*Just a little love, a little kiss, just an hour that holds a world of bliss'*. The bees hummed around him, apparently pleased by Bobby's own honey-happy song.

'If you boys want a ramble,' said John as he and Bobby made notes on the bees' comings and goings, 'There's a lovely place by the creek, under the willow tree, an easy walk even for crutches. Take a picnic lunch and make a day of it.'

Bobby, flushed and grinning, nodded. 'It's very sunny, and I noticed that willow the other day. I thought it might be nice for… picnics.' He gave John a look both sly and friendly. 'You and Mr H picnic there a lot, I reckon.'

John raised an eyebrow, mostly to cover a smirk, forgetting that the beekeeper's headgear obscured both.

'Holmes likes to swim,' deflected John.

Bobby laughed. 'Me too. A good, vigorous swim is excellent for a man.'

John took his cane on his walk into the village. The lane to the main road went past the disused lodge at the end of their quite large property. The cottage, this lodge, an empty stable and the bee hut that had once been a potting shed had once been part of a larger property.

John wore a rucksack to carry the bread and vinegar he meant to buy. Some string, too, he thought, and some long nails Davy said he needed to mend the shutter on the back window. Nails or screws, was it? It was on the list, either way, along with soap, tea, a bit of rabbit, if the butcher had some. A new bottle of lavender oil too, perhaps. The old bottle had mysterious disappeared from the bathroom, and he'd begun to suspect that the bees had been so fond of Bobby this morning less for his singing prowess and more for the scent of flowers that clung to him.

A faint tang of salt was in the breeze coming in from the sea, a few miles away. Bees hummed in hedges and gardens as he walked to the village, perhaps many from their own hives. He liked to pretend they were watching out for Sherlock's return.

He was walking home, rucksack bulging with the little household items, when the county bus rattled past. He raised his cane in a salute to Mr Fanshawe, the driver, and to his surprise the bus hove to on the side of the street.

Sherlock Holmes waved to him from the bus' open door.

'Do hurry, John,' he said, affecting impatience. 'Fanshawe's running late already and we can't let his employers berate his tardiness on our account.'

John forgot his aching leg and the weight on his back and he ran, he ran, he ran to Sherlock Holmes.

They sat side by side on the bus, almost but not quite touching. John's hands were trembling. So were Sherlock's, he noticed, from the effort of not reaching for each other. Instead, John clutched the head of his cane in both hands and tried not to stare.

He's tired. He is too thin. He's very pale. Unhurt, I think. I will examine him, when we're home. I'll touch every inch of his beautiful skin and be sure he's unhurt. I will kiss him. I'll kiss his mouth and his back and his feet. I will kiss his hands. I'll tell him he's marvellous. I'll tell him about the bees. I'll tell him how happy I am. I will tell him I love him.

John caught a laughing look in the corner of Sherlock's eye, and grinned like a giddy fool in love, and rubbed his knuckles over his moustache to hide how foolishly happy he was.

Fanshawe pulled over at the start of the little road to their cottage, and they alighted. Only then did John realised Sherlock had no baggage but a worn leather satchel.

'Holmes, your luggage?'

The bus rattled onward as Sherlock replied, 'Everything I need is at my side.'

John beamed at him. Sherlock looped a hand through John's arm and off they walked to their cosy property, past the empty groundsman's lodge they'd not yet converted to a laboratory for Sherlock, past the meadows full of flowers and bees.

'You can't say much, I know,' said John. 'But it was a success?'

'It was, and lives have been saved. Not soon enough for George Wiggins.' Sherlock became solemn. 'I did it more for them, you know, than for King and Country. They are our Country are they not, all those boys? Wiggins' boys. Robert is here, I understand, with his young friend, recovering from their injuries?'

'Yes. Using your study as a billet, I'm afraid. Your things are all upstairs.'

'Ah.' Sherlock cast John a rueful look. The nature of the regret made warmth uncurl in John's chest and stomach and groin.

'They were at the willow tree when I started for the village,' John elaborated meaningfully.

'Ah.' Sherlock smiled this time, but not as though he were surprised. He sighed, then. 'I have sometimes wished you might have had sons and daughters, but what I saw in France and Germany, John, makes me glad we had no children to feed to that madness. It's butchery, nothing more. Worse than anything I, and I daresay even you, have ever witnessed. New weapons and new warfare have created carnage absolute.'

John placed a hand over Sherlock's on his arm and squeezed. 'Even without a war, Sherlock, I have never longed for children. Not unless they could be yours too, and with that impossibility, I have been content enough with the bees.'

Sherlock laughed. 'The bees?'

'Well, we do care for and nurture them,' said John cheerily, wanting to nudge Sherlock out of his sorrowful mood. 'It's a sentimental fancy, I suppose, but what do we do for the bees that parents don't do for their children? Except clothe and educate them, and send them out into the world to seek their fortune.' John grimaced good-humouredly at his absurd fancy.

Sherlock's cheeks dimpled in an impish grin. 'They educate us instead, and help to feed us. They go out into the world and work for the hive, and so for us. You're quite right, John, only we've missed the awkward middle years of having offspring. They support us in our dotage now, as good children ought.'

'Dotage,' John snorted. 'Ass.'

Sherlock's grey eyes crinkled. 'If our lodgers are at the willow tree, Watson, perhaps you'll be kind enough to furnish me with lunch and a thorough physical examination?'

'As your doctor and your friend, I am only too happy to oblige, my dear Holmes.'

After simple bread and cheese, eaten sparingly, Sherlock opened his mouth, like a bird, and John fed him a slice of apple. Sherlock's tongue darted out to catch a fleck of juice on his lip, and John leaned forward to kiss the residue away. They didn't speak of Sherlock's absence, or its painful echo of another, long ago.

'The bees are well,' said John, cutting another slice of apple for his love. 'They seem to like Bobby.'

'Bees don't like or dislike people, John. Though it's good to know he understands how to work with them. They certainly appeared well as we passed them by.'

John fed Sherlock, kissed him again, and said, 'Thank you for the drawings.'

'You understood the messages, then?' Sherlock caught at John's wrist and licked John's apple-sweet fingers.

John hummed assent, then his lips tilted wryly. 'Not at first.'

'But by the last?'

'*I'll see you soon.*'

'Exactly.'

'I thought the carnation was simply our little joke, though I realised by the last one you meant it to establish the meaning. Green carnation. Your secret mission, and a code for none but you and me.'

'Good. And then?'

'The willow tree. You had identified your contacts and were in a safe place. It was a long time till the Southern Cross, but as it's used for navigation, I thought it meant you were on your way home. I hoped it did.'

'Exactly right, John.'

John kissed Sherlock's smiling mouth, simultaneously amused and touched by the pride in Sherlock's expression. 'I would be very dull indeed if I didn't work it out eventually.'

In their bed, Sherlock sprawled, all long pale limbs and wiry musculature. John, stockier, tanned from his afternoons in the garden, his golden brown hair now threads in the soft grey, knelt at his side. He had already run his sturdy hands all down Sherlock's arms and legs, over his skull and face, down his bare shoulders and back and buttocks, across his chest and stomach, satisfying himself that his Sherlock was unharmed, whole, and here, *oh here* . His eyes had been traitors to his knowledge in the past and so John needed to touch Sherlock's skin to anchor certainty in his head and heart and hands: Sherlock was *well* and he was *home*.

Sherlock smiled up at John from his pillow, and suckled on his apple-sweet fingers. Sherlock's hair was silvered now too, at chest and groin as well as scalp. Like John's, his skin was more lined than it had been, but they had no complaints. There were growing old together, after all. Those grey hairs, those lines of age, were as precious as the hearts and minds beneath them.

'My dear,' murmured John. 'My dear, my very dearest.' He kissed Sherlock's palm, his wrist, his forearm and inner elbow. 'I'm so glad you're here.'

Sherlock reached for John and pulled him to the mattress beside him, so that he could press their naked bodies close. He wound himself around John – leg over John's hip, an arm across his back – and brushed the tip of his nose against John's.

'Remind me,' he said huskily, 'of why I love your moustache.'

John's wrapped his arms around Sherlock's torso, pushed his legs between Sherlock's thighs, and tipped Sherlock onto his back on the mattress. He kissed Sherlock's cheeks and eyelids, his nose and mouth, and down his throat.

All the way down – throat, chest, belly, thighs – John kissed and nuzzled, brushing his moustache in ticklish sweeps against Sherlock's skin. Sherlock wasn't ticklish, though, and he arched happily into the sensation, pushing his cheekbones against it, and his clavicle, his nipples and navel and hips, all against the marvellous sensation of John's lips and teeth and tongue and moustache against his body.

Finally, Sherlock moaned and cursed and then laughed. 'John. Don't tease, I beg you.'

'You beg, do you?'

'As abjectly as you like, my dear, only, pl…aaahhh…' Sherlock bucked up into John's mouth as it slid over him, and sucked, hard, then soft. John released him, and Sherlock laugh-moaned again.

'You will manage what the Germans and Moriarty failed to do, and kill me dead, John Watson.'

'Never,' John swore, pressing down on Sherlock's body with the warmth and weight of his own. He kissed his love and bit gently on his lip and jaw.

Sherlock spread his knees so that John could settle more closely against him. 'Then give me satisfaction, you wicked fellow.'

John reached for the bottle of lavender oil on the bedside table.

'John, John, John, John…' was the breathless litany as John smeared oil over them. John took his sweet time to do it.

'Stop dallying,' Sherlock demanded imperiously, making John grin and use his hands and fingers to make Sherlock gasp.

'I don't dally,' John promised him. 'I do exactly what pleases you.'

'Yes.'

They clung to each other, and kissed, and thrust slow then fast then slow then fastfastfaster*fasterfaster* until their tight-wound passion unfurled in pulses, body against cherished, desired, beloved body.

John, panting, sagged against Sherlock, his face pressed into Sherlock's throat to hide his emotion. As though *that* would hide anything. Sherlock held John tightly against him and nuzzled at his hair.

'I'm home, John, and I'm not leaving you again. Not for anyone. Not for the King himself. You have me forever, now. You and the bees.'

John's laugh caught, a gasp-gulp steeped in joy. He smothered it against Sherlock's warm, perspiration- and tear-damp skin. 'Good.'

Bobby held the door open for Davy, who easily manoeuvred inside with his crutches and a pair of trout threaded onto a strip of willow around his neck

'Mr Holmes!' Bobby dashed towards the table, depositing on the floor the basket containing the remnants of the picnic. 'My God, sir, it's good clap eyes on you. I'd have known by Doc Watson's face that you were home if I hadn't seen you for myself.'

John rubbed at his moustache, obscuring his face, but the brightness of his eyes, the jaunty angle of his head, his whole alert and satisfied demeanour were a giveaway of his feelings on the matter. Just as the fragments of grass and willow leaves in Bobby's rumpled hair and collarbone, and a tiny leaf pressed to Davy's forearm underneath his flannel shirt attested that *fishing* had not been their only activity by the creek.

Bobby seized Sherlock's hand in his and shook it vigorously, before whirling to face Davy and relieving him of the fish. 'Davy, this is Mr Sherlock Holmes!'

Davy adjusted his crutches and thrust out a hand to shake Sherlock's. 'I've heard a good deal of you, sir, and read all of Doctor Watson's tales. Welcome home, sir, it's a great honour to meet you. I've admired your great work all my life.'

Sherlock waved his hand self-deprecatingly, but his ears were pink with a pleased flush. *Still as sensitive as a beautiful girl to praise on his art*, thought John fondly.

'John says you've been very helpful about our home, Mr MacKee,' said Sherlock, indicating the clock that had not worked since Sherlock had interfered with it for an experiment. 'And that you, Robert, are very handy with the bees.'

'We've done our best, sir,' grinned Bobby. 'And Davy can fix anything he puts his mind to. Never met anyone so clever with his hands.'

Davy flushed too, now, and looked at the pot of tea to have something to look at besides everyone's knowing faces. Bobby chuckled and at last took the trout into the kitchen.

'Tea?' offered Sherlock, and Davy took a seat.

Supper was trout and beans from the garden with fresh bread John had bought in the village. Afterwards, there was celebratory cider.

'Thanks for having us, Doc Watson,' said Bobby, 'But I guess we'd best be going back to London. The cottage is a bit small for four.' Neither he nor Davy appeared happy at the prospect.

'It's small for the long term, perhaps,' conceded Sherlock. 'You've seen the groundsman's lodge down the lane? I planned to turn it into a workshop – John has unreasonable strictures against my using the dining table here for experiments. It never used to bother him unduly at Baker Street. In any case, the old stable behind the cottage is better placed for that work.'

'We can help clear up the stable for you, Mr Holmes.'

'That would be most kind, Bobby, but I was thinking that more of your efforts could be directed towards the lodge. It can be made it cosily habitable for two easily enough. Certainly before autumn. Of course you'll stay in your billet here until then, if that's what you'd like.'

'You'd like us to…?'

'Continue to assist with us here, yes, if that suits your plans.'

'Well… if you like, Mr H. I'd be honoured. Davy?'

Davy blinked hard, as though astounded to be included in the sudden, generous offer. 'If you think I can be of service, sir.'

'You've already proven to be of service, Mr MacKee. I heard no end of it when I broke the clock and its return to working order may finally have seen me forgiven.'

Behind his cider glass, John's moustache curved up, betraying his mirthful response to that.

'Then I'd be glad to stay on, Mr Holmes.'

'Excellent.'

'A toast to the future, then,' suggested John.

John put on his beekeeper's suit and went out with Sherlock, attired in his hood, to look to the bees.

'They do like us, see? They recognise you, at any rate.'

The bees indeed flew close around them and crawled all over Sherlock's hands as though recognising their keeper had returned.

'It is known that bees recognise individuals. It will be part of my research to determine how. As to them liking me…'

'Why shouldn't they? I like you well enough, and I'm at least as clever as a bee.'

That set Sherlock to laughing, and the bees swirled around him as he did.

John grinned at the success of his joke. In the distance, he could hear Bobby singing, and then Davy's voice joining him as they turfed broken furniture and clouds of dust out the door of their new little home.

'So, Davy and Bobby in the lodge,' said John in satisfaction. 'That will be good for them. And for us, to have their help – and company.'

'Yes. Well.' Sherlock shrugged. 'We must leave this place to someone one day. Perhaps these two will suit. MacKee seems clever, Wiggins' boy is bright enough, and… the bees like him.'

John laughed again. Carefully, he removed one glove and placed his hand on Sherlock's wrist. In the sunny meadow, with none to see, Sherlock slipped his palm against John's.

The bees landed in a soft-buzzing cloud on their joined hands, and hummed and danced messages to each other for a long and lovely moment before flying off, in their industrious way, to make honey.

Author's notes: With thanks to Bobby Fries for inspiration and Britt McCombs for checking my bee facts (though any errors remain my own). The song Bobby Wiggins sings is *Just a Little Love, A Little Kiss (Un Peu D'Amour)* as sung by Maggie Teyte in 1916. English lyrics by Adrian Ross, music by Lau Silesu.

freedom is a daily practice

Lost and Found:

Practice Makes Perfect

Regan flinched at the sight of the handwritten scrawl on the whitewashed wall.

Freedom is a daily practise!

So much about it was egregious. The scrappy unevenness of the penmanship. The unnecessary exclamation mark. Most frightfully of all, the use of the verb *practise* when grammatically the sentence called for the noun. *Practice.*

Another, milder, offence was that graffiti was supposed to be bold. Regan was a Melburnian and knew street art from tagging. Regan had seen the hidden Banksy before some council dolt scrubbed it off. Regan's Instagram boasted Ghostpatrol. What was this but some hastily scribbled thought, dashed down without even the shameless flourish of a tag?

And yet.

Freedom is a daily practise!

Something in its ordinariness snagged at Regan; caught on Regan's brain like a burr on a sock. Not that ill-placed "s". Something sharper and deeper; something defiant; a needle jab to the diaphragm.

What is street art meant to do? Challenge the status quo. Agitate complacency. Spark the neurons. Light up something new.

When younger, Regan had been assertive. Regan had marched for their identity. Regan had challenged, agitated, sparked and lit up things with all their fire and passion.

Some things Regan fought for had changed. Many had not. Most, to be honest. Fighting for freedoms got tiresome then wearying then downright gruelling.

Now Regan walked in predictable, quiet ways. Regan always took the same route to work. Regan went to the same bars and cafes. Regan wore the same dark colours and too-large clothes. Regan hid in formlessness and grew selectively deaf to comment.

Past Regan was a firebird. Current Regan was a dull brown sparrow, too timid for brighter plumage, wings clipped, hopping nervously for crumbs of dreamt-of freedoms.

Sparrow Regan was safe but shackled in a prison of *don't be seen*, made years ago when it seemed that every breath had become a battle.

Sparrow Regan missed the firebird.

Freedom is a daily practise!

Not a daily *fight*, but a daily *practice*. Freedom as a daily way of *being*. Not a fire that burns bright and then to ash, but a river that runs, high and low, but constantly flowing. Even rock gave way, in time, to that patient daily practice.

Regan felt the heat stir, curling out from their heart, unspooling in their bloodstream, trickling into the whorls of their fingerprints and between the folds of their brain.

I can practise freedom and not burn, thought Regan. *I can be the water over stone. No need for declamation or belligerence. I will daily be and daily, daily, become more myself.*

Just as soon as I've made this verb a noun.

Regan knew grammar. So many people had opinions on singular "they", but Regan knew its noble history. Chaucer and Shakespeare wrote a singular "they" long before grammarians in frock coats robbed it of its full self.

Regan uncapped a thin black marker in their bag and made the unlovely scrawl unlovelier and more perfect with that assertive "c". More properly itself. Regan's first inexorable drop of self on the stone of the world.

SHADOW ON MY SHOULDER

Author's note: This story is set after the events in *Ravenfall*.

Light was a tricky thing. So was shadow. They relied on each other and competed; complemented and contrasted each other.

Which was another way of saying that Gabriel was having a bitch of time trying to get the light and shade properly balanced as he put the final touches on this portrait of Hannah. He'd been able to pay her for her sittings lately, and she'd been able to take up a room in a boarding house and get off the streets. She was too old to be sleeping rough.

The bold gaze in that portrait was not of a weak or broken person, though. Hannah was stronger than she should ever have had to be. And when he captured the light-and-shade balance properly, her strength and vulnerability would be perfectly balanced too.

A clatter beyond the art room disturbed Gabriel's concentration and he lifted the brush away from the canvas. He heard voices, and broke into an involuntary smile at the first.

'Christ, Sunil, you shouldnae taken the stairs. We'd have come down to ye.'

Sometimes, Gabriel thought, he could live on the sound of James' voice alone. As a bonus, he also had James' blue eyes, strong arms, clever hands and loving heart to live on.

'Sod that,' the second voice replied – the newly arrived Sunil. Caught up in painting Hannah, Gabriel had forgotten his planned visit. 'My physio says it's good for me.'

'Yer physio's a sadist.'

'There is that.' Sunil laughed. 'Good to see you, Jim. You look…'

Gabriel held his breath, wondering what would follow. "Well" wasn't really appropriate.

'…like a man who's wintered in London. Jim, old mate, we've got to get you in the sunshine.'

Gabriel imagined James' reply was a rueful shake of the head. It wasn't as if sunshine would actually kill him, but a tan was definitely out of the question. "Vampires don't tan" wasn't rule number one, but it was definitely in the top 20.

Gabriel inspected the canvas, decided Hannah could wait, and lobbed the paintbrush into the waiting jar of paint thinner. He emerged into the living room, wiping his hands on his paint-spattered shirt, only belatedly thinking that he should be making more effort for this first meeting with James' old army buddy.

James grinned. 'There you are. D'ye sense the prospect of a cup of tea?'

'Tea and biscuits,' agreed Gabriel cheerfully, 'And introductions, in a-'

Before he could complete the sentence, with '-minute, once I've changed my shirt', the dark-skinned man by the chair strode over to greet him, one hand thrust out for him to shake. 'Sunil,' he said, 'And you must be Jim's Gabriel.' Sunil's artificial leg gave him the slightest of limps. His dark grey prosthetic arm began at his triceps and ended in articulated fingers.

Sunil, seeing where Gabriel's gaze tracked the prosthetics, held up the fingers and waggled them. 'Not bad kit for the army, eh?'

Gabriel, shaking Sunil's other hand, wasn't sure what to say. Sunil's smile said it was joke. His eyes said something else. 'Looks good,' he said.

The other guest, a handsome, bearded fellow, hovered behind Sunil's prosthetic elbow. He gave Gabriel a distracted grimace that might have been a smile. Unlike Sunil, dressed in jeans, T-shirt and denim jacket, this man was in linen pants and a long shirt in navy blue, with a cloth scarf wound around his head.

'Jim's told me so much about you,' Sunil continued before the introductions could be finalised, 'Probably so he doesn't have to talk about himself. Tight lipped as an oyster, like always.'

Gabriel wanted to be annoyed on James' behalf, but James, in the kitchen pulling out cups, only laughed. 'Not everyone's a bletherskate, Sunil.'

Sunil leaned conspiratorially close to Gabriel. 'Sometimes it's almost like Doctor Sharpe speaks English.'

'I'll gie ye a skelpit lug!' James exaggerated his Scots lilt and accompanied it with a mock scowl, and Sunil laughed again. James grinned and continued making tea.

Gabriel relaxed. James and Sunil were old mates, even if Sunil didn't know what James was now, and James was unlikely to tell him. But they were teasing in a way that felt natural.

Sunil manoeuvred into a seat at the table, his handsome Middle Eastern friend moving with him.

'I'm Gabriel,' said the artist, introducing himself properly to the second visitor, but Sunil was the one who took and shook his hand again.

'Ah, formal introductions is it? Good day, sir. I'm Sunil Juhekar. Is that paint on your forehead?'

Gabriel wiped at the spot with the back of his hand. 'Sorry, yeah. Finishing up a portrait.'

James carried over three cups of tea by the handles, then went back for the Jammy Dodgers. Gabriel assumed three cups meant James wasn't having tea today, but after passing the biscuits around, he took up one of the cups and sipped.

James was never usually rude like this. He must, Gabriel thought, be more rattled by finally getting Sunil here to meet the boyfriend than he'd realised.

'So, aren't you going to introduce me?' he asked, with a sardonic lift of the eyebrow, half-teasing.

Sunil frowned. 'Haven't we done that bit twice already?'

'I mean…' Gabriel nodded at the man behind Sunil.

James, puzzled, said, 'All right. Um. Gabriel, this is Sunil Juhekar, former corporal in Her Majesty's Army and one time comrade-in-arms. Sunil, this is my boyfriend Gabriel Dare, amazing artist. Hmph. "Boyfriend". Makes us sound like teenagers.' Beneath James' dubious tone, though, he seemed devilishly pleased.

'Got him an eternity ring yet?' teased Sunil. 'Or are you stepping up and letting him wear your dog tags?'

'No,' said Gabriel impatiently, embarrassed on behalf of the neglected guest. 'I mean…. Oh. *Oh.*'

He looked at the bearded man again, and realised at last what he was seeing.

For one thing, he was seeing the kitchen clock faintly through the second guest's forehead. The man winced but didn't look away from Gabriel's startled gaze.

'You mean?' prompted James.

On the other hand, Sunil's face was mottled as the colour drained from it.

'I mean the man standing behind Sunil,' Gabriel said slowly, mindful of how Sunil had begun to tremble. 'He's wearing a headscarf and a long blue tunic and trousers. He has a beard. Good looking chap.'

'You can see him?' Sunil's voice was small and shaking.

James stood straight. 'Gabriel, what can you see?'

'A ghost,' said Gabriel. The ghost in question glowered at him. 'I didn't realise at first. I haven't seen a ghost in years.'

Gabriel started as he felt James' cool hand take his. 'Are ye all right, love?'

The ghost's eyes didn't leave Gabriel's, and they were dark with despair and pleading and anger.

'I don't know.'

As a little boy, seeing spirits, talking with them, Gabriel had never been scared of ghosts. They'd always seemed mostly sad and lost, the fading shadows of a terrible moment in time. His father had thought him mad and had done his best to medicate and electroshock his youngest's madness out of him. He'd succeeded mainly in making his son doubt his own sanity, and driving him to live on the streets for many years, rather than rely on that vicious, deeply conditional kind of love.

He had more than one reason to love James Sharpe. Discovering James was a vampire had released Gabriel of that self-doubt. Where there were demonstrable vampires, ghosts were hardly a stretch.

This ghost simmered with some darkness Gabriel didn't understand yet. Gabriel wasn't frightened, but he was wary.

'What does it want?' James was peering into the space behind Sunil's right shoulder, missing completely the ghost behind Sunil's left.

'Other side,' said Gabriel, wondering in a daze why James couldn't see the apparition. Surely being a vampire would give James some special insight?

James reached towards the bearded man as though he might touch the essence of it. The ghost, scowling, swiped at James fingers. James snatched his fingers back as though they'd been bitten.

'Fuck, that's cold,' James complained. He stared at his fingers then back at the air behind Sunil. 'What does he look like? He's wearing a shalwar kameez, you said? Sunil, can you see him?'

'Not always,' said Sunil in a whisper. 'But he's always there.'

'Who is he?'

'I don't know.'

'You do,' said Gabriel, because the look the ghost gave Sunil was full of offended rage.

'No,' insisted Sunil, then, 'maybe. Maybe I do. I can't. I never see him properly, I hear him. He says things. He makes it cold. He makes the lights turn off, or on. He makes the walls bleed.' Sunil buried his face in his hands. 'I thought I was mad, but you can see him.'

Gabriel reached for one of the sketch pads that were always lying around the flat, fetched a pencil from his pocket and dashed down a lightning portrait. A quick, undefined shape for Sunil, and behind him in much more detail, the ghost: a young man with an oval face framed in short, dark hair and a neat beard, a long straight nose, a mouth that might have inclined to smiling that was set now in a grim line, pale but intense eyes that stared out of the picture in an unnamed challenge.

James tapped on the image in sudden recognition. 'That's Wali Marwat, isn't it? He was serving the unit as interpreter when I got… invalided out.'

Killed, you meant, Gabriel thought. *Turned into a vampire.* There was so much to that story that James wasn't prepared to share yet.

James continued: 'Sunil, what happened to him?'

Sunil lurched out of his chair and dashed towards the door in panic. He stumbled on his prosthetic, and only didn't fall because James caught him and held on, even when Sunil began to struggle.

'No,' protested Sunil. 'No. It's not. It's not Wali. Wali wouldn't. He was my friend. He wouldn't. He wouldn't do this to me. He wouldn't… haunt me.'

Gabriel heard but wasn't paying attention, because what he'd seen as Sunil leapt from his seat and staggered away from the table was how helplessly the ghost was dragged along in his wake. It twisted as though anchored to Sunil's body by unbreakable tethers; it wrenched itself about but couldn't escape. It was forced to follow Sunil's every jerky movement, even when Sunil was being held in James' firm grip. As Sunil swore and writhed, so the ghost was flung to and fro around Sunil.

The ghost opened its mouth and howled, making every molecule of air around it vibrate like the skin of a beating drum.

Gabriel and Sunil clapped their hands over their ears – only James was unaffected. Then Sunil's panicked panting breaths became visible puffs of fogged air in the suddenly freezing cold room.

'James,' said Gabriel, alarmed, eyes wide, his breath fogged too. 'He's–'

The ghost's jerking gyrations turned into a jagged blur of colour, blue and red and black. A linen-clad arm would appear then vanish in the distortion; dark hair would swing and smudge; droplets of blood flew in a spray before smearing through the twitching, warping haze.

James' sparing breaths were cooler than a human's, but even they now fogged on the icy air that had inhabited their living room. He still didn't see or hear the wildly blurring shape of the ghost as it fought to free itself, but he saw well enough when Sunil was raised off the ground, ice frosting the surface of his prosthetics. Sunil fought against the ghost's whirling grip, unable to speak except for helpless gasps of terror. The ghost could not break free; nor could Sunil.

Gabriel instinctively reached for Sunil and the ghost, thinking to help. He was flung violently aside, repelled by the energy of the writing ghost. James' reaction was instant: his fangs descended, his every predator instinct rose up, and he snarled, eyes fixed on the blue-black-red blur behind Sunil that had very clearly become suddenly visible to him.

'I see ye noo, ye bastard!' He leapt at it with a hiss.

Gabriel staggered upright, using the wall that he'd been pitched against for support, and watched his Jamie pounce into the centre of the distortion and disappear.

'*Jamie*!'

And as suddenly, James was flung outside the vortex. With his supernatural reflexes, James tucked and turned, landing on his feet like a cat. A cut across his face closed up as he judged his next attack.

The maelstrom twitched in Gabriel's direction and instantly, so fast the transition wasn't visible to the human eye, James was standing between Gabriel and the disembodied rage with his teeth bared.

'Ye'r nae the only deid thing in this house,' snarled James. 'Sae git yer scabby claws away frae my lad or I will send ye tae hell, Wali Marwat, do ye hear?'

And abruptly, the flat fell silent and there stood Wali beside Sunil, his blue tunic and dark hair matted with blood, his expression full of grief and defiance.

Sunil was shuddering in shock, wild eyes darting from vampire to ghost, back and forth, back and forth, James to Wali.

James closed his eyes and willed his fangs to retract. Rather than face Sunil, he turned to Gabriel and drew him up into his arms, looking into his eyes to check dilation and focus, listening to his heartbeat to determine his pulse.

'I cannae scent any blood, love. Are ye hurt?'

'I'm fine, Jamie.' Gabriel smiled a reassurance. He took James' hands in his and kissed his knuckles, then James' face where the cut was already healed. 'Are you? God, I was terrified when you disappeared inside there that you wouldn't come out.'

'It was cold, then hot and full of pain,' said James grimly. He shuddered. For a man who had seen and done the things he had, that shudder spoke of all the things that James was refusing to articulate. 'That poor man did not die easily, and he did not die fast.'

They turned together to see Sunil with his back pressed to the wall. The fingers of his prosthetic arm twitched as he stared at the ghost that stood wearily over him.

'It's not my fault,' he said in a jagged voice. 'Wali, it's not my fault.'

'What's nae yer fault, Sunil?'

Sunil stared wildly at James. 'What the fuck are you?'

'You can see ghosts, Sunil,' said James gently, 'Ye can probably guess what I am. What Major West turned me into.'

'You were looking for West.'

'Aye, and I found him, and that's done with. Tell me about Wali.'

'He died. He's haunting me.'

The ghost shook his head, angry-resigned.

'How did he die?' James pressed.

'I tried to tell them we had to get Wali out of Kabul. All the terps were at risk. Getting letters. Disappearing. Turning up tortured. Dead.'

'Terps. Interpreters,' James explained to Gabriel. 'Like all of the Afghans who worked with us, they were targets. The Taliban likes to make examples.'

'He got a letter, saying they were after him. I was trying to get someone to help get him out of there.'

James frowned at him. 'Was this before or after you got blown up by the IED.'

Sunil, never taking his eyes off the silent ghost, said, 'After. I was in rehab. Nobody listened.'

'No. They didn't. They don't.' James narrowed his eyes. 'It's a fucking disgrace, the way they've left those men behind. It wasn't your fault, Sunil. Wali, it wasn't his fault.'

Gabriel could have sworn the ghost of Wali rolled his eyes in exasperated agreement.

'Sunil?' James went to his old friend, placed a hand on his shoulder. 'Tell me what happened.'

Sunil began to weep. 'He was my friend. Wali and I both had Iranian grandparents – odd enough for the region; when we found out we talked a lot about our families. We'd speak Farsi together. I'm not English enough to have left that part of me behind, and he was

Persian enough to be a kindred spirit. Neither of us a perfect fit for our homelands. I loved him like a brother. I said I'd find out how to take him home with me and keep him safe. I didn't.' Sunil stared helplessly at Wali.

'That wasn't your doing,' James said. 'You were in hospital.'

'They tortured him for days, Jim. That's what they said when they found his body by the road. *Days*. He couldn't tell them anything they needed to know. The Taliban just wanted to make his death a punishment. A warning.' Sunil squeezed his eyes shut. 'That's why he's haunting me. I didn't keep my promise. I didn't keep him safe.'

The ghost tried to move away from Sunil, only to come to the end of the unseen tether and be jerked back into Sunil's orbit. Spectral blood soaked his hair and was now splotched all over his tunic, back and front. It leaked from his mouth. Wali kept shaking his head.

Suddenly, Gabriel understood. 'He's not haunting you. You're haunting him.'

Sunil and James both gaped.

'What? No,' protested Sunil.

'You pull him around like a balloon on a string,' said Gabriel. 'Whenever you move, he gets jerked along. He keeps trying to leave and he can't.'

Wali's ghost looked like someone had finally whispered the secret he'd been trying to tell. His pale eyes finally looked less angry than hopeful.

'That doesn't make sense.'

James nodded though, ruefully aware. 'It does, though Sunil. We carry them, you know. The ones we failed.'

Sunil's desperate gaze left Wali and found James' blue eyes.

'Who did you fail?'

'A lot of people,' said James quietly. 'When West made me what I am, I woke up savage and I… I hurt…people who relied on me. People I was supposed to protect. But I couldn't. Not then. I had no control. I was an unthinking beast.'

'And you're not now?' Sunil was wary.

'No.'

'You're a… a vampire.'

'Aye, but I'm not a monster. Not any more. Gabriel taught me that. He gave me back a soul. I choose to have one, whatever it is.'

Sunil took in a sobbing breath, and turned back to the ghost. 'It's my fault he's dead.' The out-loud admission of the guilt he felt made the ghost more solid for a moment.

'No, lad. It's the Taliban's fault.'

'I promised I'd look after him and I let him down.' Sunil reached towards Wali with his right hand, and the metal fingers of his left twitched. 'I'm sorry. Please. Please let me go.'

'He wants to,' said Gabriel. 'But you have to let him go first.'

'I. I don't.' Sunil took a shaking breath. 'I don't want to. I want my friend. I want my brother, Wali. I want to save him.'

'You can't,' said James softly. 'We can't save the ones we lost. We have to accept that. Terrible things happened out there, Sunil. Some of them were choices we made and some of them were consequences of what we did. And some happened regardless of any choice or action of ours. The only thing you can do is look it all in the eye, acknowledge it, and accept it. You can't lay it to rest any other way.'

'Have you?' demanded Sunil. 'Laid the things you did to rest?'

'Aye,' said James. 'I've made amends where I could. I've tried tae do better every day, for the unforgiveable things. Gabriel forgave me, and I forgave myself in the end. I don't carry them any more. I remember them, and I choose tae do better than I've done. It's all I have to offer. I choose, every day, tae be human. I let them go.'

'You make it sound easy.'

'It's really not,' said James. 'But what else is there? Ye can bury yourself in guilt and grief, or you can make yer peace, and try to be a better man.'

A soft voice whispered out suddenly from Wali's blood-specked lips. 'Let me go.' The plea was in English, but simultaneously in Farsi. The air fogged where he spoke.

Sunil's fingers finally touched Wali's shoulder. The hairs on Sunil's hand lifted up and frosted.

'I'm so sorry, Wali. I didn't try hard enough. I let you down.'

The ghost's expression was kind but stern. 'You lost your arm, your leg. Almost your life.'

'I lost *you*.'

'But you are alive. You must let me go, my brother, to find out what is next for me. Please. Do not keep me bound to your suffering. You cannot bring me back with your own pain.'

'I deserve it.'

Wali become more solid still. 'You don't, any more than I deserved mine. The only ones made happy by our continued pain are the ones who killed me, and I've given them enough of my torment. So have you, Sunil. My brother. Let me go.'

Sunil's cold hand found purchase on the back of Wali's neck. He pulled the ghost towards him, heedless of the slick of blood between his fingers, the tangled of bloodied hair at Wali's temple. He kissed Wali's forehead, then each cheek.

'Forgive me?'

'I never blamed you.'

Sunil pressed his forehead to Wali's, smearing his own skin with blood. 'I'd have saved you if I'd known how.'

'I know.'

'I'm going to try to help the others. All your comrades, your countrymen who helped us. They should be bringing them here. You risked so much for us.'

'Turn your grief to action,' said Wali, and now he had begun to fade. 'Try. It is all you can do.'

'I will. I'll try, Wali.'

Sunil raised his head and the ghost-blood on his face and on his hand faded. Wali looked as he had when Gabriel first saw him: unbloodied; a handsome Afghan man, but no longer surly or in despair. He seemed peaceful.

And then Wali Marwat faded like a drop of ink in water, washing out to nothing. Sunil raised his two hands as though seeking him. He twisted to look all around him, but saw nothing.

'He's gone.' He blew out a breath, then took several more to steady himself. Finally, he looked James in the eye. 'So, mate. You're a vampire.'

'Aye,' said James, non-commitally.

'And do you, ah…?' Sunil snapped his teeth together, then looked ashamed to have done so.

'I dinnae drink unwilling blood, Sunil.' That reply didn't put Sunil at any kind of ease, so he added, 'I dinnae eat people.'

Gabriel thought it wise that James didn't explain how it actually worked.

'That's not why I haven't come to see you. I don't come tae the pub with you and the lads because I cannae drink anything but tea.'

Sunil didn't ask for clarification but his wariness abated. 'Well, we don't all drink beer anyway. Hoffman's two months sober himself. We drink squash and play darts, and try not to jump at loud noises.' He thought a moment. 'And what's Gabriel?'

'He's an artist, like I said.'

'I see ghosts,' added Gabriel helpfully. 'It's not exactly a superpower.'

Sunil frowned and peered at his prosthetic arm. He used his sleeve to wipe the condensation from it. 'This'll be a story for pub night.'

James started. 'Don't tell the others what I am, Sunil. It frightens people.'

Sunil gave him a sardonic, lopsided grin. 'Yeah, well, you were scary as fuck when you thought Wali had hurt your boyfriend. But you're not scarier than carrying a ghost around on your back who can make your walls leak blood.' He huffed out another breath, without the fogging. He scratched a hand through his hair.

'If it's all the same to you Jim, I think I'd like that cup of tea now.' He grinned awkwardly at Gabriel. 'And I can find out more about your feller, who may have just saved my sanity.'

'I also paint portraits,' said Gabriel, deadpan.

'He's rare canny, my lad,' agreed James, kissing Gabriel on the cheek and then the tip of his nose before gathering up the cups of cold tea and returning to the kitchen.

'Sounds like a keeper,' said Sunil, sinking onto a chair at last.

Gabriel could see he was shaking, but that mottled look had vanished. Sunil was starting to smile again.

'He wears my dog tags,' admitted James.

Gabriel patted the place under his shirt where the metal was warm against his skin. 'And his face is tattooed on my arse.'

Sunil spluttered on the tea James had just brought him, and then realised he was being laughed at.

'Eternity rings are better,' Sunil advised. 'You can show those off.'

'Gabriel does have an excellent arse, though, don't ye mae bonnie?'

'Know Your Artist dot com gives it an eight out of ten.'

'You were robbed,' said James. He sat opposite Sunil. 'We all right, Sunil?'

Sunil considered. 'You and your sweetie un-haunted me, and helped Wali find some peace. Yeah, Jim. We're good.' He raised his cup of tea in a toast and they clinked cups. He'd almost stopped shaking.

Gabriel joined in the toast too, and dropped into a chair beside Sunil.

An eternity ring for a vampire was probably more eternal than most people considered, but he liked the idea. Next commission payment, he was going to take James shopping.

He also wondered if Sunil would let him paint his portrait.

Lost and Found:

Long Live the King

Elizabeth leaves white roses at the statue's feet. A sharp little spur of sorrow takes her every time.

Workers dug up his mortal feet, all unknowing, before anyone learned the rest of him was buried here. Distal and proximal phalanxes. Metatarsals and cuneiforms and taluses. The foot bone connected to the ankle bone, the ankle bone connected to the shin bone. The small king with the bent back connected to the hard earth.

Once this little hole into which he'd been thrown had been the floor of a priory. Then it was car park. Elizabeth supposes it's a miracle he only lost his feet, poor Richard.

Shakespeare transmuted him into a grand old villain, charming and treacherous. These days new battle lines are drawn: good king or bad? Child-killer or slandered Christian?

Elizabeth thinks he's both; she thinks he's neither. She thinks that method, motive and opportunity were collectively very murky 530-odd years ago and a lot of questions remain unanswered.

She thinks maybe he didn't deserve to be hacked at after his death, the post-mortem blows so hard they cut grooves in his bones. Maybe he didn't deserve to be dumped with his hands still tied, his head bent up against one end of the hole, before they piled on the dirt (in his grave and on his reputation) and tiled him in. Tarmacked him in.

Elizabeth's sister Celia thinks she's foolish, with this *tendresse* Elizabeth has for a long-dead king. What does it matter if he killed his nephews or not (and he probably did)? What possible difference does it make now?

Because it's so unfair, Elizabeth wants to say.

She can't honestly say why this King's pitiable end moves her so much she brings him flowers every month. She read a story once, perhaps, where all the truths are questioned, or where all the truths were repented. A story where he was a fully textured human and not a cautionary tale about tyranny.

Richard was brave, in his time. The scoliosis that twisted his spine didn't keep him from honours on the battlefield. A good administrator, by all accounts. Perhaps he did one truly terrible thing. Perhaps he was only blamed for it. Henry had more motive, some say. *Cui bono?* Who benefits? Henry certainly would never have gained the throne had the boys lived.

Elizabeth lays the York roses at Richard III's metal feet. Behind her is the story of his life in one tourist attraction. Opposite, his bones (minus his feet) lie in the cathedral, stained glass streaming coloured light onto the limestone tomb when the time of year is right.

'In another world,' Elizabeth tells his statue, 'someone loved you for exactly who you are, and you loved them back in just the same way. In some other when and where, you're the best version of yourself. And you're happy.'

In some other when and where, a short man with a bent spine pauses by a statue. He's slight and his eyes are kind. A little boy grips his father's fingers with one hand. In the other is a posy of daisies.

Richard lifts his son up in his arms and holds him while the boy places the daisies at the statue's feet. They look up at her face, the sun shining behind her like a halo.

'I don't think Queen Bess killed her sister,' says the boy.

'Nor do I, Neddy,' says his father. 'Some say so, but she was so wise in other ways. Perhaps she made a terrible mistake. Perhaps she was only blamed for a terrible thing.'

Neddy climbs up and stands on the plinth by the posy. He wraps his skinny arms around the statue's hips. He closes his eyes.

'What are you wishing?' asks Richard, smiling indulgently at his son.

'I wish for her to be happy in some world somewhere,' says Neddy. His cheek rests on the metal hip of the queen. 'Jack says it's silly, that I like Queen Bess.'

Richard leans against the long metal skirts of their favourite monarch.

'It's not silly to be kind, or to try to see both sides,' says Richard. 'It's a good hearted thing, to want to be fair. But do you know what else is important?'

Neddy nods. 'To be your best self every day.'

'The attempt is as worthy as the achievement,' says Richard. 'And forgiveness is a kindness when we can't quite manage our best. We can always try again tomorrow. And what is our motto?'

'Loyalty binds me!' laughs the boy, and he trustingly topples from the base of the statue into his father's arms.

Neddy is almost too big for this game, but not yet. Richard catches his son and swings him around, puts him on the path again.

'Be loyal to your promise,' says Richard. 'Be your best self.'

'Every day,' agrees Neddy.

Half way home to Anne and the girls, his sisters, Neddy wants to feel what it will be to walk like his father. He stands upon his father's feet, his upraised hands held in his father's strong grip, and Richard takes strides just long enough to make his little son feel big.

A Song for Hell

This is the story of Orphea and Eurydice. It's a little like the old story, except that Orphea was a kickass rock goth queen and her Eurydice was a poet who danced with her words as well as her body. Orphea's eyes were grey as stormclouds and her dark hair hung in ringlets around her face. Dainty Eurydice's eyes were green as spring, her cropped dark hair a pink-streaked nest.

Orphea and Eurydice were almost like their namesakes, except that Eurydice was famous as a songwriter-advocate, with her fierce lyrics calling those who heard to stand up for Gaia and her sisters – and people listened.

Orphea wrapped Eurydice's lyrics in music of gold and stars, her guitar a translator, sending Eurydice's call direct to the hearts and minds of everyone who heard. Orphea and Eurydice taught all who heard their songs about love in the face of hatred, about unfailing courage in the face of rage, about how to act in the face of fear.

Orphea and Eurydice loved each other not only with passion but with audacity. They married in their hearts and exchanged golden bands without needing official sanction, though they had that too, eventually.

Their story is almost like that of the oak nymph and Apollo's son, except that the snake that killed pink-haired Eurydice was an angry, jealous, spurned man with a knife for a fang.

Orphea held Eurydice in her arms and sang to her, soft and weeping, as she died. *My love, my love, my love.*

It's a terrible, terrible thing, to feel the cherished body of the woman who owns your heart grow cold.

Grief is not one thing. It's many things, cascading one after the other, or crashing down all at once. Hollowness and burning; shrinking to smallness and also towering wide; tears and snot and cursing and spitting. It is debilitating. It is galvanising. It is the thief of action. It is the match lighting the fuse.

Orphea's grief was sharp and hot and deep, like a compressed sun burning underneath her heart. Instead of consuming her, it fuelled her, and armoured her, and made her impervious to all attempts to *get over* her unjust loss. She closed her lips and sang no more, spoke no more, keeping that ferocious power inside her body, behind her biting teeth.

Orphea walked in bare feet up the side of a volcano, over fire and ash. At the top she fell to her hands and knees on the earth and opened her mouth and keened her anguish and her rage into the mouth of the volcano. She sang a note that could have shattered moons and cracked the ocean floor.

Eurydice!

Gods heard. Let's call them Hades and Hephaestus, though they've always had many names. Hades and his brother kept the world from cracking open with the force of Orphea's cry, but the sound with which she might slay the world kept pouring out of her until Hades said:

> *Stop! You may have her back, if you come to claim her, and pay the price. You may walk into the Underworld, and she may follow you back, but only if your faith and hers are unconditional and complete. You may not speak to each other. You may not look at each other once you begin. Only when you and she have returned to the realm of the living will you be reunited, there to live a long and fruitful life. Only then.*

Orphea didn't even think it over. She never even asked the price; she was prepared to pay anything.

She walked into the Underworld, bare feet on ice as cold as death, on stones as sharp as blades, on coals as hot as the burning sun under her heart.

She walked until she met Eurydice, waiting under the shadow of Hades' hand.

Orphea nodded at Eurydice. Eurydice nodded at Orphea.

Orphea turned and walked, over coals, over stones, over ice.

This story is different to the old one. Orphea, unlike cursed Orpheus, did not look back. She trusted that Eurydice followed. She trusted that Eurydice *chose* to follow. Sometimes she stopped to listen. She could hear no breath, but Eurydice was still dead – there'd be no breath yet. She could hear no footfall, but Eurydice was still part of the Underworld – her feet were soundless yet.

Orphea felt a disturbance in the air. A presence. Eurydice? She longed to turn and look, but the fire under her heart made her strong.

Also, being practical, Orphea stopped to tear a strip from her clothes, and made a blindfold for herself. She was faithful and strong, and now blind too. Though her hands shook and her heart raced, she wouldn't fail Eurydice now.

Orphea crept in darkness and her feet burned, and bled, and froze, until at last she felt soft ash beneath her feet, then softer grass. Where she'd felt shadows press against her skin, now she felt the light of morning, and it felt like the sky touching her face.

Orphea sat on the grass with her hands on her knees, and after all her courage, she was afraid to take off the blindfold.

She felt someone sit beside her. Someone solid and warm. Someone silent.

'Eurydice?'

The person beside her placed their hand on Orphea's wrist, and it felt like Eurydice's hand, but she spoke not a word.

Orphea untied the cloth from her eyes and opened them wide, but she saw nothing at all – for she was blind.

'Eurydice?' she whispered again.

The person beside her took Orphea's hands and placed them, soft as a lullaby, on their own silent lips. Those lips kissed Orphea's fingers, and Orphea knew. She *knew*.

'Eurydice. Oh love, oh my love, you're here.'

Eurydice kissed Orphea's fingers three times, yes yes yes. She kissed Orphea's cheeks three times. Yes yes yes. She kissed Orphea's lips, one time, a long time.

Yes.

Orphea took Eurydice's hands and pressed them to her blinded eyes.

'Hades took his price,' she murmured.

Eurydice took Orphea's hands and pressed them to her cheeks. She nodded. Yes.

'I don't have to see you to know you're my Eurydice. I know your scent, and the silk of your hair. I know the shape of your hand in mine and the arch of your foot against the calf of my leg. I know the taste of you and the shape of your soul, and how it fits with mine.'

Eurydice kissed Orphea's hands. Placed them on her throat. She made no sound at all, and they knew the other price they'd paid to the king of the Underworld.

Orphea held Eurydice's face in her palms. 'I don't have to hear your voice to know who you are,' she whispered. 'Your voice is in my head, in my heart, in my blood, in my soul. I hear you breathing. I hear your heart beating. I hear you.'

She wept anyway. Eurydice kissed the tears dry and placed Orphea's fingers against the curve of her lips, so that Orphea could touch the happiness in them. Eurydice's soft laughter was silent too, but loud with joy.

They kissed then. Eyes closed, voiceless but for tiny hums of pleasure, as they'd always done, and they'd lost nothing at all now that they'd found each other again. Eurydice's dainty fingers threaded through Orphea's ringlets; Orphea's guitar-callused fingers stroked the short strands of Eurydice's still pink-streaked hair.

Orphea smiled. 'Poor Hades. He's the god of the Underworld. He thinks silence and darkness are our worst fears. He thinks it is a curse to have lost the sun. But you've always been my light.'

Eurydice took Orphea's palm and wrote on it with the tip of her finger. She wrote: *You have always been my voice. I will be your eyes.*

'Thank you for coming back to me.'

Eurydice pressed Orphea's palm to her cheek, and kissed her wife's wrist. *Thank you for bringing me home,* she wrote in Orphea's palm.

Eurydice wrote a song on Orphea's skin. Orphea wrapped it in music of gold and stars and sang their gratitude to the gods and to their own strength for taking the chance that was given, for having faith.

> *You gave me darkness; it's a fair trade,*
> *You gave me silence, a choice gladly made*
> *If hell for you is quiet and black*
> *Let us give you colours back*
> *A daisy chain of thanks we sing*
> *We'll weave for you an endless spring*

This new legend is different to the old.

It's said that when blind Orphea sings mute Eurydice's words, garlands of wildflowers hang on Hades' gates, and that sometimes he wears them in his hair.

THE CHRISTMAS CARD MYSTERY

On a squally day in the second week of December, and being in the neighbourhood to visit a patient, I called upon Baker Street to convey my regards to my old friend, Mr Sherlock Holmes. Mrs Hudson ushered me into the hall with warm greetings and the news that Holmes was out on a case.

'I shouldn't intrude, then…' I began.

'No intrusion, Doctor Watson,' she promised me. 'And it's wet enough out there, and cold enough, for you to stop by the fire a while. You're a busy man and mustn't make yourself unwell with a chill.' Mrs Hudson deftly relieved me of my hat, scarf, gloves and coat so gently and relentlessly that I was in 221B and before the fire without offering a single protest.

In truth, I was glad to be out of the blustery, sleeting wind, and with my wife away a week, visiting the lately mourning Mrs Forrester, her old employer and friend, it was lonely at home. I missed, too, the old days of mysteries and liked to see, from time to time, if I might be of assistance again. Perhaps if he was on a case, I might be so fortunate again today.

I stood in front of the hearth warming my hands, noting that Holmes had left my old chair exactly where it had always been, beside his. I dared fancy he might at times miss my company in his endeavours, too, and hoped that I might visit.

The mantelpiece was as cluttered as ever with pipes and the Persian slipper, a few stray plugs of tobacco held against his morning smoke, unopened correspondence, the clock, a collection of curved wooden shapes of obscure function, and a retort containing pale yellow fluid sitting in a cradle – some half completed or completely forgotten experiment, no doubt. The morocco case in which he kept his syringe was thankfully not to be seen. An engaging conundrum, then.

Sitting among all of this habitual detritus were five Christmas cards, each depicting scenes of a macabre humour. A frog that had stabbed its fellow, two naked-plucked geese with a man on a roasting spit, a wasp chasing two children with the unlikely subtitle *A Joyous New Year*, a savage white bear crushing an explorer in *A Hearty Welcome*, and a dead robin which read *May yours be a joyful Christmas*. The latter at least hearkened to the Christ story, the rest to a certain black wit about Holmes' profession.

It seemed likely to me that one card had been sent by Lestrade, others by Gregson or Jones. I took up the card depicting the frog-murder but found it inscribed merely with *To my dear friend* at the top and *Mrs Inke Pullitts* underneath. The script was disorderly, as though done in haste, and struck me as more a masculine than a feminine hand.

I was startled out of my examination when the door flew open and Sherlock Holmes strode through it, a dozen newspapers under his arm.

'Ah, Watson, I see you are making yourself at home! No, no, my dear fellow, go right ahead, and tell me what you make of my Yuletide correspondence while I pour us a brandy. It's a cruel day out, and my blood's in need of warming.'

He abandoned the papers over the arm of his chair. His pale cheeks were rosy with the cold he'd just escaped, and his grey eyes sparkled with the merriment I had long associated with an intriguing case.

'I had thought our friends at Scotland Yard were sending you cards,' I admitted, 'but I realise I must be quite wrong. They've never sent you any before now.' In fact, Holmes rarely received such personal missives, except from me and Mary or his brother Mycroft Holmes. 'Did you retain the envelope?'

Holmes placed two glasses on the table and fetched five envelopes from beneath a book on folklore. The topmost he gave to me. I examined it closely – it was addressed in the same untidy hand as the card to the attention of Mr S Holmes, though scrawled so untidily as to appear to read "Mrs Hulmes". The paper was inexpensive, matching the quality of the card, and bore no return address. The corner of the envelope was marked, fore and aft, with a peculiar indentation, as though it had contained something other than the greeting. I saw a similar mark upon the matching card. I sniffed the paper, as I had seen Holmes do in his investigations, but it told me nothing and made me feel foolish. I couldn't bring myself to dab the tip of my tongue to the paper, another of Holmes' investigative techniques.

'What was in it?' I asked.

He selected two of the wooden shapes from the mantel and held them between thumb and forefinger for me to see. The first was like a misshapen peg, three inches long, and almost a teardrop shape when viewed from the end that was rough with bark. The piece tapered slightly here – perhaps the top of the piece – though the other end was only a fraction thicker. The second piece, when viewed from the bark end, formed a rough U. They appeared to be carved from oak, as did the other pieces on the mantel when I examined them, though the wood was marred in places with a dark stain.

The remaining cards and their envelopes were alike in their particulars: addressed *To my dear friend* as from *Mrs Inke Pullitts* and variously dented from the inclusion of the odd peg.

'Who is Mrs Pullitts?' I then asked. With a broad smile, he told me he knew no such lady, and all his enquiries, made with advertisements in the papers and the gossip-gathering prowess of the Irregulars, had uncovered no person of that name who might seek him.

I was tempted to dismiss it all as a meaningless prank, but was too wise to say so. If this prank had stirred Holmes to the point of broad smiles and the spark of merriment in his eye, then it was a puzzle worth his attention.

A puzzle. I turned again to the mantel and took up the wooden pegs and U-shapes that lay there in a pile so that I might examine them more closely. Holmes beamed his approval at me as I set them on the table, and I confess I felt it as a high praise. He sipped on the brandy, but I ignored mine in favour of the puzzle of the pegs.

'These pieces seem to fit together,' I said, 'And this third.' The three pieces indeed sat snugly together, bar the slender gaps created by the tapering. The grain of the wood and gnarled pattern of the external part betrayed their origin. 'Hewn from the same oak log.'

'Splendid,' said Holmes. 'What else?'

'Mrs Pullitts is sending you this puzzle in a strangely piecemeal fashion, though for what reason I cannot surmise, unless it's to keep the sending of it secret from a member of her household – Mr Pullitts perhaps? She has even attempted to disguise your name, unless it's simply that her handwriting is terrible. It would be so much easier to send a discreet letter, so I must conclude it's a vital secret.'

'Well done, Watson, though as I've said, I know of no Mrs Inke Pullitts, or of anyone of the name of either Inke or Pullitts. I don't think this letter comes from a woman at all.'

'I did wonder at the more mannish stroke of the pen. A pseudonym, you think?'

'Perhaps, or a clue in itself.'

'A clue?' I frowned. 'How so?'

Holmes clapped me on the shoulder. 'Drink your brandy and I'll show you.' He fetched fifteen squares of paper from beneath the book of folklore to show where he had written the individual letters of his correspondent's name.

'Having ascertained that I knew of no *Inke*,' he said, 'I thought to look at the name in the light of one of the simplest codes. The little scenes on the cards and what appears to be parts of a child's wooden puzzle led to me think along a certain path.' I must have looked quite blank for he added, 'Consider it an anagram, Watson, and it may lead you to my own conclusion.'

I placed my brandy aside and spent some time shifting squares of paper about the table. It was only by separating the letters of the word "stilts" that the solution came to me. The letters spelled out *Rumpelstiltskin*.

'This really makes it no clearer to me, Holmes,' I said, exasperated.

'No?'

'No. A fairy tale character is sending you macabre Christmas greetings and a child's wooden puzzle, but to what end? Your Rumpelstiltskin may be simply trying to test his wits against yours to pass the tedium of the season.'

'Oh, Watson.' His disappointment was palpable. 'Taken alone, these cards may signify a certain pawky sense of humour, but taken as a collection, sent by the same nameless person taking such pains to keep their communiques secret, I fear it adds up to something sinister. Don't you recall the story of Rumpelstiltskin?'

'Yes, yes. The girl whose father swears she can spin gold from straw, and the King threatens to kill the girl if the boast isn't proven. Rumpelstiltskin uses magic to accomplish the feat for her, and demands her firstborn. But Holmes, this is mere childish nonsense. In any case, Rumpelstiltskin is the villain of the piece.'

'That story has several villains in it, Watson, but for our purposes, I think we may reasonably hypothesise that our correspondent doesn't identify as the goblin, but uses the name to signal to us his dilemma.'

'Which is?'

'What's the crux of the story, Watson?'

'A girl's held prisoner until she performs an impossible feat. She dupes her way out of death with fairy assistance, and then has to outwit her helper to save her child.'

'Exactly!'

'How does this help?' My confusion was leading to annoyance.

Holmes shook his head at me. 'You are a teller of tall stories, Watson. You should surely see the artistic licence in this one.'

I was too used to his teasing references to my stories to be stung, but a reminder that I was sometimes required to alter details in my chronicles to protect certain parties (occasionally ourselves) suggested the solution.

'Your correspondent is held against his will – perhaps to achieve some difficult feat – and has found a way to send to you this plea for assistance.'

Holmes clapped his hands and grinned. 'Indeed! He must be held under some very tight scrutiny, to be unable to send a clearer message, yet with sufficient freedom to slip a card into the mail. He's very careful to disguise its destination, so he must feel certain that his gaoler would intercept anything that's too obvious.'

I frowned and picked up one of the pegs. 'I can't see how this will help you find the poor fellow.'

'Have faith, Watson! And patience, and if you'll be kind enough to help me examine these papers, you might join me in a rescue mission. If you have the time, of course.'

'All the time in the world, my dear fellow,' I declared. I took up several of the papers, flung myself into my old chair, and opened the *Bromley and District Times*. 'What am I looking for?'

Holmes sat opposite me with the *London Evening Standard*. 'Anything that may strike you as relevant to a wooden puzzle, Watson, or any other unusual feature.'

We began to go through each newspaper. I scanned smaller items as well as large, and even the advertisements, my efforts going much more slowly than Holmes'. He whipped impatiently through each page. He flung each paper aside with a grunt of irritation as he completed his search, while I folded them more neatly to drop on the floor beside me.

'These are all local papers, I see,' I said after a moment, 'What if he's from farther afield?'

'No, no! The postmark, Watson!' He softened his irascibility a little. 'Though you couldn't know when each card arrived. I do, however, and the time between the postmark and delivery is so short that the sender *must* be within the metropolis. Oh, this is promising.' He tore the page from the paper and rose, thrusting it at me. As he reached once more for his coat, hat and gloves, I read the obviously related story, a small piece in the corner of page five of *The Echo*.

> Would anyone knowing the whereabouts of Mr Silas North, cabinetmaker and carpenter of Chester Street, Lambeth, missing now for fifteen days, please make this known to his employer, Mr Abel Sudbury. Mrs North would also be pleased to hear from her husband.

Our hansom deposited us before a row of three smart terraces that had once been more uniform, but now displayed a variety of railings, eaves and other decorative touches. The first's embellishments were primarily in woodwork, the next in ironwork and a third, ceramics.

'This will be Mr North's home, I think,' said Holmes. This house was trimmed in intricately carved wooden eaves and elegant window frames and shutters.

'These terraces are all owned by Abel Sudbury,' explained Holmes as we headed for the door painted in fine, fresh blue. 'Accommodation for the master craftsmen in his employ in the building trade. You'll note how he uses the buildings to showcase the skills he can offer his clients. This particular house offers the finest examples of woodwork. The right home for a master carpenter, wouldn't you say?'

Holmes' knock was answered by a harried looking woman of middle age. A small child with a round, sticky face hung upon her skirts and an older girl bustled towards them. 'Here, now Bess, what did I say? Leave Mam alone for the door.'

Little Bess gazed widely at us. I smiled at her and she ran away to hide behind her sister.

Holmes gave the woman a small bow. 'Mrs North. My name is Sherlock Holmes. I…'

'Oh, I know of you, Mr Holmes!' said Mrs North with a breathy sigh of relief. 'Judy, my eldest, read out that story in Beeton's! Have you come to tell us where Silas has gone?'

'I'm afraid not, Mrs North – but I have come in an endeavour to *find* him.'

We were welcomed into the tidy little home and shown to the parlour while Mrs North went to instruct the maid to prepare tea. Beyond the door, I heard the piping of young voices, and a motherly admonishment to hush and be good children.

While we waited for refreshment, Holmes prowled around the parlour, gleaning all he could about the family and their missing patriarch.

My efforts to follow Holmes' methods led me to conclude that the Norths had five children – two girls and three boys – and that Mr North was a highly skilled craftsman, if it was his work that had furnished their home. The joinery and finishes were the best I had ever seen, and through my association with Holmes I had been in a good many exquisitely furnished apartments. The parlour was also filled with beautiful hand-made toys, many scuffed with loving use and age. On the top of a small bookshelf – filled with books by the likes of Ballantyne and Stevenson – was an unusually designed wooden castle and a regiment of painted soldiers.

The parlour spoke of a warm and loving family life, and I confess I felt a pang of envy. Mary and I had hoped before now to have our own home so filled with happy children.

Mrs North and her maid returned with tea, and Holmes remained remarkably patient until all was settled to our hostess' satisfaction. Mrs North sat on the edge of a chair commonly used for needlepoint, judging by the basket of work to one side. Her hands were clasped tightly together in an attempt to settle her agitation. Holmes sat opposite her, touching her wrist briefly in a gesture of reassurance, before leaning forward attentively, elbows on knees and fingers steepled.

I sat across from them with my tea and my notebook.

'When exactly did your husband disappear?' Holmes began, ignoring the cup at his elbow. 'Tell me everything you recall about that day.'

Mrs North pressed her lips together, met his gaze with resolve and told her tale.

'He left us fifteen days ago today, on November the 29th. He had his breakfast as usual, waved us goodbye on the stoop and walked towards Kennington Station – he was catching the tube to a house in Islington, where he and Mr Sudbury were to meet with a client, a Mrs Babcock. Silas never arrived at the house. I knew nothing of it until Mr Sudbury came to the door, very cross too, to see why he hadn't come.'

'What did you do?'

'I sent Freddie with Mr Sudbury to walk to the station, but nobody there knew anything, nor had they seen Silas.'

'What steps did you take then?'

'We went to the police of course, but they've found nothing. Someone near the station thought they'd seen Silas get into a hansom with someone, but they couldn't be sure, and one hansom looks much like another. The police haven't found a cabman who'll own it they picked him up, and there's been nothing since. Except this.'

Mrs North rose to pluck a Christmas card from her mantelpiece. It depicted two owls on a bench, one in a top hat, the other in a bonnet. The inscription read "Maudie" at the top and "I'll be home soon, God willing, S." at the bottom.

Holmes examined the card minutely then held it out to me. The only thing clear to me was that the handwriting matched that of Holmes' mysterious Rumpelstiltskin.

'When did this arrive?'

'A week ago, only the police could make nothing of it. They say it only means he has run off for his own reasons and will be back or not as he pleases. They gave up looking. But Mr Sudbury, who is a good man, knows my Silas as well as me, and we know he wouldn't just take off like this. There must be a reason he's away, and if he could come home he would. Only I've no notion why he can't!'

Her harried look, kept at bay, returned, heralded by anxious tears. 'If you can only tell me where he is, Mr Holmes, I'll go and fetch him myself, or Mr Sudbury will send a lad. This isn't like him! Please don't tell me, like that Inspector Bartle did, that Silas has run off. If he'd done so, why would he write?'

Holmes hushed her with a pat on her wrist. 'I can assure you, Mrs North, your husband is trying to return to you. Do you have the envelope this card came in?'

'No. Oh! Should I have kept it?'

'It may have been instructive, but I shall persevere without it. Now, can you tell us of the days before your husband disappeared? Did he seem preoccupied or anxious?'

'He was his usual self. He's a man of few words, my Silas, and soft-spoken when he has something to say. Though there was the gent, came to the door the week before. Silas wasn't pleased with his being there, but no hard words were exchanged that I know. I heard none of their conversation, and when I asked, Silas only said, "The persistent fellow offers a fascinating commission, but I work for Mr Sudbury, and that's that".

'His contract with Mr Sudbury is very watertight on that point – Silas isn't allowed to work for others.'

Mrs North was unable, however, to describe this "persistent fellow" beyond that he was tall and pale and, 'had the most penetrating blue eyes.'

'One last thing, Mrs North,' said Holmes as we rose to leave. 'The toy castle on the shelf – is this your husband's work?'

'Oh, yes. He learned the trick of it from his grandfather, and makes them for all the children around here who want them.' Mrs North brushed her fingers over the turrets of the toy, and all of a sudden the towers collapsed with a friendly clatter into the base. Then she lifted the base block and with a flick of her wrist, the carved pieces shot out, creating a concertina of shapes that built three extending layers of tower.

'Made all from a single piece of wood, I see,' said Holmes, showing it to me. The tower pieces all had that peculiar curved shape, teardrops and U-shapes, tapering finely so that they fell snugly into place when flicked out, yet would collapse neatly into the base after. 'Thank you, Mrs North. You have been most helpful. I expect to have news for you within a day or so.'

She pressed a hand urgently to his elbow. 'He'll come home, you think? He isn't…' she steeled herself, 'hurt or ill?'

'Not at this moment, and I've every hope he'll continue in good health until found. Come, Watson!'

As we strode back to Kennington Road in the wind, but thankfully not the rain, Holmes withdrew a wooden peg from his pocket. It was one of those sent with the cards, oak bark still attached to the crown of it.

'That castle design shown to us by Mrs North is most unusual, Watson. Rumpelstiltskin is undoubtedly this vanished Mr Silas North, and wherever he is, and if he willingly went, he almost certainly did not willingly stay.'

'Perhaps he took on that fascinating commission,' I ventured. Holmes flagged a hansom for our return to Baker Street.

'I'd be surprised if that persistent gentleman were not involved. The timing is too close to be a coincidence.'

'Then perhaps Mr North decided to take on the job, and keeps his silence as a way of avoiding questions from his regular employer, Sudbury.'

'In that case, why send me these cards and castle pieces? Which, you'll note, are not carved as smoothly as the toy he made for his son. No, Watson. Silas North is held against his will, although not yet, I think, in any real physical danger. He has freedom enough to both make and send these tokens, but not enough to send a clear message. He has been allowed to reassure his wife, too, which means his warder isn't beyond humanity.'

'You think he'll be released in due course, when whatever this commission is has been completed?'

'I'm not as certain as all that, Watson. If the report of Mr North willingly getting into a hansom cab is correct, it's likely he was tricked into entering the vehicle, perhaps on the pretext of getting a ride closer to his intended destination, and waylaid that way. If no driver has come forward, either he has been paid well for his silence, or laid up in some fashion. Any legitimate business offer would surely not involve such secrecy, and would certainly not keep Mr North from communicating with his family. No, Watson, I fear there may yet be some threat to Mr Silas North, once he has completed whatever work is required of him.'

'What can we do?'

'I must examine those cards and envelopes again, Watson, and consult a directory or two. You are most welcome to join me, if you have no other calls upon your time.'

'None at all,' I assured him. 'Though, Holmes, do you think I should return home for my revolver?'

'I don't believe it will be necessary,' he said thoughtfully. 'But you should be ready with that strong left hook of yours, as needed.'

Once more at Baker Street, we found a new delivery from the Royal Mail, and a new card. This, like all the others, was postmarked Bethnal Green, and was addressed scrawlingly to either Holmes or Hulmes. Within was a Christmas card depicting the head of a dog which threw a distorted shadow of a policeman. The inscription was identical to the previous missives, addressed *To my dear friend* and signed with the anagram of Rumpelstiltskin. Holmes put the enclosed U-shaped peg with all the others and gave them to me.

'See what you can make of the addition, now that we know what they're for.' He dashed to his shelves to withdraw several business directories and a map of Bethnal Green, and flung the lot over the table.

I sat in my old chair, placed the small side table in front of me and arranged the wooden castle pieces on it. This sixth piece filled the gap and now all six fit, with that slender fissure that showed how the pieces tapered towards the top.

Of course, these pieces lacked the unifying base that had held the North's toy castle together, and replicating that foundation might prove tricky. Of course, I need not have the solid base in order to flick out the towers and turrets as Mrs North had done. It would be sufficient to have a pedestal that could hold the towers steady.

'Do you still have a plentiful supply of putty in your disguise kit, Holmes?' I asked.

He waved me towards the box where he kept such things, intent as he was on his directory. I retrieved a largish selection of putty and sat once more with my puzzle. As I considered it, Holmes leapt to the door, called for Mrs Hudson and sent her away with a telegram for Billy to take. 'Tell him to wait for an answer!'

It struck me, turning over the pieces of carved oak and remembering the intricacies and layers of that toy castle, that surely Mr North was only part way through sending his message to Holmes. Nevertheless, I slotted the pieces together and then, using the putty to hold each layer steady, I made the pieces jut up as intended.

Looking from above, the puzzle meant nothing. I was disappointed, having hoped for some secret message to be spelled out in the bark.

Holmes crouched by my side. He peered at the result – a crude selection of rising towers. I could imagine what the base must be like, and reckoned it'd be a handsome thing when completed, quite a neat little carpenters trick to make turrets that could stack high and then compact down again like that.

'I'm sorry, Holmes,' I said. 'I thought there might be more…'

But Holmes grinned and clapped me on the shoulder. 'Look again, Watson. I believe we have found our missing carpenter.'

He rose as I peered at the pieces. It was a moment before I could see with new eyes, to find the clue I had missed, but there it was. Parts of the curved shape were stained a slightly darker colour, and now that I looked at the thing front-on, it was possible to read those marks as more than flaws in the wood. With a little imagination, I could see the letters F and O.

'I still don't see how this helps.'

Holmes dropped a directory into my lap and leaned over my shoulder to jab at an entry with a long, elegant forefinger.

> FOX BROS: Toymakers. Artful Constructions, Tricks and Trinkets
> for the Curious Child.

The address was in Bethnal Green.

'And here,' added Holmes, dropping the second directory on top of the first. 'By the fine print on the back, all of our cards and Mrs North's owls were printed by Fox Brother's neighbours, Calico Press. I think we can be on our way and learn more of the why once we have located our Rumpelstiltskin!'

The day had become dark, though the wind had dropped, as we made our way by hansom to the fringes of Old Nichol Street Rookery, a slum filled with workhouses and dilapidated tenancies. The rookery was notoriously crowded, damp and unsanitary, and I had professional cause to know that a child contracting whooping cough or diphtheria within its boundaries were significantly more likely to be lost to the disease than their counterparts a mere half mile away.

The toymaker's store with its cheerful green door stood at the corner of Bethnal Green Road and a row leading to the warren of the rookery beyond. Its windows were crammed with all manner of bright and colourful trifles – dolls and sailing boats, tops and tea sets, tennis rackets and drums, puzzles and hoops, and books and soft felt rabbits. Nothing like the unusual castle we had seen at the North home could be seen, but Holmes was undeterred.

'That isn't why Mr North's liberty has been taken from him. No, Watson, there's clearly a much bigger game at stake.'

We didn't enter the toyshop, as I imagined we would, but turned down the row to the shop's perpendicular neighbour, Calico Printing. Its goods, too, were on display: posters for concerts, magic shows and theatrical events, as well as prettily spread fans of pamphlets and monographs. A wide range of its fantastical and humorous Christmas cards were hung upon a string in its window.

'Be a good fellow,' said Holmes, 'and take a turn along this adjoining lane. I'd like to know if the Fox Brothers have a workshop at the back of their shop premises. We'll meet again at the corner.'

I drew my coat and scarf closer against the cooling day and did as I was bid. I concluded, from the depth and height of the building that the shop front and living quarters above it concealed modest space at the rear for at least some of the toy-making labour of the business. I met again with Holmes, who smiled in satisfaction at my report.

'Calico did indeed supply a modest number of cards to the Brothers Fox, which perforce have been delivered only to their premises here. So come, Watson, let's go shopping.'

His ebullience was infectious, and we strode through the front door of Fox Brothers together, as two friends seeking Christmas gifts for their families. It was not so much pretence for me, as we had hopes, Mary and I, that this time she would carry to term. Her health was robust enough for her week away with Mrs Forrester, early as she was in her condition, and from there I would ensure the best of care for her confinement. As Holmes spoke to the proprietor, I lingered at the blocks, dollies and felt rabbits, thinking, *perhaps one day for my sons or daughters*.

'I understand your workshop can make special items on commission,' Holmes said to the man at the counter, undoubtedly one of the Fox brothers. He was a slender fellow with a jolly face and gingery side whiskers that suited his name.

'It's possible,' jolly Mr Fox conceded. 'It may depend upon your needs. We buy from local craftsmen around here of course – one tries to support good local workers – but we can arrange special requests too.'

'I was thinking of a type of toy castle,' said Holmes, 'carved from a single piece of wood. The interlocking pieces unfold with a flick of the wrist to make towers…'

'Oh, I do believe I know the design you mean. My youngest boy has a friend with the very toy. The other boy's father is a carpenter and makes them for local children. My brother approached the carpenter in question, North by name, to see if he'd make them for us, but he declined.'

'That's a shame.'

'Very much so, but you know, the fellow works exclusively as a cabinet maker for Sudbury Furnishing and Trimming, if you've heard of them.'

'I believe I've heard them highly spoken of,' offered Holmes cautiously.

'Their reputation is unparalleled,' Mr Fox assured him. 'But Sudbury aims to keep it that way. He snatches up all the best craftsmen and their contracts are very strict.'

'Surely the making of a trifle like a child's toy wouldn't constitute a problem.'

'Constantine offered very generous terms, but North refused to work around his obligations. A very conscientious fellow, it seems.'

'Ah well,' said Holmes, feigning disappointment. 'Perhaps North might consider a one-off wouldn't violate his honour. Do you think he would?'

'Possibly,' said Mr Fox agreeably. 'Although he also declined Constantine's request for another one-time commission.'

'A pity,' said Holmes. He looked to me. 'Has something caught your eye?'

I placed a felt rabbit on the counter, which may have been precipitate of me, considering our previous loss, but I chose to look on it as an act of faith. 'These seem well made.'

Holmes gave me the most searching look, but I was well used to being under his scrutiny and it rarely bothered me.

'Our sister makes those,' said Mr Fox proudly. 'She has a very fine hand and their little faces are very dear.'

The felt rabbit did, indeed, have a very dear little face, and I happily handed over my coin for it.

'Are all your magnificent toys crafted by your talented family?' asked Holmes with generous admiration.

Mr Fox beamed. 'Not all, no, but they all contribute something. Well, Constantine isn't a craftsman, it's true, but he often designs some of our more clever toys for the artisans to make. He's a magician, you know, and does conjuring tricks for the customers. He's a great admirer of Maskelyne and would dearly love to follow in that great man's footsteps. He has been engaged for some house parties, and has hopes of gaining a following. He has hired a week at the Piccolo Theatre for the spring.'

'Didn't we see a poster for *The Astounding Constantine*?' I asked Holmes: the poster had been displayed in the window at Calico's.

'Did you?' asked Holmes, though I knew full well we both had.

I turned to Fox. 'My wife likes magic shows. Perhaps I should take her. What's his act?'

'My friend's wife is something of a connoisseur,' expanded Holmes. 'She would hope for something more than card tricks and disappearing coins.'

Mr Fox seemed mildly offended. 'My brother's only starting out, but he takes the craft very seriously. Levitation, mind-reading, all of the best expected from the province of magic.'

'A Cabinet of Wonders?' suggested Holmes. 'I myself am fond of a good disappearing act.'

'The very thing he's perfecting over the winter.' Mr Fox's familial pride had returned. 'He saw a most excellent disappearing act last summer and has been designing an ingenious cabinet for the purpose.'

'Oh, I'd like to see such a thing. These devices are splendid pieces of engineering. Would he let us see his workshop, do you think? Is it far?'

Mr Fox shook his head. 'He works in the shop behind the house, but he won't even let me see what he's up to. It's very secret stuff.' He waggled his eyebrows at us, showing how charming he found his brother's eccentricities.

'You haven't seen him working?'

'Oh no,' Mr Fox assured us. 'He's been nigh on living there for two weeks now, though he comes out to eat with the family. Many days he even sleeps in the workroom. Apparently, rival magicians are apt to sneak about and steal ideas.'

'And you don't see him otherwise? He must be very dedicated.'

'Oh he is, though he doesn't neglect his family duties. I told Constantine, "if you must spend time sequestered on your art, you must, but at least you can address all the festive cards for our customers, clients and suppliers, and save me the time!" and so he has done.'

Mr Fox's affectionate enthusiasm for his brother's preoccupation with magic and the making of a cabinet bordered, I thought, on the foolish. Certainly, he had a fool's propensity for wittering on about the brother with strangers as though Constantine Fox was a precocious child who deserved to be indulged.

Holmes beamed upon the garrulous Mr Fox. 'I have friends in theatrical circles,' he said. 'Should your brother be in need of an agent. I shan't be this way again for a while, but I'd be happy to exchange a word with him now to confirm if he would like a letter of introduction.'

Mr Fox was so tickled by my friend's generosity and kindness, that he felt sure, he said, that Constantine would spare him a moment.

Holmes cast me a glance which spoke volumes. I tucked the felt rabbit, which Mr Fox had wrapped in brown paper, into my pocket and followed the two men behind the counter, beyond the shop door to a corridor. The passage led left to stairs and the living quarters for the Fox family, and right to a firmly shut door.

Mr Fox tapped on it. 'Constantine! I have a visitor for you! A wonderful fellow who can recommend an agent for your show.' He turned the handle, but the door was locked.

A sudden flurry of noise behind the door included what seemed a throttled cry, a dull thud and the sound as of a door slamming.

'What say you, Ezekiel?' came a strained voice. 'Haven't I told you not to disturb me at work?'

Mr Fox gave us an apologetic look, as though to excuse his brother's rudeness. 'You have, but this man may be of great benefit to your career, and I thought you might make an exception.'

Silence greeted this pronouncement, broken at last with a querulous: 'You know an agent for a magic act?'

'Certainly,' said Holmes with a flourish. 'The great Allendale himself, who I am sure you know, acts on behalf of many of the great stage artists. He's a personal friend of mine, and was saying only the other day that he wished he had some new up-and-coming performer for whom to play Midas. *His* words. He tends towards vanity, though it seems well founded upon his successes.'

'Yes,' came the voice. 'I've heard he's a bit of a peacock, but he's very good.'

'He is,' said Holmes. 'And it'd delight to me to deliver him a new protégé. I owe him a good turn.'

The key turned in the lock. The door opened a fraction.

A wan face looked out at us. Younger and shorter than his jolly brother, his thinness speaking of frailty, Constantine Fox had anxious blue eyes and a trembling mouth. Had he come to my door for professional services, I would, on that face alone, have prescribed bed rest in the country for a month. He seemed a man on the verge of nervous collapse.

Holmes acted on the instant, placing his foot in the narrow space between door and frame and pushing his shoulder against the door itself. With a yelp, Constantine Fox tried to slam the door shut. The violence of the action must have caused Holmes some pain, but he held fast and at the next moment I was using my own strength to push the door wide.

Ezekiel Fox shouted an ineffectual protest as Holmes and I stumbled into the room beyond. For his part, brother Constantine shouted at us about the invasion of his privacy while standing before a great wooden box placed on a wooden platform.

'It isn't any good, Mr Fox,' said Holmes sternly. 'We know that you are keeping Mr Silas North a prisoner here, and it's very easy to see the work you have been making him do.' Holmes gestured grandly towards the box – the height of a man, with a pyramid roof, sturdily built and covered in chalk marks outlining so-called mystic symbols. I supposed this was the sketch for later decoration.

Constantine Fox went pale as a ghost and stumbled so that Holmes reached to catch him, but he righted himself and drew himself up defiantly.

'What nonsense!' Fox declared. 'Ezekiel, who are these impossible intruders? I warned you about my rivals who would try to steal my idea!'

'I'm not your rival, but a detective,' said Holmes crisply. 'My name is Sherlock Holmes and you, Mr Fox, are in dire trouble. If you tell me where you are keeping Mr North prisoner, and you have done him no harm, I may yet persuade him and the authorities to press no charges.'

A strange spark came into the magician's eyes. 'I challenge you to find such a man, Mr Holmes.'

I could have warned him how foolish it was to issue such challenges to my friend, but I confess I rather enjoy the effect of their learning such foolishness for themselves.

Holmes immediately strode around the raised platform, heading for the back of the workshop. Constantine Fox appeared very smug about it, until Holmes, having walked a semicircle around it, leapt lightly onto the planks to investigate the box.

'I shall call the police this instant!' cried Ezekiel Fox.

'That's up to you,' I said, watching as Holmes circled the cabinet now, his hands trailing across the four panels. 'But I expect that will obviate Mr Holmes' efforts to have no charges pressed, once he finds Mr North.'

'You are offensive, sir,' said Ezekiel Fox haughtily. 'Constantine hasn't seen Mr North since approaching him about the toy castles. Have you, Constantine?'

'Of course not!' But there was something furtive about his reply, and as I had failed ever to keep a secret from my late brother Henry when we were boys (and indeed, ever from Holmes now), the elder brother knew instantly that the younger lied.

'Oh, Constantine, what have you done?'

'Nothing. Nothing!'

Holmes pressed the front panels of the cabinet and it sprang open. It was empty. Holmes immediately fell to his hands and knees and explored the floor of the thing, but no trapdoor was revealed. With a snarl of disappointment, Holmes stood inside the cabinet and felt all the walls of it, again without satisfaction. He fell still and closed his eyes, thinking, and when he opened them again, the gleam in the grey told me that he had solved it.

Holmes reached up to the ceiling of the box, which came some 14 inches below the peak of a square hip-roof atop it. The four sides of that little pyramid were chalk-marked with symbols and the name *The Astounding Constantine.*

Holmes pushed. The ceiling clicked. Constantine Fox cried out in horror and fainted as the ceiling section yielded.

At that moment I suddenly had three patients on my hands – Constantine Fox in a swoon, and Sherlock Holmes on the floor, half under the man who had fallen from the tiny cavity in the roof of the cabinet – no doubt Mr Silas North.

It was a simpler triage than many I had made on the battlefield, and I leapt at once to Mr North's aid. His breathing was laboured with him, a tall man, having been folded up into so small a space for some minutes. He was curled in on himself with a bruise on his forehead.

Holmes scrambled out from underneath him, following my instructions to stretch out the patient on the floor. I set about raising North's arms above his head before bringing them down to his chest and repeating the action until his breathing regained regularity. North groaned and I checked his pupils. He'd have a very nasty headache, and perhaps a slight concussion, but would recover.

'Rest easy, Mr North,' I said in my most soothing tone. 'You are rescued and will be home soon.'

'Constantine!' I heard Ezekiel Fox cry in despair. 'Constantine!'

I knelt by Constantine Fox's side, but there was nothing more wrong with him than exhaustion and the fear of the consequences of his own selfish madness. Already he was moaning, rather more theatrically than his condition warranted.

'That's enough of a fuss,' I told him sternly. 'You'll sit up and confess all.'

Strangely, this is precisely what he did. He sat, pale and trembling, and told us the story as though seeking, if not absolution, then at least validation.

'Silas North is the best cabinet maker in London, and he refused to help no matter how much I promised to pay, so I *made* him do it,' he said. 'That cabinet is the only thing I needed to begin my career. I designed it so *perfectly*, but I don't have the skill to make it myself. Twice North refused me. I took a hansom to see him, to ask again, and offer more money, and again he refused. Well, I had gone prepared for his stubbornness. I offered him a ride in my hansom, since he was heading over the river anyway. Once he was inside the cab, I overpowered him with chloroform, as I once read about in a book. When we were near home, I told the driver my mate was taken ill and carried North right in here with hardly a murmur. I didn't even pay the cabman extra, as that would have drawn attention to us.'

Constantine Fox looked at us with a shining, beseeching face, but none, not even his indulgent brother, could give him absolution for his actions.

'I was good to him,' he continued. 'I let him write to his wife so that she wouldn't think him dead in a ditch. I told him he could go home when the cabinet was done, but he couldn't get it right. The floor, you see, is false. At the compression of the concealed switch, it springs up to become the ceiling, while I curl into the space, vanishing in a trice! Then my assistant closes the doors, the ceiling drops, and once again I appear in the box, to the amazement of all. Wonderful, don't you see? But the spring mechanism is supposed to be soundless, and lift very quickly, and North couldn't get it *right*. So I made him stay until he could. I'd have let him go after. *I would have*.'

'You have nearly *killed* him,' said Holmes darkly, which wasn't much of an exaggeration. Another few minutes in that crushing chamber and Silas North may have suffocated.

This observation set the elder brother to roughly shaking the younger by the shoulders.

'That is enough from you, Constantine!' snapped Ezekiel Fox, all jollity vanished, as Constantine might say, in a *trice*. 'And enough of this ridiculous business. You have spent all your savings on this madness and it is done. You'll be lucky if you don't go to prison for this! Oh, you wretched idiot. I've been too forbearing with your stage-struck follies.'

Constantine Fox wept, but it was very difficult to summon any sympathy for him.

We agreed to leave him in his disapproving brother's care until Mr North was in a condition to choose his next steps. Scotland Yard should perhaps have been called immediately, but Mr North wished only to return home to Lambeth, to his long-suffering wife and his little ones.

Holmes escorted Mr North home, where I completed a second examination to satisfy myself that he suffered no permanent injury.

'My messages reached you!' Mr North said to Holmes, throat still hoarse from his ordeal.

'They did indeed,' said Holmes. 'Though I wonder how you smuggled them out. Even a man as overtaken with obsession as *The Astonishing Constantine* should have noticed what you were doing.'

Mr North shook his head. 'He left me alone many nights, chained like a dog in the workshop and gagged so that I couldn't cry for help. But then he brought in boxes of cards he was to address for his brother's business, and decided that it was good use of my time to aid him with this so that we could together resume work on the magic box sooner. When he left to eat in the evening with his brother, he'd leave me to work, under the most dreadful threats if I made any sound. I was able then to work on the castle pieces that I sent you, from a piece of firewood, but it was very hard going.

'Still, he wasn't very observant. I took some of the cards and was able to slip them and their contents among the many piles of cards to post – some of which contained little trinkets. I disguised the messages, of course, in case someone in the household read them. I had no idea how many of them were in on the scheme. I'm lucky it is so successful a toy business that my little messages were able to leave my prison so easily and often.'

'It's a clever man who can make the use of a good opportunity,' Holmes assured him, and we left Mr North in the embrace of his wife and loving family.

In truth, Holmes didn't try particularly hard to persuade Mr North against pressing charges, but Ezekiel Fox paid a handsome compensation to him and gave many boxes of toys to Mr North and all his neighbours. He also sent his wayward brother to South Africa to see if that made him more sensible.

Within the week, Mary returned home, looking bright and healthy for her time in the country. I showed her the felt rabbit. She exclaimed upon its pretty face and said, 'I do feel quite strong this time, John. I'm certain all will be well.' She placed her hand over her belly, which held our hopes, and I kissed her cheek.

We invited Holmes to join us for Christmas lunch, and I was honoured that he came, bearing a box of fine chocolates for Mary, whose sweet tooth had become insistent since she was with child. I hadn't told him of her condition, so he must have deduced it – along with the fact that I had changed my brand of tobacco only a month before, as he brought me a tin of the new blend. Mary had knitted him a fine scarf, which he admired with all sincerity. He smiled too, at my gift to him of Kendal Mint Cake, which I knew he carried with him for quick energy while working on a case.

After an excellent roast dinner, Holmes played carols for us upon the violin. And so we three kept our Christmas together with an excellent meal, good cheer and much hope for the future.

DEATH'S DOOR

Samira found it unsettling to have Death stalking her. She would have been more terrified, except Death was being such a jerk about it. You'd think Death would be more subtle than to stand behind her on the tram, leaning over to see what she was writing in her journal. Death trying to pilfer her good pen at the library was also really inappropriate.

(Death, realising that Samira was watching, had slipped the pen back onto the desk with badly feigned nonchalance and sidled behind a rack to stare.)

Irritated and confused, Samira had jammed her journal and pen into her backpack and left the library at a brisk pace, but was aware of Death at her heels the whole time. In desperation, she ducked into a too-cool-for-anyone café in a narrow side street.

Now she sat in a corner, warily watching Death, who had taken a table near the door. She couldn't work out if it was comforting or disturbing that even Death failed to be cool enough to warrant service from the painfully hip staff. It's not like they didn't know Death was right there. They'd watched it take the chair and Samira could see them talking about it from their fortress behind the counter.

The lack of service was not her problem. If no-one here wanted her money, fine. Screw 'em. Scowling, Samira tugged her journal out of her pack, slapped it open and ferociously made notes. Her free hand with its chipped black nail polish splayed across the page, shielding it in the unlikely event anyone approached for her order. Her black, frizzy hair draped like a curtain over her right eye. The hair on the left was cropped short and bleached a piebald yellow and russet, showing off the multiple piercings in her ear and eyebrow.

'Excuse me.'

Samira's pen skidded across the page at the voice, dark and uncomfortably ticklish, like ants in her ear. She looked up at Death. It wasn't a skeleton, she already knew that. It was… a space. A concept. An idea in a dark woollen cowl that draped over its not-face in a peculiarly hopeful way. It was a very Western image of Death. Personally, she blamed that Halloween episode of Simpsons, which seemed to be the only one on when she stumbled across the show.

'What the hell do you *want* from me?!'

'I'm really sorry to interrupt,' said Death. 'But I have to ask. Are you writing another poem about me?'

'I'm…' she began, then looked down at the page. Then up. 'Yes.'

'Can I read it?'

'I'm not done yet.'

'I can wait.'

Samira opened her mouth to protest. Closed it. Looked back at the page, filled with ink. Some letters ended with dark splotches, where she'd held the pen too long, making the full stops into lazy scribbles as she contemplated the next line. She returned her gaze to Death's cowl. 'I've lost my flow.'

'Oh.' The cowl's folds moved in a disappointed fashion. 'Oh. Sorry.' Nevertheless, it seemed to peer with diffident hope.

Samira sighed and moved her arms so Death could read.

Dear Death,
    You come, a shadow in a reflection
    dressed like a B Grade movie.
        I don't want to walk with you to the Gate,
Not yet.
I finally got my driver's licence,
And I want to have gone somewhere, anywhere, before everything ends.
    Hey Death
If something kills me in the next fifteen minutes
Can you hold off on collecting me until after Soundwave?

'It isn't one of my better ones,' said Samira.

'I can't imagine you'd write a *bad* poem,' said Death encouragingly. 'No-one understands me like you do. So many people write like I'm some mad, callous killer, coming along with a metaphorical scythe to reap the living.'

'Most of them have no idea,' said Samira.

'But you do,' said Death, its itchy-ant voice a little warmer.

'I met you once,' said Samira.

Death's cowl had a kind of question mark in it. 'I don't remember that.'

'It was only for a moment. I suppose we didn't really meet. I was in a car accident. I saw you. You were with my brother, Bashir. You said, sorry, it's time to go, and he went with you towards this gate. You waited and he went in, and I woke up in the ambulance. They said I died for fifty two seconds.'

The cowl seemed thoughtful. 'Sorry. I really don't remember.'

'Well,' said Samira, disappointed. 'I guess you see a lot of people.'

'Hundreds simultaneously, usually,' agreed Death.

'This was last year. The tenth of August.'

Death considered it. 'No. Sorry. Nothing.'

'Never mind.'

'It's nothing personal,' said Death. 'I was probably focused on your brother.'

'Yeah.'

'I'm sorry.'

'No, that's cool. You were busy.'

'But I've noticed you since then. I read your poems.'

Samira frowned. 'How?'

'On your blog.'

'On my…? Oh. I didn't know you knew about things like blogs.'

'I try to keep up with the times,' Death assured her, modestly. 'And your poems are addressed to me after all, so they came to my attention. It was so refreshing to read them, and know somebody understood. To be frank with you,' Death leaned close to Samira, 'I got quite emotional.'

Samira considered her reply. 'It must be upsetting, to have people think that you're a killer.'

'I ignore it most of the time. Sticks and stones and all that. I was surprised at how your poems made me feel. I didn't realise how much it bothered me, that people think I'm murdering their loved ones, when all I do is escort them to the Gate.'

Samira had written all about the Gate. It was news to her it was an actual place. Or perhaps an actual metaphysical place, anyway. She'd always assumed her brain had just fired up some fitting allegory in those fifty two seconds while she watched her brother leave.

'The gate to the afterlife…' she said in a thoughtful tone. 'To the life, after. Heaven or Hell, or just where energy goes to convert back to matter.' She cocked her head at Death. 'That's where you took Bashir.'

'Yes.'

In a small voice, she asked, 'Was he scared?'

'No,' said Death. 'He seemed excited, as though it were an adventure.' The cowl shifted in a shrug. 'It takes some people like that. They think it's a great escapade.'

'Oh.' Samira's brow knitted briefly. 'Bashir was always like that. Everything was always an adventure to him. I loved him for that.' She scowled and pushed at her eyes with the heel of her hand. Her eyes were red but dry when she lifted her chin.

'Did he get it?'

'What?'

'Did Bashir get an adventure on the other side of the gate?'

'I don't know.'

'What do you mean you don't know? Don't you know what's on the other side?'

'No,' said Death, uncomfortably. 'I don't get to see through the gate. Not my job. My job's to get everyone there, that's all.'

'What's the use of that?'

'Well, if I don't make sure people find the gate, they… drift off. Interfere.'

'Become ghosts, you mean?'

'Sometimes. Or they try to inhabit other bodies. Possess them, I suppose. That's unpleasant for everyone.'

Samira shuddered.

'Don't worry. It hardly happens any more. These days it's just… collect and guide. It's very straightforward.'

'It must be frustrating.'

Death shrugged. 'A bit. Mostly, it's dull.'

'How could it possibly be dull?' Samira was astonished.

'How could it be otherwise? I spend all of my time in between the dead and the gate, and that is very busy, as you can imagine. It's not like I have time to develop a hobby.'

'But you meet all those people!'

'We don't talk much,' said Death. 'I'm not sure there's a point. Getting to know them, I mean.'

'You're taking the time to follow *me* around like a creeper.'

Death flinched at the description. 'I've been working up the courage to talk to you,' it said. 'And it's not *easy*. Parts of me are working particularly hard at the moment, covering for this bit of me here, talking to you.'

'Oh.' Samira tried to imagine Death's daily routine: picking people up, taking them to the gate, watching them go. Pick up, go to gate, watch them go. Pick up, gate, watch. Rinse and repeat. Endlessly.

'You don't talk to anyone else?'

'Not much. As it was, Bashir was the one who started the conversation, and then he had to leave, and so did I.'

'Sounds like Bashir. Ever the talker.' Samira thought she remembered seeing Bashir chatting, now, hands and face moving with bright animation at the dark, caped figure at his side. Fifty-two seconds of her brother's last moments, and he was talking. Typical.

Her heart bloomed warm at the memory. Bashir's typical chattiness had been the beautiful cornerstone of her life. She had grown up with that lovely buzz of thoughts and ideas and jokes and silliness and good humour wrapped around her. Their mother had been a silent and sad woman, and with reason, but Bashir's voice had been like the lazy buzzing of summer bees, like the birds bustling in trees in the morning, like the radio playing all her favourite songs somewhere in the background. Bashir's voice had always made her feel loved and safe.

The world was too quiet now. Quiet and lonely and more daunting than it had once been.

'You miss him,' said Death.

Samira shrugged.

'It was nice of him to talk to me,' said Death, as though still slightly shocked by the development.

Samira thought Death's reticence with his charges was a shame. People were like books – everyone had a story; it should be shared at least once. Bashir's life had been full of stories.

Bashir had been young, but his life had been worth knowing about. The hopeful start and the horrible blow that forced their family to flee. That big, awful adventure to find better things, and all Bashir's little adventures too; his hopes and plans. Samira had been part of his story's telling, and she still missed him, every day. She missed all the things they'd done together. A year wasn't long enough to have erased the vividness of all the things they'd never now get to do.

'He did say one thing,' said Death.

'What was that?'

'He hoped that you'd still go backpacking around Thailand, as you'd planned. Did you?'

Samira shrugged again. She contemplated her notebook. Death contemplated the hem of its robe.

'Would you… like to watch me work?' Death asked shyly. Its cowl dipped like Death was hiding its face. It was kind of dorkily endearing.

'Sure,' said Samira, and she packed her notebook away, 'I don't have to be anywhere till tonight anyway.'

Death's job was a lot duller than it had to be, Samira decided, and that was nobody's fault but Death's. While the two of them flitted about, meeting spirits and guiding them towards the gate, Death said not a word. It would gesture and nod, and sometimes chivvy people along a bit with a waft of the cloak, but it didn't talk. Samira didn't think she could do it on Death's behalf. She was only an observer, after all, and whether the dead were surprised, resigned, grateful or enraged, none of them seemed to see her.

Death didn't notice any of it. It treated each and every person like a tedious chore to be dealt with as efficiently as possible. It never asked any questions, and harried each person to the gate as though on the clock.

'Do we have to be in this much of a hurry?' Samira asked.

'What? Oh. No, I suppose not. But what is the point of loitering?'

'You don't have to loiter, but you don't have to bolt everyone through the process, do you?'

'I don't bolt.'

'You do,' said Samira. 'You shove them along like parts in a factory. It's rude.'

The cowl took on an irritated angle.

'Maybe not rude, exactly,' she amended. 'But you're all they get in those first few moments. It's kind of important, don't you think?'

The cowl fell forward over the shadows inside in a more embarrassed angle. 'I never know what to say,' Death confessed. 'It is a rather large moment, and most conversational openings are not helpful, I found.'

Samira wondered what conversational openings Death had tried before, and how long ago it had last made the attempt.

Then she noticed they'd moved again.

Death stood by a hospital bed, unseen by the staff or the family of three ranged around the old man's bed. The old man saw it, though. Far from afraid, the guy looked relieved. The mask on his face kept him from speaking – breathing was clearly hard enough – but his hazel eyes spoke volumes about his pain and his being done with it.

Samira lurked by Death's elbow (she thought it was its elbow; she wasn't sure if it had a body, really, but whatever was under the cloak, that part was elbow-*ish*). She felt a bit like a little kid with a parent on Take Your Kid to Work Day. The old man didn't see her, or if he did, she didn't really count.

The man closed his eyes, and the harshness of his breathing in the mask developed a stronger rattle, and then it faded away altogether.

Then the man stood beside them, wan and translucent. For all the relief he'd shown while in his body, now he was uncertain.

Death began to walk away, expecting the spirit to follow, as they usually did. The old man hesitated, accordingly, then took a step. Took another. He looked like he was being dragged along by fishing wire in his navel, and that he was fighting it.

Samira extended a hand to him. 'It's all right,' she said. 'It's taking you to the Gate.'

The old man finally fixed his gaze on her. 'Will it hurt?'

'I don't know,' she confessed, 'But I don't think so. My brother was killed in a car accident that crushed his legs and his ribs and the side of his head, but his spirit looked fine. Death says Bashir talked a lot. I don't think it hurt once he was out of his body.'

The old man considered this. He shifted, flexing his body as though testing it and finding it surprisingly pain-free, then nodded and took her hand. 'It's not so bad. I can breathe without it hurting now. Well. I suppose I'm not actually breathing. That probably makes the difference.'

But he held Samira's hand and they walked together in Death's wake. The hospital room faded around them and coalesced into a gate. It was made of shadows and wrought iron, Samira thought. Either that or smoke and old wood. Or maybe onyx and ice crystals.

Death stood meaningfully by the gate. The old man stood before it, bewildered. He frowned at the gate, at Death, and at Samira. He took a step towards the gate, which was swinging open.

'What…?' Samira blurted out, startling the old man to stillness. She grimaced. 'I'm sorry. Only, I meant to ask, what's your name?'

'Piotr,' said the old man.

Beside them, Death stifled an irritated sigh.

'What happened?' Samira asked.

'Life.' He frowned, then smiled. 'I married a beautiful woman. Helena was a wonderful cook, and a wonderful lover. She always held me afterwards and kissed my cheek and she made me feel safe. Will she be waiting on the other side?'

Samira hated to admit she didn't know, he looked so wistfully hopeful. 'She might be,' she said, deciding that it wasn't a lie, exactly.

Piotr smiled and stepped through the Gate. He, the Gate and whatever misty stuff surrounded it vanished.

Samira sensed Death regarding her. 'What?'

'Nothing.' The cloak shifted, not quite a shrug, and then they were at a driveway and a small boy stood, confused, by his own small, shattered body while an adult screamed and screamed and screamed, kneeling on the verge at his side.

The little boy looked up at Samira, and she held out her arms. He stretched his own up and she scooped him into her embrace.

'I had an accident,' he said. 'I didn't stay where I was supposed to.'

The screaming adult was sobbing and cradling the boy's broken body.

Samira shielded his little face against her own body, so he didn't have to see. She looked at Death with huge, anguished eyes.

'I can't,' it said to the unasked question. 'I don't have the power.'

'No, I know,' Samira whispered. 'It's just so sad.'

'It often is. I try not to think about it.'

The boy wasn't too distraught – Samira wasn't convinced he understood – but he told her his name when she asked. Shui, he said, and giggled, and he told her all of his favourite toys. When they got to the gate, Samira put him down on the ground (if it *was* "ground"; a surface of some kind anyway). Shui asked for his mother.

'She will come for you later,' said Death gently, and ushered Shui through the gate.

Samira stared at Death as the gate faded. 'Do you mean what I think you mean?'

Death shrugged. 'Everyone comes to the gate, eventually. Perhaps it won't seem long to him. Depending on what happens on the other side. Maybe he'll wait. Maybe he'll be born again before she comes. I have no idea, really, but she'll certainly get here one day.'

The next spirit they collected was a teenage girl named Claire who should have got *the hell off* that balcony ledge when her sister told her to.

Claire was shocked, and stammered her name when Death diffidently asked what it was.

'Am I dead?' Claire asked.

'I'm afraid so, yes,' said Death.

Claire turned to Samira for confirmation, and Samira nodded.

'Well, that sucks,' said Claire.

'So I'm told,' said Death. Samira gave it a dirty look.

Silence settled while it led her to the gate, but just as the gate was forming, Death turned to Claire again. 'I'm sorry. I don't mean to make this more difficult for you. But… was there anything you wanted to get off your chest before you go?'

'Like what?'

'I don't know. A secret you wanted to tell. Some last thought to share. Perhaps your favourite colour?'

'Purple,' said Claire. 'Not that lavender shit. Royal purple. Like an iris, you know? Really deep and bright. I was going to get a tattoo with a royal purple iris, right on my shoulder here, and Trudy, my sister, she was going to get a rose. I suppose she'll have to get hers without me, now.'

'Yes.'

Claire nodded. She peered beyond the gate. 'Oh well. I suppose I have to go, then.'

'Yes.'

'Right.' And she stepped through.

Death shuffled a bit at Samira's ongoing glare, until she said, 'I know it must be blasé to you by now, but dying's probably a big deal for most people. You could try to be nicer.'

'I'm not unkind,' said Death, stung.

Samira sighed. 'I know. Not really. But your bedside manner is shit. I hope you weren't that cold when Bashir was talking to you.'

The cowl shifted a little. 'I liked talking with your brother. Well, listening to him. He seemed… nice.'

Samira blinked rapidly, and the tears stayed in her eyes. 'He was nice,' she said. 'He was lovely, and I miss him. And I hate to think he was afraid.'

'He wasn't,' said Death.

'Good.'

After Claire, Death tried more often. Over the next hour, as it met the dead, Death tried to ask a question or two. Sometimes the dead were too angry to speak, or too sad, but most of them… most of them broke out of their surprise and shock and spoke to it on the way to the Gate. Some told it secrets. Most just seemed glad to get a few words in before departing for the unknown.

At the end of two hours, Death had developed some gentle patter, and a softer, kinder tone. He learned names and a lot of favourite colours before it eased into the questions that intrigued it the most.

'What did you want to do that you never tried?' it asked most people, and then, 'What will you miss the most?'

And some of the dead cried. Some of them were angry. Most of them were tenderly wistful, and told Death about people and pets and places, about sunsets and music and recipes for *really good* cannoli.

Samira missed the band she meant to see that night. Instead, as she flashed from soul to soul, and watched Death grow more interested in its charges, and more intrigued by their answers to its questions, she began to feel uncomfortable.

When it's my turn, she started thinking, what am I going to tell Death? That I wrote poetry and thought about dying a lot? That I missed Bashir so much, I didn't want to get on with my life? That the thought of having adventures without my brother hurt too much, so I didn't have any at all?

I want to have adventures. I don't just want to write poems about how much I don't want to die. When I was little I wanted to learn how to ride a motorbike, and I wanted to meet the Little Mermaid. I wanted to go backpacking with Bashir and make one of those stupid YouTube videos with us dancing at all the famous places. I want to see where my Grandmother came from in Somalia. I want to write songs and tell stories and tell people about Bashir, now that he's not here to show people who he was.

I want to have a story to tell Death when it comes to take me to the Gate.

'I have to go,' she blurted out.

'Oh.' Death was surprised. A little disappointed too, Samira thought.

'Sorry. I just, I need to do some stuff. You know how it is.'

'Not really,' said Death.

'Well, I do. But I've had a...' *A good time? A lovely evening? A very weird couple of hours where I re-evaluated my life?* '...a really interesting night. Thanks for having me along.'

'You're welcome. I liked having your company. Thank you again for the poems.'

And they were at her flat, just like they'd suddenly been in a lot of places that night. No gate appeared, only her usual front door in its usual frame, sealing off her usual life beyond it.

'Well. Good night, then.'

'Goodbye, Samira,' said Death. And then it was gone.

Samira sold everything in her flat that wasn't of sentimental value. She bought a backpack. She went to Thailand. She went to Japan after that, then Singapore and Malaysia. Europe came next. The Americas after.

Samira stopped writing poems about Death, though she never stopped writing. She started having adventures, big and small, and wrote about those instead.

She filmed a stupid little dance in all the famous locations, twice in each place in different clothes. With clever editing she made it look like she was dancing with herself in all of them, only on one side she was Samira and on the other she was dressed like Bashir. She made the video a tribute to her brother, and got a few million hits, and she wrote poems and then a story and finally she got a book deal and wrote about how Bashir's life and death had become part of hers.

She wrote blogs and newspaper articles and books. She travelled everywhere. She climbed mountains and explored cities. She volunteered at animal sanctuaries and at soup kitchens, though she didn't tell anyone much about those. She fell in love, and out of love, and in love with someone new. She yelled for justice in protests in New York, Sydney, London, Auckland. She was arrested for breaching the peace in some places.

She still wrote to Death sometimes, though the poems were more like letters, keeping him up to date. She kept the letter-poems to Death in a special notebook.

Once, it replied to her.

Dear Death,
The sun striking off snow makes me think of you,
Because all you ever saw was
The cold, the frost, the frozen dead,
You saw those mountain climbers
Who fell from the slopes like stones in the avalanche
(Aoraki's crags selfishly holding onto the bodies
of those who died in the act of living)
Their skin burnt red by sun and ice
Bodies crushed to sleep
Lying under the soft, killing layers
You didn't see the rainbow light
The crystals sparkling
The blue, blue sky of all those who made it alive
To the summit,
And back to the base, too
And even those sleeping, frozen climbers saw shining light
Rainbows and the dome of heaven
Before the living high and wide and loud killed them.
What will you ask them?
What will they answer?

The day after she wrote that letter, she found Death's reply underneath, inscribed in an old-fashioned script.

I ASKED THEM WHAT THEY HAD LOVED AND WHAT THEY WOULD MISS.

ONE OF THEM WOULDN'T STOP CRYING,

AND ONE OF THEM COMPLAINED ALL THE WAY TO THE GATE.

AND ONE OF THEM LAUGHED, AND SAID EVERYTHING.

I ASKED – WHICH QUESTION DOES THAT ANSWER?

AND SHE SAID, BOTH.

Samira didn't live to ripe old age, though she was ripe enough with living by then.

At the age of fifty-seven, after a night camping in the back yard in a tent with her grandkids, she was bitten by a spider. The bite got infected at the same time she got the flu, then complications set in, relating in part to the internal injuries she'd carried since the car accident, and that was that.

Death came for her.

'Hi,' she said. 'Long time, no see.'

'Oh well,' said Death. 'People to guide, questions to ask. You know how it is.'

Samira laughed. 'Yeah, I do, actually.'

'I have something to confess,' said Death. 'When I met you that last time, and I said I didn't remember you – I was lying.'

'Oh?' Samira wasn't offended, although she was puzzled.

'I'd seen you a few times, actually,' Death continued. 'When the soldiers came and shot your father, you were there, though you were very small. Your mother hid your face against her breast so you couldn't see, and to keep you quiet. Bashir was hiding against her, too, though he witnessed everything. I saw you again later on the boat when your neighbour's mother drowned, and you nearly did, except the naval ship arrived in time to get you out of the sea. Then at the car accident with Bashir.'

Samira frowned. 'You knew me pretty well, then.'

'No,' Death said. 'I'd just seen you a lot. But when I came for Bashir, you saw me for the first time. It wasn't your time yet, but you saw. You were like a hot spark in my path. I probably would have forgotten you, really – a lot of sparks cross my path before their time – but when you were in hospital, you started to write those poems.'

'I was trying to understand.'

Death's cowl shifted in a nod. 'You wrote to me. You didn't blame me, but you didn't like me very much.'

'I like you now,' said Samira, and she patted Death's cloak where she thought its elbow might be.

'I'm glad.'

By now, the Gate had formed, all smoke and dark metal and velvet night and stars.

'Before you go,' said Death, 'Is there anything–'

'Everything, and everything,' said Samira, smiling. The folds of Death's cloak implied that it was smiling too.

'Tell me,' said Samira, 'does anyone ever ask *you* anything?'

'No-one ever does,' Death confessed.

'All right, then, I will. What would you like to do that you've never done?'

Death was quiet for a long time, and when it spoke, its voice was hushed. 'I'm curious about what's on the other side of the Gate. I never used to wonder before, but now I wonder all the time.'

'Why don't you go, then?' Samira suggested.

'I'm kind of busy,' said Death.

'Oh, I could do that job for you,' said Samira. 'It's not that hard. Pop up where people die, try to be a bit kind on the way to the Gate, have a little chat, choof them off through to the other side. That's all, isn't it? I mean – you don't have to do any spooky magic thing to make the Gate appear, do you?'

'No,' said Death cautiously. 'It just… manifests.'

'Cool. Well, I can do that, and you can go satisfy your curiosity.'

Another long silence.

'Seriously?' asked Death.

'Sure. Why not? I got done with my life a bit sooner than I expected. Maybe I can do this for a millennium or two. You go and have a big adventure. If you see my brother, tell him I love him and I miss him.'

'I don't know if he's there. I don't know where he is.'

'That's all right,' said Samira. 'You don't make the rules. So do you want to go or not?'

'I want to go.'

'Right then.'

Death's cloak moved and the shape under of it of an elbow, an arm, a hand, extended towards the Gate, and then stopped.

'Do you need the cloak?' it asked.

'Seems a bit unnecessary,' said Samira. 'I'll be fine like I am.'

Samira was in dark green cargo pants, a multi-coloured tank top and walking shoes. A necklace with a B hanging from it adorned her neck, and a bright orange and blue bandana held her curly, salt-and-pepper hair away from her face.

Death shrugged and stepped through the Gate, which vanished.

At once, Samira felt herself fragmenting, although she remained peculiarly whole. In her own head and out of it at the same time, her vision became like bees' eyes, multi-faceted, seeing everything all at once, but her brain understood all the many pieces.

Like a roaring waterfall splash, she separated into droplets and sprayed like a mist, light, soft and fresh, throughout the world.

Samira took all the dead souls she met by the hand and led them to a Gate, simultaneously and yet individually.

She didn't know what was beyond the Gate – adventure or peace or something terrible or something beautiful. But it wasn't her purpose to fret about that. Her purpose was to be the bridge from one place to the next, to make sure everyone who needed the Gate found it, and found a gentle touch and a kind word on the way.

Samira asked every single one of those souls, before they stepped through the Gate: 'What did you love? What will you miss?'

And some cried, and some complained, and some were confused or angry or scared.

But some of them laughed and said, *Everything, everything*!

CONSTANT

When I see you,
in light that has taken eight
minutes to race from the Sun to the Earth,
and then Einstein-fast into my retina,
I think:
*   a million million years of evolution brought me here.*
Me to you. This single moment.
The sun was born 4.5 billion years ago,
and so too the Earth,
and you and I are less than blinks in the eternity of spacetime.
But here you are,
and here I am.
Standing on four and a half billion years of rock;
in four and a half billion years of light.
In the now *of one another.*
Let us burn our own little lights bright,
and light up other lives in
the blink-blink-blink-blink-blink of a universe,
*   like my heart,*
*   expanding.*

Acknowledgements

This collection has come together with the encouragement and support of many wonderful people.

First of all, thank you to all the editors and publishers who first published my stories 'Scar Tissue', 'The Christmas Card Mystery', 'Long Live the King' and 'Death's Door'. My forever-thanks also to Pulp Fiction Press, Improbable Press and Clan Destine Press who have published my novels and supported my writing these many years.

Extra special thanks to Clan Destine's Lindy Cameron for her unfailing support and assistance, and for kindly agreeing to publish *Scar Tissue and Other Stories* under the Clan Destine banner.

My love always to Tim, who stands by me with encouragement, kindness, good planning and patience.

Thank you to my dear damsels, Wendy, Janet and Dimi, who are always there when I need them. Bear hugs to Dimi and Wendy especially, for their knowledge and assistance in editing several of the new stories.

Another callout of gratitude goes to Wendy C. Fries for editing this collection, and Tim Richards for proofreading, and the Clan Destine team for putting this book together.

My love and thanks also go to my wonderful Patreon supporters, who encourage me with word and deed.

And you, dear reader. Thank you. May your scars ever be badges of your strength.

This book was made possible by my Patreon supporters. Thank you!

Sarah Remy
Holly
Carey Handfield
Clarenight
Lycia Severson
Linda Ertley
Kizzia
Barbie Jett
Donna Sams

Kim Fasching
Stephen Harris
Jane Tisell
Sally Beasley
Mary K Hostetler
Andrew P Street
Grant Watson
Sarah Drosendahl
Jehni Thomas-Wurth

Isabelle Rowan
Dimitra Stathopoulos
Sally Koetsveld
Tim Richards
GreenEyedGal
Graham Williams
Tansy Rayner Roberts
Mike Thompson

https://www.patreon.com/NarrelleMHarris

NARRELLE M. HARRIS

Narrelle M Harris writes crime, horror, fantasy, romance and erotica. Her 30+ novels and short stories have been published in Australia, US and UK.

Award nominations include *Fly By Night* (nominated for a Ned Kelly Award), *Witch Honour* and *Witch Faith* (both short-listed for the George Turner Prize), *Walking Shadows* (Chronos Awards; Davitt Awards).

In 2017, her ghost/crime story *Jane* won the Athenaeum Library's Body in the Library prize at the Scarlet Stiletto Awards presented by Sisters in Crime Australia.

Her work includes vampire novels, erotic spy adventures, queer romance, traditional Holmesian mysteries, the Holmes/Watson romances *The Adventure of the Colonial Boy* (2016) and *A Dream to Build a Kiss On* (2018); the queer paranormal thriller-romance, *Ravenfall* (2017); andthe spec-fic romance, *Grounded* (2019).

Narrelle is releasing her Duo Ex Machina series of gay romance crime stories through her Patreon in partnership with Clan Destine Press.

Find out more: www.narrellemharris.com
Subscribe to her blog, Mortal Words: www.mortalwords.com.au
Support Narrelle M Harris on Patreon:
   www.patreon.com/NarrelleMHarris

Narrelle M. Harris
with Clan Destine Press

RAVENFALL

British soldier, Dr James Sharpe, returned from Afghanistan a changed man. Like most war veterans haunted by deadly choices and the horrors of battle, James struggles against his demons.

Unlike other ex-soldiers, his demons are real. Transformed in the heat of a desert battlefield, James Sharpe is now a vampire.

Struggling London artist, Gabriel Dare, has his own secrets – like who he really is, and why he lived on the streets before lodging with Dr Sharpe; like the ghosts he used to see, that made others question his sanity.

James knows Gabriel is the best thing in his life, but questions his ability to love and fears he's a danger to all. Gabriel knows there's something different about his enigmatic landlord, but can't deny his attraction.

When some of Gabriel's street friends go missing, he discovers that London is full of monsters – real, vicious, otherworldly monsters. The two men join forces with a clairvoyant cop and a Peer of the Realm to uncover the truth, for it seems the vampire who sired James is back in London – with a diabolical agenda that threatens the entire nation.

WALKING SHADOWS

Lissa Wilson's life hasn't been the same since people she cared about started getting themselves killed. By vampires. Lissa learnt that the opposite of life is not always death.

On the plus side, she made a new friend. Gary Hooper may be the worst best-friend a librarian could have – and easily the worst vampire ever – but he has taught Lissa the real meaning of life.

Gary's worldview has also improved remarkably since meeting Lissa, but all that could be lost if she discovers what services he provides Melbourne's undead community.

Meanwhile, as their friendship brings him closer to the humanity he lost, it also puts them both in grave danger.

And there's a big chance that the evil stalking them could them both killed – in Gary's case, for good this time.

Narrelle M Harris
with Improbable Press

THE ADVENTURE OF THE COLONIAL BOY

1893: Dr Watson, still in mourning for the death of his great friend Sherlock Holmes, is now triply bereaved, with his wife Mary's death in childbirth.

Then a telegram from Melbourne, Australia intrudes into his grief. 'Come at once if convenient.' Both suspicious and desperate to believe that Holmes may not, after all, be dead, Watson goes as immediately as the sea voyage will allow.

Soon Holmes and Watson are together again, on an adventure through Bohemian Melbourne and rural Victoria, following a series of murders linked by a repulsive red leech and one of Moriarty's lieutenants. But things are not as they were. Too many words lie unsaid between the Great Detective and his biographer. Too much that they feel is a secret.

Solve the crime, forgive a friend, rediscover trust and admit to love. Surely that is not beyond that legendary duo, Sherlock Holmes and Dr John Watson?

A DREAM TO BUILD A KISS ON

John Watson, invalided army doctor and sometimes artist, and Sherlock Holmes, consulting detective, become flatmates and friends in contemporary London.

Love grows too, despite past betrayals and present dangers – for where you have Holmes and Watson, there too are Moriarty and Moran.

A Dream to Build a Kiss On explores love and family, trust and betrayal, brothers and brothers-in-arms, forgiveness and revenge, in an ongoing tale told 221 words at a time.

Other fiction by **Narrelle M Harris**

SHORT FICTION

Sky High, Bone Deep
Birds of a Feather
Near Miss

COLLECTIONS

Showtime
Scar Tissue and Other Stories

SERIES

Talbot and Burns Mysteries
Homecoming
A Paying Client

Duo Ex Machina
Fly By Night
Sacrifice
Coming soon in this series:
Number One Fan
Kiss and Cry
Little Star

Secret Agents, Secret Lives
Double Edged
Expendable
Wilderness

Narrelle also has short crime, romance, science fiction and fantasy stories in over a dozen anthologies.

See all of Narrelle's novels, shorts stories and anthologies at

www.narrellemharris.com
or
Narrelle M Harris on Amazon Author

www.ingramcontent.com/pod-product-compliance
Lightning Source LLC
Chambersburg PA
CBHW041746010726
47507CB00008B/304